PURITY KILLS

ANDY MASLEN

TYTON PRESS

ALSO BY ANDY MASLEN

Detective Ford

Shallow Ground

Land Rites

Plain Dead

DI Stella Cole

Hit and Run

Hit Back Harder

Hit and Done

Let the Bones Be Charred

Weep, Willow, Weep

A Beautiful Breed of Evil

Death Wears A Golden Cloak

Gabriel Wolfe

Trigger Point

Reversal of Fortune

Blind Impact

Condor

First Casualty

Fury

Rattlesnake

Minefield

No Further

Torpedo

Three Kingdoms

Ivory Nation

Crooked Shadow

Brass Vows (coming soon)

Other Fiction

Blood Loss – A Vampire Story

You're Always With Me (coming soon)

WHO IS TARA WOLFE?

Tara Wolfe was born in Hong Kong to a British diplomat and his half-Chinese wife. Her older brother, Gabriel, would grow up to become first a soldier in the Parachute Regiment and then the SAS, before joining a British Government black ops unit called The Department.

When still just a baby, Tara was kidnapped by gangsters, under the direction of a corrupt officer in the Royal Hong Kong Police. The kidnappers botched things and Tara was spirited away to the mainland by the widow of a triad enforcer. She renamed the child in her care Wei Mei – 'Beautiful Plum'.

This is what happened next.

For Jo

"Respect yourself and others will respect you."
Confucius

1

1998 | A SMALL VILLAGE IN GUANGDONG PROVINCE, CHINA

The fish was a giant: Wei Mei had first seen it when her gang had been swimming in the river. An expanse of silver scales that flashed in the sun as it rolled over a few centimetres below the surface and dived for the bottom.

She planned to catch it and then sell it at the market. Think what she could do with the money someone would pay for it.

'You're twelve, Mei,' her best friend, Ping, had said when she'd shared her plan. 'You can't have a stall. The authorities won't permit it.'

'Who cares about the authorities? I'll do it anyway,' she said, folding her arms. 'By the time they find out, it'll be too late.'

Squatting by the edge of the slow-moving water, she pictured the fish snaking along the bottom looking for something tasty to eat.

'Come along, beast,' she murmured, eyes fixed on the softly rippling surface of the river. 'Come and get your dinner.'

So engrossed was she in the hunt that she failed to notice the older boy creeping up on her through the reeds and broad-leaved plants that thronged the bank.

Tan Hu was fifteen. A good head and shoulders taller than Mei and all of her friends except Beanpole. But Beanpole was too skinny to defend himself against the village bully.

Because that's what Tan Hu was. Actually, Wei Mei thought 'bully' wasn't strong enough to describe the kind of boy who would beat up little kids for fun. Throw sharp-edged stones at them when they were playing quietly in the dirt. Or steal their snacks right out of their hands and run off laughing as they cried.

Mei kept the line nice and taut against the current. Behind her, Tan Hu grinned as he manoeuvred into position. Keeping low, he slid a knife from a nylon sheath on his belt. As he watched her, he pressed the palm of his left hand against his groin, enjoying the hot, fluttering sensation it produced in the pit of his belly.

Mei blinked as a flash of sunlight bounced off the water. When she looked again, the tip of her fishing pole was dipping sharply.

With a cry of triumph – 'Got you!' – she jerked the rod up to set the hook in the beast's great bony-lipped mouth. Immediately the rod seemed to fight back, almost pulling free of her hands.

'Oh, no you don't!'

She heaved back and felt the fish resisting her, a surge of power like when you tried to lead a mule with a rope and it didn't feel like coming with you.

Straining every muscle, she levered the rod upright and was rewarded with a flash of silver as the fish broke the surface, rolling and thrashing in the dull green water.

She leaned backwards, and the combined strength of her arms, the bamboo pole and the heavy fishing line brought the beast curving and bucking towards the bank.

Leaning over and trying to avoid the gaping mouth with its double row of ugly, needle-pointed teeth, she stuck her thumb and fingers into its gill slits and clamped down hard. It was cold in there and slippery, but she squeezed tighter and readied herself to yank it out of the water.

She could already imagine what she'd shout at the weekly market.

'Come on, ladies and gents! Who wants this beautiful fish? One-hundred-and-fifty yuan and it's yours.'

She knew she'd have to haggle, but even a hundred would be a fortune.

Then another hand gripped the rod and pulled the giant fish closer. She whirled round, ready to thank whoever was helping her land the beast. And a cold tremor flashed through her.

Still holding the rod, Tan Hu swept his knife out in a wide arc and cut the line.

The fish folded itself double then disappeared back into the green-dark depths, showering the two children with water from its scimitar-like tail fin.

'What did you do that for, you idiot?' Mei shouted.

She punched Tan Hu in the face, drawing blood from his lower lip.

In response, he brought the knife up where she could see it.

'Do what I say or I'll cut you open like a fish belly,' he said. 'Take your clothes off.'

'No!'

He grinned; an oddly disjointed expression as if his lips had forgotten to tell his eyes something was funny.

'My friend here says you will.'

The knife was small, but the blade looked sharp. If she tried to take it off him, he'd probably stab her or give her a good cut. Mei wanted neither. Instead, she meekly said, 'OK, Hu.'

His eyes widened. 'Really?'

'Yes, really. Just turn around.'

'You'll run.'

'No I won't. Anyway, you can run faster than me, you know that,' she said, holding her hands wide. 'So what would be the point?'

He nodded. And, like the stupid brute he was, he did just that.

Mei launched herself at him, grabbed a handful of his thick, shaggy hair and pulled back hard. His head snapped back and he howled with pain. Then she dug her fingers into his throat, choking off the sound.

'Try that again and I'll come to your house at night and castrate you with your own knife. I mean it,' she muttered into his ear.

Then she shoved him, hard between the shoulder blades. With a cry, he pitched forwards into the swirling green water of the river they all called Little Mekong, even though the real one was way, way, *way* over to the west.

But as Tan Hu toppled in, Mei's foot slid in a patch of clay where the weeds had been torn away in the scuffle. She went in straight after him.

His head broke the surface a few seconds later. Ten metres downstream from where she was treading water.

'I'll kill you!' he screamed, spraying river water from his mouth.

'Try it!' Mei yelled back. 'Next time maybe I'll slit your belly open.'

He opened his mouth to shout something back but swallowed river water instead. Coughing, he went under again, only to reappear another twenty metres downstream, now facing in the direction of the current and striking out towards an overhanging tree branch.

Mei reached the bank easily: she was a strong swimmer. She hauled herself out and clambered to her feet, careful not to slide straight back in on the slippery red mud.

Laughing, she ran back the way she'd come, through bamboo and the pink-berried plants with long, sharp-pointed leaves that had earned them their nickname: Devil's Tongue.

Halfway back to the village she looked over her shoulder, just to check Tan Hu wasn't after her. Maybe he'd try it on again later, but she'd be ready for him this time. Probably she ought to take a knife from the kitchen just in case.

She looked forward again and crashed into Ping, who was running the other way.

Mei jarred her ribs as she tripped and fell onto the hard-packed red earth of the track. Ping stumbled, but stayed upright. Hurriedly, she pulled on Mei's wrists, dragging her to her feet.

'What is it?' Mei asked her friend as she rubbed her elbow. 'You look like a demon's chasing you.'

Ping's eyes were wide. 'There's a man at your house. He's got a gun! He was pointing it at your mum and shouting.'

Mei's heart was thumping in her chest. She'd forgotten all about the pain from the collision.

'What about? What was he shouting? Tell me!'

'You!'

'What do you mean, me?'

'He said she had to tell him where you were. He said he was taking you away. And he's wearing a suit!'

This was bad. Nobody from round here wore suits. The only people who had guns *and* suits were Party officials. Mei had seen them now and again when Mummy had taken her into Shenzhen. Mummy would delight in pointing them out.

'See those two over there? They're Party. Secret police, most likely. If they don't like you, you just disappear. Turn up three weeks later in a ditch outside the city limits with a bullet in your brain.'

At the time, Mei thought Mummy Rita was doing a poor job of frightening her. But one was actually here, in the village. And looking for her.

Mei took Ping by her narrow, bony shoulders.

'Listen, Ping. Listen to me really carefully,' she said. 'Go back to the village. Just act normal. If he asks you, say you haven't seen me.'

'Why? What are you going to do?'

'I'm going to get a better look at this guy without him seeing me.'

Ping's eyes widened.

'That's a really bad idea. What if he spots you?'

Mei grinned.

'He won't!'

With Ping gone, Mei turned off the track. She knew the woods round the village like her own skin. Every animal track, every fallen tree, every patch of boggy ground that would swallow you whole if you fell in.

She started working her way back to the village using every bit of her skill. She'd come out in a stand of bamboo just behind the house. Dense enough to hide in, but with enough light coming in between the thick green stems to spy on the house.

She wanted to get a good look at whoever was threatening her mum. Eventually he'd leave and then Mei would have a think about what to do afterwards. But, for now, she just needed to see him.

Reaching the house meant pushing through some dense patches of spiny shrubs. They had inch-long thorns hidden amongst gaudy orange flowers with black centres. It didn't seem fair that such pretty flowers concealed those evil little spikes.

By the time she reached the stand of bamboo, her arms, legs and face were scratched and bleeding. But that was fine. Scratches healed.

She peered through. At first she couldn't see either Mummy Rita or the Party man. Then she heard him. A deep, boomy voice riding over the top of Mummy's higher one.

'Where is she?'

'I told you already, Jian! I don't know. She's a naughty girl. Always running off. Never in school when she should be,' Mummy said, repeating the complaints she usually threw in Mei's direction. 'She spends every day by the river or in the forest. Why don't you look there?'

'Oh, I will. Maybe for now I'll just sit here. Bring me some jasmine tea.'

Mei frowned. Not at his rudeness. In her experience, men were usually rude to women. Party men, especially. But because Mummy Rita had called the man by his name. Jian.

That was weird. As far as Mei knew, the village headman was the only Party official Mummy knew. And this wasn't him. And why did she sound cross with him and not frightened?

She decided it didn't matter. She'd ask Mummy later. What mattered was making sure the fat Party man with the gun didn't catch her.

And anyway, she had no idea what she might have done to attract the attention of the Party in the first place.

Sure, like Mummy said, she skipped school most days. But

honestly, what was she going to do with all that stuff about fractions and minerals and the history of the People's Republic of China?

The stuff she really needed to know? How to fight off boys like Tan Hu? How to snap a chicken's neck? How to milk a goat or tell which berries in the forest were OK to eat? Those, she either knew already or could ask real people in the village, like the blacksmith or one of the farmers.

She took one last look at the man with his shiny silver gun and his slicked-back hair. *See you later, Mr Party Man!*

Something crackled in the dry grass behind her. Maybe a rat. Too loud for a mouse or one of the big purplish-black beetles that trundled around the place pushing balls of cow dung. She prepared to go.

The pincers that suddenly clamped on the back of her neck made her scream. A giant stag beetle had got her! She felt herself rising to a standing position without using her legs.

'Got you!' a man said from behind her.

With his fingers still digging into the soft flesh at the sides of her neck, the man marched Mei over to her house.

The fat man got to his feet, a broad smile on his face revealing flashing gold teeth. He put the gun away in a leather holster inside his suit jacket.

Mei was terrified. She started gabbling.

'Look, I don't know what I've done, OK? But I'm sorry. I love the Party. I love Chairman Mao. And all the ones in charge now. I know I've skipped school, but I can explain. Just, please don't hurt my mum. I'm a disobedient girl. I never do what she says, it drives her mad, she can't control me. I'm—'

The torrent of phrases, most of which had come originally from Mummy Rita's own lips, dried as the fat man burst out laughing.

'Wait! You think I'm with the *Party*?'

He laughed harder, only stopping when a fit of coughing seized him. Bending double, hands flat on his wide thighs, he shook his head until the coughing stopped.

He pulled a red handkerchief from a pocket and wiped his streaming eyes.

'You hear that?' he said to the man gripping Mei's neck, 'She thinks we're with the Party!'

'Fat chance,' the man said, chuckling deep in his chest.

The first man cleared his throat and sighed out a big breath.

'Listen, Mei, I'm about as far from being a Party man as you can ever imagine,' he said. 'You won't remember me, but I've known you since you were a baby. I'm here to take you back to Hong Kong.'

'What?'

Mei couldn't believe what he was saying. Hong Kong? Why? And if he wasn't a Party man, what was he?

'Hong Kong,' he said. 'A place of opportunity, still, despite the handover.'

Mei had no idea what he was talking about. What handover? But she did know there was no way she was going to Hong Kong with him. She wasn't going *anywhere* with him.

She slapped at the man's hands around her neck.

'Get off me.'

Mei watched the fat man signal something with his eyes over her head. The other man let go of her neck.

'Do you need to get some things before we leave?' the fat man asked.

'I need to pee. Your bully-boy frightened me,' she said.

Fat man laughed again. 'Fine. But don't even think of running off. We'll only catch you.'

Mei shrugged. 'Who said I was going to run? Hong Kong sounds fun. And I hate it here anyway.'

Mummy Rita reappeared just as she said this. Mei watched her face crumple. Her lips trembled as she handed the small china cup of tea to the man she'd called Jian. Mei felt guilt wash through her. But she couldn't explain she'd only said it to get the fat man to relax.

'Fine,' he said. 'But be quick. We've got a long journey ahead of us.'

Mei nodded. She walked off around the side of the house. As soon as she was out of sight, she ran. She ran as fast as she'd ever run in her life.

She found Ping playing down by the stream that fed the Little Mekong.

'Ping!' she hissed. 'I have to go.'

'What? Where?'

'Shenzhen. That guy's not from the Party. I don't who he is, and I don't care. But he's not taking me to Hong Kong.'

Ping's lower lip trembled.

'You're coming back, though, right? When they've gone, I mean.'

Mei smiled. 'Of course, silly.' She had an idea. 'Look, if you really, really need to find me, leave a message somewhere only we know about.'

'But where?' Ping asked, crying properly now.

Mei looked up. Where would be a good place for a secret message? Mummy always took her to the big city on the bus. Yes! That was it.

'The bus station,' she said. 'Where the bus from here pulls in. Queue number seven. There's a stand selling *People's Daily*. All decorated with red-and-yellow banners. The hammer and sickle.'

Ping smiled tearily, wiping her snotty nose with the back of her hand.

'I know it. We went to Shenzhen last year. Dad bought a copy off the sales lady.'

'Put your message inside an empty drinks can and squash it flat,' Mei said, 'then leave it at the back of the stand. I'll check every week.'

Ping nodded, gave an almighty sniff, then turned and ran back towards the village. Just before she disappeared out of sight, she turned and raised a hand in a farewell wave.

* * *

Three months passed. As did Mei's thirteenth birthday. Every week for her first month in Shenzhen, she checked round the back of the *People's Daily* stand at the bus station.

But soon after arriving, she fell in with a group of street kids and found she enjoyed the life. Stealing food from stalls, and wallets from head-swivelling tourists. Running from the cops if a daring raid caused too much commotion. Sleeping on the top floor of an unused carpark, warm in the humid night air of high summer.

Little by little, her memories of the village faded as the thrills of city living took hold of her.

2

THREE YEARS LATER, SHENZHEN MEGACITY, CHINA

With her practised thief's eye, Wei Mei spots the three rich kids before Binyan does.

She picks out her mark. The one on the left, nearest the road. She can hit him, snag his wallet, chuck an apology over her shoulder – '*Sorry, mate, wasn't looking where I was going!*' – then escape through the traffic.

He won't follow. His threads look too new, too fancy, too damned expensive. No way he's going to risk a chase across nine lanes of traffic. He might fall down and get his wuvvly wittle blazer dirty and then what would Mummy and Daddy say?

She snorts. Who is she kidding? They'd probably buy him two more to replace it. His mates'll cluster round him, when any fool knows you leave the fallen man and go after the attacker.

Has Binyan even noticed? Probably not. He's probably daydreaming about setting his next fire. It's how he got his nickname.

Spark just about sums him up. Show a normal kid an empty car or an abandoned building and they look for stuff they can sell on. Spark starts looking for matches.

Weirdo! But she likes him, just the same. They hang out together every day. Binyan calls her Juice.

'Because you've got the juice. You know, the rush, the swagger,' he exclaims, when she presses him for an explanation. 'The juice!'

But Mei knows better. She heard him once, talking to another member of their gang. 'Plum juice, man. It's my favourite.'

Her name means Beautiful Plum. Spark's in love with her. Or so he thinks. That's OK. He never tries anything. Good job, too, 'cause he'd have to learn to piss like a girl if he did.

She nudges him.

'I spy dinner,' she murmurs.

Spark nods. 'I got your back,' he mutters.

It's a tried and tested routine. She goes in for the kill, Spark lingers, ready to trip a pursuer or generally get in the way: whichever'll give Mei time to get away with the loot. Then they find somewhere quiet to divvy up the spoils.

The snazzily-dressed trio are about five metres away now. They've got that look. Not just the money. The confidence.

It comes from knowing they're protected. Not by bodyguards, nothing so obvious. Though she and Spark aren't averse to rolling the odd executive or tourist dogged by some shaven-headed goon with a bulge on his belt.

No. These kids have *protection*. The only kind that really matters. Their parents are high-ups in the Party. You fuck with them, the Party fucks you straight back. But, like, a thousand times worse.

Last year a girl – who they called Panda, on account of her striking black and white hairdo – pulled a knife on a Party kid and took his wallet.

'Total result,' she crowed later, round the fire on the top of an abandoned building as she showed them the genuine dollar bills the kid'd been carrying around.

Panda turned up dead three days after that. Slung onto a pile of stinking rubbish behind a cafe. Eyes crudely gouged out. Fingers removed. A Party pin hit so hard into the skin of her forehead it had lodged in the bone beneath. Her mouth stuffed with a crumpled sheet of glossy, coloured paper that, when they hooked it out, depicted a smiling Chairman Mao.

In blood-red writing, someone had added an unofficial slogan:

THIEVES NEVER LAUGH FOR LONG

Poor Panda. Mei had stretched out a hand and stroked her cheek. The dried blood gave her skin a sandpapery feel. They couldn't bury her. It wasn't their style, in any case. They just left her and moved on. You had to.

The Party kids are only a couple of metres away now.

Mei's heart is racing. It's mostly excitement. She's never been caught and doesn't intend to start now. Mostly excitement, sure. Maybe a little jag of fear running through the middle of it all like a guitar string vibrating.

'Ready?' she hisses.

'Ready,' Spark hisses back.

Mei takes a step to her left and then, as the Party kids draw level, stumbles sideways and gives the nearest one a hefty bump on the shoulder.

'Hey! What the fuck?'

He spins round. Shiny, well-fed face a mask of righteous indignation. *Where do they learn that expression?* she has time to wonder.

'Sorry, man,' she says holding him by the shoulder with her left hand, while her right snakes inside his Burberry bomber jacket. This style has the inside pocket on the right. 'I tripped. Are you all right? Did I hurt you?'

He sneers. Behind him, his two friends are watching with smirks on their faces.

'Yes, Ren,' one says sarcastically, 'did the street rat hurt you? Shall we call a private ambulance? Shall we get her friend here to fetch you a glass of water?'

'Piss off, Ching!' he snaps. He glares at Mei. 'Of course you didn't hurt me, you little street whore. Now fuck off.'

Which Mei is happy to do, his fat leather wallet nestling inside her own jacket. She and Spark are halfway across the road when a shout goes up.

'Hey! The little bitch stole my wallet!'

'Get her!' the one called Ching shouts.

Without turning her head, Mei shouts, 'Run!'

It's force of habit: Spark doesn't need telling. Together they dart through the traffic, zig-zagging between cars, motorbikes, vans and trucks.

Ignoring the parps and toots from the drivers' horns, Mei streaks for the pavement on the far side of Shennan Avenue, almost bumping into a drably-dressed woman fiddling with oversized sunglasses.

Mei's grinning. The Party kids won't dare chase them into the stinking, smoking traffic; once she and Spark are safe on the other side, they can dodge into an alley and make their way home via the back streets.

There's a loud bang. And a scream. A boy's scream.

Spark's scream.

She looks back, just for a second. Through a gap in the traffic she sees her friend lying in the road. Something's happened to his neck. His head's at completely the wrong angle.

Beyond him, she sees the three rich boys charging towards her. The leading boy, the one she rolled, actually leaps over Spark. His teeth are bared.

'Come here, whore!' he yells.

Tears streaming down her cheeks, Mei sprints away. Poor Spark. She hopes he's just injured. That some kind person will gather him up and take him to hospital.

Yes. That's what will happen. And once he's better, he'll discharge himself and come and find her. But for now, she needs to put some serious distance between her and the rich kids.

Mei reaches the safety of the pavement, although it's choked with people and keeping ahead of the rich kids is proving hard. Now she can feel it. Fear. She doesn't want to end up like Panda.

She weaves through the oncoming shoppers like a snake,

twisting and turning her body while keeping her balance as she races down the street. She's got a destination in mind. A place where she knows every square centimetre: every climbable fence, every blind alley, every elevated walkway, every nook, cranny and hidey-hole.

She reaches the side street that leads to the building site and – *Oh, thank you, thank you!* – it's almost deserted. Just a couple in drab, much-washed, old-people clothes gumming their way through coconut cakes they're eating out of a paper bag.

She skips round them and hurtles through the gates into the deserted site. The workers have all been redeployed to another city project. It's why she and Spark like to hang out here.

She risks a look over her shoulder.

Shit! The lead boy is only twenty metres away.

A lump of concrete the size of a mango whizzes past Wei Mei's head and bounces harmlessly off a corrugated-iron sheet with a loud clang.

'Come back here, bitch!' he screams after her. 'I order you!'

Yeah, like she'd follow *his* orders.

Mei runs on, deeper into the huge building site.

A fire is burning in a blue-painted oil drum. Three peasants from the countryside are gathered round it. They're passing a bottle from one brown hand to another.

They look over, mouths agape. Like they've never seen a sixteen-year-old girl fleeing three Party kids for her life before. Idiots!

Another lump of concrete flies past her head and strikes the oil drum with a boom like the world's most out-of-tune gong. She laughs. He might be rich, he might be protected, but he's got a shit right hand.

Mei streaks around a huge red-and-yellow crane and through the slit in the chain-link fencing she and Spark cut last month. This is the supply yard and it's the perfect place to lose them. Huge piles of stone slabs, bricks and bamboo scaffolding poles everywhere.

She vaults a stack of wooden pallets and skids sharp-left down a narrow corridor between two temporary cabins the workers use.

Then her heart stops. One of the rich kids appears at the far end, turning the light to dark.

'Got you now, bitch,' he says with an evil smile.

Mei turns, intending to run back the other way. Then her hopes explode. Ching is standing at the other end. She's trapped.

3

They advance on her. Walking. More of that confidence they get spoon-fed from the moment they're born.

'I bet she's a virgin,' Ching calls out to his friend.

'Not for much longer!' he calls back.

Mei looks up. The cabins are about two and a half metres tall. Their sides are smooth.

She turns sideways onto the two boys, braces her back against one cabin and her left foot against the other. She's done this before, in the hills where she and Spark found a really cool cliff for practising being famous mountaineers.

With a grunt, she lifts her right foot off the ground and sticks it against the wall at her back.

Now she starts climbing. Push up, reposition left foot. Lift hands and stick the palms against the hot metal. Push up again. Reposition right foot.

The boys have reached the spot where she was standing a moment ago. The one called Ching stretches up a hand and manages to grab her dangling right sneaker. She jerks her knee up, pulling her foot free of his grasping hand, then kicks out and catches him a glancing blow across the face.

'Shit! You broke my cheekbone, bitch. You're going to pay for that,' he screams up at her.

What is he *talking* about? She's wearing knockoff Nike Air Jordans. How the fuck does he think she broke his bone with a squishy lump of foam?

He's jumping up, but she's safely out of range. Another couple of pushes and she's on the roof of the cabin.

She runs to the far side and looks over the edge. It's a big drop to the ground, but there's a pile of empty sacks about two metres out from the cabin. In the distance, she sees the peasants still round their oil drum. The rising heat makes their faces wobble. One looks over, smiles and waves. She sighs. How do they ever think they're going to survive in the city, acting like dumb cows?

The boys are shouting. Calling out. The usual names. Bitch. Whore. Cunt. Mei grins. They're down there and she's up here.

She backs up a few paces, gets into a sprinter's crouch, then hurtles towards the edge, leads with her right foot and leaps, arms outstretched, sailing over the gap, over the hard concrete strewn with cigarette butts and broken glass, and lands with a perfect roll on the pile of sacks.

She rolls to the edge and stands…and comes face-to-face with the third boy. Who she totally forgot about.

He's holding a stave of wood. He swings, but he telegraphs the move with an exaggerated backswing and Mei ducks as the club whistles towards her face.

The wood glances off the side of her head, spinning it round. Her vision darkens and tiny red fireworks pop around the edge of her vision. She staggers, but then is on her feet and running.

'Come back here, you!' he shouts.

Now she hears two more sets of running footsteps. The side of her face is warm. She puts up her hand and her palm comes away covered in blood. It's fine. She's had worse.

Hoping to throw them off by a metre or two, she tips her hips to the right, then suddenly jinks left, scooting round the back of a cute yellow dumper-truck, its scoop full of red sand.

But she's miscalculated.

She's boxed herself in between tight-packed pallets of bricks. She leaps towards the first stack and starts climbing. The toe of her Air Jordan misses the lip where one brick stands proud of its fellows and drags her fingertips painfully out of the crack she's wedged them into.

Searing pain shoots up her left arm, all the way from her fingers to her shoulder. She looks. Two nails have torn down to the quicks.

Then a hand grabs her right shoulder and spins her round. The incoming blow knocks her over, her head narrowly missing the edge of a column of bricks. A kick to her midsection drives the wind from her and she curls into a little ball.

'I've got her,' her attacker shouts. 'Here! I've got the little bitch.'

Groaning with the effort of pulling air into her bruised chest, Mei levers herself into a sitting position, but he kicks her arm out from under her.

'You're going nowhere, cockroach,' he says with a triumphant smile.

Sweat sheens his round face, which is the bright red of a ripe tomato like the ones Mummy Rita used to grow back in the village.

For a second, Mei wishes she'd never left. That she was back there now, wandering the hard-packed red-dirt roads, singing to herself, or helping one of the farmers drive oxen to a new paddy.

The two other boys arrive, out of breath. Panting. Their sleek haircuts are properly mussed up now and they've got smudges on their soap-washed faces. As for the clothes, Mei reckons Mummy and Daddy might have a few sharp words on *that* score.

'You stole Dalei's wallet,' the boy says.

She's identified him as the leader. That makes him the most dangerous. But also it makes the other two vulnerable. They'll look to him for a steer on how it's going to go down. And they get their courage from him, too. So he's the one she needs to deal with first.

'He can get more money. I can't,' Mei spits back, pushing herself away from them with her hands and heels.

He puts his hands on his hips.

'Do you know who we are?'

She thinks of the famous clowns from the State Circus. 'Are you Piggy, Ducks and Uncle Sam?'

He scowls. 'Ha, ha. Our fathers are members of the Shenzhen People's Governing Committee. They're very powerful. You picked the wrong boys, men, I mean, to tangle with.'

The one called Ren looks at his leader. 'Come on, Dalei, I thought we were going to fuck her. I'm as horny as a goat.'

That's when she pulls her knees up to her chest in a lightning-fast crunch, braces her hands against the gritty concrete beneath her and shoots her right leg out. Her heel connects square-on with the front of his expensive American denims. He emits a high-pitched squeal, like a pig when the village butcher draws his long, sharp blade across its throat.

He falls sideways and Mei rolls onto her belly and is on her feet in a second. There's nowhere to escape to, and she's had it with running, anyway.

The one called Dalei looks panicked. His eyes are wide and Mei sees the fear in them. Good. He's not used to his victims fighting back.

He swings wildly at her. She doesn't even have to duck, the blow is so poor. She just leans back a little as his fist passes harmlessly in front of her face. Then she lunges and gives him a faceful of clawed fingers, aiming for the eyes, but content to hit him anywhere on that expanse of fat, pork-fed flesh.

She catches him across the nose and one fingertip slips, disgustingly, inside, but the real damage happens when her index finger, tipped with a torn and dirty nail, scrapes across his eyeball. He screams and his hands fly to his face. Mei shoves him hard and he trips over his own feet and tumbles to the ground.

She turns and meets Ching's incoming fist which chops her across the neck: a vicious blow that sends a spear of agony lancing across her chest and making her feel sick.

Staggering, she lets herself stumble sideways as if she's hurt worse than she is. She crashes against the nearest pallet of bricks, but the sound is mostly where she shoves them with her right hip. She straightens and swings her right hand across in a fast, tight arc.

When she connects with the side of Ching's head, he emits a short, grunting groan. His eyes roll up in their sockets. Mei drops the sharp-cornered brick to the ground. Blood is coursing down his face from the wound to his temple. He is still on his feet.

He groans again; an odd, disconnected sound as if it's coming out of his body and not his mouth. Then he falls sideways, slamming into the pile of bricks before coming to rest on the ground. A pool of dark-red blood the colour of ripe plums spreads out beneath his head.

A hand grabs her ankle. She looks down. Dalei, is it? The one whose eye is closed and weeping a slimy mixture streaked with red. He's trying to pull himself to his feet using her leg as a support.

'I'll kill you, you little whore,' he croaks.

'Not today,' she says.

She stamps hard on his other hand and hears a crackle like dry twigs snapping.

Yowling like an alley-cat, he lets go of her ankle. Mei turns to see Ren, still rolling around, both hands clutching his private parts. Funny. She'd have thought he'd be feeling better by now. But time slows down when you're fighting. She thinks about braining him with a brick, then shakes her head. They've learned their lesson.

She's about to go, then smiles. Taps her forehead. *Silly me!*

Bending, she relieves the other two boys of their wallets and sprints away from them. She stops briefly at the group of peasants round the improvised brazier. Hands them one of the wallets.

'Here. No need to go to work today,' she says with a grin, then runs off back towards the street.

She fails to notice the new arrival among the group, a woman dressed in a dowdy blue smock and loose matching pants. Perhaps because the adrenaline is messing with her perception. Or maybe just because the woman seems so utterly insignificant, even among a boring group of country bumpkins.

4

Mei took the long route back to the rooftop she shared with Spark and half a dozen others.

Halfway down Glorious Leader Mao Street, she ducked into a shop and headed for the darkest corner. There, enveloped in the smells of spices, freshly picked herbs and salty dried fish, she watched the door for a while to see if she'd been followed by Piggy, Ducks and Uncle Sam.

She stifled a giggle. Those idiots. All that money, all that privilege and they were out of their depth the moment you took them away from the high-class shopping streets or fancy academies where they learned to be good Party capitalists.

'Hey, you!' the shop-lady cawed. 'You buying? I didn't think so. Go on, get out before I call the cops on you. Dirty creature.'

'Yeah, yeah,' Mei shot back, 'I'm going, Grandma. Don't lose your drawers.'

The old woman's toothless mouth dropped open and Mei felt a delicious thrill. Being rude to adults was pretty much her go-to way of talking. But to show such disrespect to an oldster like that? She'd fry in the afterlife for sure. Yeah, well, she wasn't there yet, was she? And she had a lot of living still to do.

She emerged, blinking, into the sunlight and turned left, relaxing into a stroll now she was sure she'd thrown off the clowns.

What would Mummy Rita think, if she could see Mei now? The thought made her laugh.

Her route would take her past the bus station. Maybe she should check for messages, like old times. Shaking her head and still grinning, she detoured into the bustling central departures hall, thronged with people rushing in every direction.

Lots of confused-looking peasants worried they'd miss their bus back to the countryside. Office workers strolling along, reading the newspaper, smoking or just striding around, heads held high, like they were the most important people in the whole of China.

The guy at the news-stand by the Number Seven bus queue was working flat out. Handing passengers their newspapers, taking crumpled bills and making change, or counting coins dropped into his palm, blackened from the cheap newsprint the Party used.

Mei sneaked round the back and crouched behind the tall red banner advertising the *People's Daily*. She bent sideways and saw a crumpled beer can. Her heart fluttered. No. It couldn't be! Most likely just an empty someone had crushed under their heel and kicked out of sight.

She stretched out an arm and retrieved it.

'Hey, you little thief! What are you doing under my stand?'

It was the news-stand guy, scowling at her and already raising his right arm, palm open.

Mei jumped to her feet.

'Just you try it,' she growled. She patted her pocket. 'I've got a knife in here. I'll use it to slice your balls off.'

The man's mouth dropped open into a round O that made Mei laugh. She sprinted away, dodging through the crowd like a little rabbit evading a wild dog.

Outside, she slowed to a walk. Running kids who looked like her always attracted the attention of the cops, and right now that was the last thing she wanted.

She turned right down a side street and found a quiet spot between two bins about halfway along. It took a little bit of effort, and sliced the pad of her thumb, but Mei managed to tear her way into the beer can.

And there, soggy from the dregs, was a slip of pink paper. She unfolded it. It was a candy wrapper. Pioneer Mint-Toffee, the writing said. And it had a picture of Chairman Mao, smiling.

Mei turned it over. On the back it bore today's date and a message.

Mei. Those men came back. They came to our house. They said if I didn't tell them where you were, they'd kill Mummy and Daddy and then me as well. I had to. I'm sorry. Ping.

Frowning, she screwed the candy wrapper into a little ball and flicked it away from her.

'Hey, honey, have you got the time?' a man asked.

She turned in surprise. Seriously? Did she *look* like the kind of girl who wore a wristwatch? She caught a flash of black. A long tube of some kind.

… *oh, shit* …

The cop's swinging baton smacked onto the top of Mei's skull.

The little red stars when Dalei had clipped her with the stave on the building site were just the warm-up act. Here was the main attraction. A glorious, agonising fireworks display: scarlet and tangerine chrysanthemums, purple streaks like jet trails, and, the big finale – the blue-black sky was torn apart by giant, taloned hands, admitting a boiling yellow fire that scorched the inside of Mei's skull and ripped her brain into tiny pieces.

Then.

Nothing.

5

'Wake up!'

Mei opened her eyes just as the toe of the cop's boot drove into her belly. She cried out, still caught halfway between sleep and waking. The pain wasn't *that* bad. It wasn't a full-fat kick. More of a wake-up call.

She realised where she was. A cell. *Been there done that*, she thought as she curled into a ball before righting herself. She shuffled her bottom along the floor until she could get into a sitting position and then stand.

'Yes, Sir,' she said, keeping her eyes down. 'Sorry, Sir.'

'Don't give me that,' he snapped. 'You're the shit on this city's boot soles, do you know that?'

'Yes, Sir.'

She risked a look up at his face, trying to see if he was one of the bored rule-followers who could be placated with politeness. Or was he one of the sadists who got off on inflicting pain? She'd been arrested by both. The trick was knowing who you were dealing with before you tried to work yourself into their good books.

His eyes were slits in a pallid, doughy face, like a steamed dumpling. He reeked of body odour and fried chicken. He grinned, revealing crooked teeth stained brown by tobacco. Her heart sank. Not a rulebook guy at all.

Outside the barred front wall of the cell, a woman sat in a chair, watching them. She looked vaguely familiar. A dusty blue peasant jacket, brown hair scraped back from a face free of makeup. Long, pointed nose like a crane's beak. Mei imagined it stabbing a fish from a shallow pond choked with reeds.

The cop looked over his shoulder and made a questioning sound in the back of his throat.

'Uh?'

The woman nodded and crossed one trousered leg over the other. Mei had time to notice that she had beautiful slim ankles.

Then the back of the cop's hand lashed out like a snake striking and caught her across the mouth, splitting her lip. She tasted blood.

Mei staggered back, but managed to stay on her feet. That was important with the beaters. On your feet, you had a chance to survive. You could roll with the punches, stagger a little as the kicks came in to absorb the worst of the force. If you fell, you were done. Diceman got caught like that the year previous; he ended up puking blood for a week.

The cop bunched a fist and smacked it into her face. She felt something go wrong in her nose. The crack sounded loud, but maybe it was only inside her head she could hear it. Now there was more blood, flooding out of her nostrils and over her top lip. She couldn't breathe through it anymore and had to open her mouth.

She fell back against the wall, spreading her arms out to keep herself from sliding sideways. It wasn't all an act. The bastard was a hard hitter and she could see from the way his mouth was slack and his eyes were shining, that he was enjoying himself.

Behind him, the woman looked on, as if she were watching a play at the theatre instead of some musclebound arsehole getting his kicks beating the shit out of a sixteen-year-old girl.

The cop grabbed her by the arms and wrenched her into an upright position. Then he delivered two fast slaps, left, right, to each side of her face. She screamed as his hard fingers dragged over her injured nose.

'Please!' she screamed, afraid, suddenly.

There was something about the way the cop was going about it that frightened her. Like he might not stop. That he might just keep going until she was dead. It happened.

Everybody knew at least one kid who'd ended up beaten to a bloody pulp and dumped in some back street for the rats and the crows to feast on. Not even for crimes like Panda's, either. Grab a bag of apples from the wrong stallholder, maybe one with a brother in the police, and you could be zipped – that's what they called it, when the cops killed one of you – for it.

He laughed, releasing another garlicky gust from between those horrible brown and grey teeth.

'Oh, you're nice and polite now, aren't you, cockroach?' he mocked. 'Should have thought of that when you stole from the children of important Party men, shouldn't you?'

He closed with her and punched her, hard, over her left breast. The pain was agonising. Tina, one of the older girls in the gang, had taught Mei how to make a sort of plastic armour out of a bucket that went between her bra and her T-shirt, but it was hot and stiff and it cut into her armpits so she didn't always wear it. Only if she knew they were meeting a rival gang for a fight.

She wished she had it on now.

'Did you like that?' the cop asked, leering at her.

Then he pinched her other nipple. Really hard. Like he wanted to pull it right off. Mei screamed. But while the cop was laughing at her, she decided she needed to fight back.

'Yeah,' she gasped, trying to ignore the pain. 'How about I give you something in return?' she asked.

That was when she lunged forward, ripped the ring of keys from the chain connecting them to a frayed belt-loop and stabbed them into his face. One, two, three – rapid, darting jabs. The first one opened a tear in the skin on the side of his nose and brought forth a scream. But the second and third ones were better. She'd got her aim in and the long shaft of the cell door key punctured his right eyeball. She pulled it back to hit him again and the eye came out, lodged on the key like a lychee on a bamboo skewer at New Year's.

Now he was roaring with pain. He staggered back, clutching his ruined eye socket. Blood was running out from between his fingers.

Mei grabbed the front of his tunic and yanked him toward her, swinging him round at the last second so he tumbled forwards, into the cell. She tripped him and sent him sprawling onto the concrete floor. His head hit the wall with a loud smack and he went still.

Mei looked down at the slimy gobbet of fibrous tissue stuck on the end of the key. With a shudder, she prised it off and dropped it to the floor then jammed the key against the lock with shaking fingers. It bounced and skittered off the metal a couple of times before, swearing and using her other hand to steady it, she slotted the key home and turned it over twice.

She spun round, ready to give the perverted bitch in the chair a good slap to keep her from running and raising the alarm. If that happened, Mei reckoned she'd last about two minutes before the other cops shot her or kicked her to death. They probably wouldn't even bother wasting bullets.

But there was no need.

6

The beaky-nosed woman had stood. But she wasn't running. Wasn't screaming. Or looking around for an alarm button to push.

Instead, she was looking at Mei the way farmers did at the livestock market. Like she was wondering whether to buy Mei, or shake her head, spit on the ground, and move on to the next deal.

Mei's chest was heaving, and it still hurt from where the cop had molested her. She was breathing through her mouth still, and wiped a hand across her nose, which came away streaked with blood and snot.

'Get away from me,' she hissed, brandishing the bunch of keys at her. 'Or I'll blind you like I did him.'

She jerked her head over her shoulders.

The woman smiled.

'No need for that, chicken,' she said, and took a step forward.

Then something strange happened. The keys disappeared from Mei's hand and reappeared in the woman's. Mei's fingers stung where the thin wire ring had dragged across the already tender skin.

'What the fuck?'

The woman nodded towards the door.

'Come with me.'

'Fuck you.'

She shrugged.

'Fine. Stay here with the dead pervert and see what that gets you,' the woman said. 'I'd say his colleagues will gang-rape you, then kick you into the next world.'

'Who are you?'

'Why do you care? I'm offering you a way out of here.' The woman nodded towards the door. 'Coming?'

Mei looked over her shoulder. The cop was face-down in a big pool of blood. The woman was right. Only someone with a death-wish would stay. And whatever the woman had planned for her, it couldn't be any worse than what the cops would dish out. Plus, she needed to get somewhere where the men from the village couldn't find her. The cop shop was the first place they'd look.

She bobbed her head once, a quick up-down.

The woman opened the door with a key of her own and strode through into a dimly-lit corridor, buzzing with flies. Mei followed her, trailing her fingertips along the painted wall, damp with condensation.

As soon as they were outside, she'd give old Beaky-nose a punch to the throat and be off on her toes, back to the gang and the sanctuary of the car park that served as their base. Then she could figure out how to keep herself hidden until the fuss with the fat man and his friend blew over.

They ascended an echoing staircase of riveted steel steps and crude welded railings. Mei looked down. In the centre of the floor at the bottom, a large dark-red stain spread out like a map. Here and there, dark lumps of something that looked like porridge were stuck in the slick.

The woman used another key to open the door at the top of the stairs. Mei took in the painted notice on the wall: STREET LEVEL. She readied herself, though the pain from her face and chest was growing worse now the buzz of the fight was gone.

They emerged into a bustling reception area. There were cops everywhere! How was Beaky-nose going to get them through that without getting arrested?

She wasn't, turned out to be the answer.

A cop with a big pistol on his belt spotted Mei and came bulling over, shoving a couple of civilians out of the way.

'Hey! Who let you out, you little—'

Beaky-nose held out a leather wallet in front of the cop's red face. He stopped dead and stared at it. Beaky-nose muttered something. Mei couldn't hear much of it, but she caught one word – 'Bureau'.

The cop turned white, like he was about to lose his lunch. He stuttered out an apology, turned on his heel and pretty much ran away.

Mei looked at Beaky-nose with a new kind of curiosity. Who the hell was she? And what kind of bureau would cause an armed cop to split like a little kid before a gang of bullies?

As if sensing that Beaky-nose wielded some serious clout, the people thronging the public area of the police station got out of her way without her having to ask.

Mei stuck close behind her, keeping her head down and trying not to bleed onto the floor. She kept dabbing at her nose: the blood seemed to have congealed on her top lip. The lip itself was still bleeding. Lips were bad, almost as bad as cuts to the scalp. *Those* bled like pigs with their throats cut, dangling over the butcher's bucket.

She peered round Beaky-nose's right hip and saw the double glass doors that led to the steps down to the street. Perfect. They were nearly out. Then a quick tap to Beaky-nose's nut and Mei would be off, running faster than she'd ever run in her life.

A hand landed on her shoulder. She whirled round. Another cop, this one with a wispy moustache and a bunch of medal ribbons and gold on his green uniform jacket. A boss-cop. Maybe the station chief. Shit! It was over.

He put his hand on his gun butt.

'Who are you, young miss?' he asked.

Mei's mind emptied. Normally quick-thinking as well as fast on her feet, her brain just checked out, like she'd forgotten how to speak. She thought back to Beaky-nose's threat. About what the cops would do to her. Felt sick.

'She's my daughter.'

Beaky-nose had turned and laid a protective hand on the top of Mei's head. They were almost the same height – everyone said Mei was tall for her age – so it felt kind of weird. But none of that mattered. Not right now.

'Has she been attacked?' the boss-cop asked, his brows creasing.

'She was knocked down by a motorcycle. We've made a complaint. Thank you.'

But the cop wasn't finished with them yet. Mei wanted to scream at him. Tell him that everything her 'mum' said was true and they just needed to leave. Her legs were trembling. She looked at the doors and briefly thought about making a run for it.

Beaky-nose slipped her hand off Mei's head and slid it around her waist. It might've looked motherly to the cop, but there was plenty of steel in that grip.

Mei didn't think Beaky-nose would have much trouble keeping her there. Something about her made Mei think her original idea that she was just some rich bitch out for kicks was way wide of the mark.

'She needs medical attention. We have a doctor here,' Boss-cop said. 'Let me take you to see her.'

Beaky-nose shook her head. 'That won't be necessary. We have an excellent doctor already.'

Boss-cop frowned. Mei watched his fingers unsnap the strap holding his pistol in place. Her belly flipped, and she felt a strong need to pee.

'You seem to be in a hurry to leave,' he said. 'Are you sure this girl is your daughter? The way you talk, you are clearly quite high class, whereas she, forgive me for saying, looks like a street kid, you know? Scruffy.'

Beaky-nose squared up to the cop. She narrowed her eyes and to Mei the expression made her look even more like a crane spotting a nice fat carp to spear.

'What is your name?'

'Pardon?'

'Your name, man! I want your full name, rank and ID number.'

Wow! Beaky-nose had stones, that was for sure. Fronting up to a station chief like that. Mei felt growing admiration for her.

Most civilians were terrified of the cops. Pretty sound, given they could snatch you off the street and throw you into a cell for just about anything they fancied. From spitting your chewing gun out in the street to not bowing when you passed a portrait of Chairman Mao, even though the old fart had been out of power since way before Mei had been born.

But Boss-cop wasn't impressed. The gun came out of its holster. It dangled by his side, but Mei could see how this was going to go down. She got ready to run.

First she'd have to get Beaky-nose's claws off her waist, then she could sprint for the doors. She would shove a couple of people on the way out, get them screaming and panicking, running around like chickens with their heads chopped off and getting under the cops' feet.

Boss-cop raised his pistol and shoved it into Beaky-nose's midriff.

'My name is Mr I'm-In-Charge-Of-Everyone-And-Everything-In-This-Police-Station,' he said.

Beaky-nose glanced at Mei and mouthed a single word. *Ready?*

Mei nodded.

Boss-cop grinned and shoved the gun into Beaky-nose's belly a second time.

'My rank is so high, I could take a shit over your head and it would take an hour to land.'

Beaky-nose mouthed another word. *Balls.*

Mei nodded. She sensed they'd be leaving very soon. At speed.

Boss-cop waggled the pistol in Beaky-nose's face.

'And my ID number is—'

Without looking down, Beaky-nose nodded.

Mei drew back her fist and punched Boss-cop as hard as she could, right in the nuts. He yelled out and clutched his groin with both hands. Which he could do because, somehow, Beaky-nose was now holding the pistol by the barrel.

As he crumpled in front of them, Beaky-nose smacked the butt down onto the top of his head. He crashed to the floor as all around them, people screamed and scuffled, some fleeing, others crowding closer, trying to see what all the fuss was about.

Mei gave him a kick in the face for good measure, then she turned and quick-stepped after Beaky-nose, who was firing the cop's pistol into the air as she strode towards the doors. She pushed through, sticking the pistol into her waistband. Mei followed and they were free.

She thought she'd stick close to Beaky-nose until they were well clear of the cop shop. She had some impressive street-fighting skills as well as a borrowed set of balls as big as an ox's. But once they were out of danger, Mei intended to get herself gone.

A minute or two later and Mei was sure it was time to go. She timed her moment perfectly. They were in a quiet stretch of the street, between two blocks of down-at-heel shops. Beaky-nose had her back to Mei.

Mei focused on her target. A magic spot just underneath the back of the skull, where it dipped in towards the top of the neck. Hit somebody there with enough force and they went down like a sack of coal.

She bunched her fist.

And she swung.

7

She'd used the strike before on rival gang members and it always worked like a charm. But not this time. Her fist flew wide of the target. Like it had a mind of its own.

Then she saw Beaky-nose's clawed hand clamped tight to her wrist.

Mei's hand kept on travelling and then pulling her down. She found herself bent over with her right palm flat on the pavement, Beaky-nose's left foot crushing it into the hot concrete. Her face was almost touching the ground. She was close enough to see the dirty blobs of used chewing gum, greyed with the passage of many feet.

Beaky-nose squatted beside her. Up close, she smelled of lavender. Something glinted in between Mei's eyes. This close it was out of focus, but she knew what it was all the same.

'I could take your eyes out with this a lot easier than you did with that key,' she said in a conversational tone. 'Try anything like that again and I will. Run and I'll catch you. Then I'll slit you open like a fish and pull your guts out on the street. Are we clear?'

Mei grunted, trying to free her trapped hand. The knife actually grazed Mei's left eyelid, making her draw in a quick breath.

'I said, are we clear?'

'Yes.'

'Good girl.'

The knife vanished. The shoe came off Mei's knuckles. She got to her feet, rubbing the back of her hand and glared at Beaky-nose.

'Who the fuck are you?'

The woman smiled.

'I bet you're hungry. Let's get some noodles.'

Mei's mouth dropped open. Was she for real? This was like one of those dopey comic books Spark liked so much, where starving peasant children met a Party official or maybe a kindly soldier in the PLA and they gave them food to eat and medical supplies and everyone sang patriotic songs at the end. At the thought of her friend, tears sprang to her eyes.

'Is he OK?'

'Who, the cop? He'll be fine. Does them good to remind them who's in charge from time to time,' she said. 'Not sure your gaoler's going to be dipping his wick again though. You did for him good and proper.'

'No,' Mei said. 'Spark. My friend, I mean. He got hit by a car. Were you following us?'

Beaky-nose pooched out her thin lips. 'Was that his name? Spark?'

'Yes.'

'Sorry, dear. I'm afraid his spark went out.'

Mei knew it, really. Had done since she saw him lying there with his head all funny. But she hadn't been able to give up hope. Not until she knew for sure. The tears over-ran her eyes and tracked down her cheeks, hot despite the sun on her face.

They all swore there was no point having friends on the street. It was just asking for trouble. One minute you'd be best mates, nicking fruit off market stalls or rolling business types for their wallets and watches; the next, one of you would be lying in the gutter, stabbed by a rival or shot by the cops. Or just dead of some illness. It happened. It was life.

But with Spark, it had been different. They'd met on Mei's first morning in Shenzhen after leaving the village.

She'd arrived after walking and hitching rides on farmers' trucks and ox-carts all night. In a single day she'd gone from sharing living space with Mummy Rita, a cat and two mangy dogs, with chickens and pigs wandering freely in the mud outside, to living on her wits in a concrete megacity that stretched to the horizon.

She'd been eyeing up the hot, sugar-dusted doughnuts on a cart beside a pedestrian crossing, then Spark had grabbed her by the elbow and drawn her back.

'Not that one,' he'd whispered with a ferrety grin. 'He pays protection to the cops. Steal a doughnut off him and you'll end up drinking soup through a straw for the rest of your life.'

He'd taken her to a different street and pointed out a different snack vendor.

'You like soft-shell crab?' he'd asked.

'I don't know. What is it?'

He smiled. 'Delicious! Here's what to do.'

She'd bent her head closer to his as he explained her job. Smiling in anticipation and feeling a squirm of excitement replacing the hunger gnawing at her insides, she nodded eagerly.

She looked around and saw what she wanted. In the gutter lay a round pebble the size of an apricot. She picked it up and weighed it in her hand, enjoying the sensation of the warm, smooth stone in her hand.

She advanced to within five metres of the crab-man and yelled at him.

'Hey! Do you scratch those crabs off your diseased prick before you fry them?'

Then, for good measure, she hurled the pebble. It struck him dead-centre in the chest.

Eyes wide, he swore at her: a stream of filth that made the cussing at the village bar seem like nursery-school rhymes.

He rounded the stainless-steel cart and came after her, waving a cleaver. Laughing, and sending more insults flying over her shoulder, she dashed down the alley the boy had pointed out. She could hear the crab-man's heavy footsteps slapping on the pavement. Halfway down the alley, she dodged down an even narrower passage, little more than a slot between two drab, grey buildings. He'd never get himself down here and, besides, he'd want to go back to his cart.

She shimmied down the passage and pushed her way clear at the far end, into a little courtyard surrounded by tall apartment blocks, festooned with drying laundry and straggling plants in brightly-coloured plastic pots.

Panting, she sat with her back to a grimy white dumpster and waited.

When after two minutes the kid didn't appear, she started to think she'd been tricked into helping the kid rob the crab-man for his own ends. Then he appeared, grinning triumphantly, fists clamped around bundles of shining, greasy, battered…things. Long jointed legs. Flat bodies.

He scooched down beside her and opened his hands. Up close, the snacks looked even *more* like…she shuddered. She didn't want to think about it. She hated those scuttlers. Always had. Mummy Rita used to chide her for it, but it was no good.

'Those are soft-shell crabs?' she asked doubtfully.

'What else? Try one, they're delicious.'

'They look like,' she inhaled sharply, 'spiders.'

He laughed, showing white teeth all the way to the back of his mouth.

'Oh, man, you kill me. They're crabs! Look, I'll show you.'

He picked up one of the fried creatures and bit off a leg, chewed vigorously while rolling his eyes and making '*mmm*' noises, then swallowed. He took another bite, then another, saving the body till last. He popped it into his mouth and chewed for a while, actually closing his eyes and groaning.

'Let me try one,' she said.

He held out his cupped hands, and Mei selected a small one. She raised it to her lips and at once caught the delicious aroma of salt, soy, and seafood.

She hadn't eaten much fish at Mummy Rita's. They tended to eat land animals off the farms. Duck sometimes. Maybe the odd catfish or eel if someone had gone out fishing. But once, a traveller had come to the village with a plastic tank of salt water on a trolley.

They'd gathered round while he showed them these crazy-looking animals jostling at the bottom of the container. They were spotty, blue and cream, with whip antennae on their heads like beetles had. And they had millions of legs with two super-big ones at the front with claws like the tools the butcher used to castrate the pigs.

Mummy Rita had exclaimed happily and bought a fat one. She boiled a big pot of water on the fire and when it was steaming and the bubbles were just plopping to the surface, she dropped the creature in.

It made a loud, hissing sound. Mei asked if it was angry, but Mummy Rita explained it was just steam escaping from its shell, and that a lobster – that's what she called it – didn't have feelings, anyway.

Mummy Rita showed Mei how to crack the shell and pull out the meat. The legs were fiddly, but, once she'd tasted that sweet, succulent flesh, Mei got down to business with a pair of pliers and a skewer.

The soft-shell crab reminded her of the lobster. The batter was crunchy and flavoured with garlic and chilli, but that just added to the delight she felt as she ate her first meal in Shenzhen.

She sniffed.

Poor Spark. All he wanted to do was light fires and hang around with Mei, and now he was dead.

She rubbed her eyes and looked at Beaky-nose.

'He was my friend,' she said.

'You'll make other friends,' she replied. 'Now, we can't go and eat with you looking like that, can we?'

She pulled a packet of hygienic wipes from her jacket pocket. The kind that came in a flat plastic pouch printed with yellow flowers and were soaked in disinfectant, or perfume, or whatever. Stinky, anyway.

Holding her gently under the chin, she tilted Mei's face up towards the sky and started wiping her cheeks. Mei caught the tang of whatever the tissue factory had put on the wipe. Lemony. Maybe a bit chemical-y too.

'Hold still, this might sting a little.'

She dabbed at Mei's lower lip. Mei winced, but didn't make a sound. You didn't show fear, and you didn't show pain. They were weaknesses an enemy could use against you.

'Good girl,' Beaky-nose murmured as she worked, and Mei felt an odd sense of pride, as though this woman's praise mattered to her.

She moved onto Mei's nose.

Mei winced.

'Is it broken?'

'No. He just caught you a good one.'

'But I heard something. In my head.'

'Just the cartilage moving. It's fine. Now, hold still.'

In this way, using swift, efficient, but not unkind strokes, Beaky-nose cleaned Mei's face and finished off by wiping her palms with a fresh tissue.

Mei smiled at her.

'Thank you.'

'You're welcome. Hungry?'

'Starving.'

8

Beaky-nose took Mei into a small cafe. She walked confidently, like she owned the place. Head high, looking left and right, picking out a table. She led Mei to the back and sat facing the door and gestured for Mei to take the chair opposite her.

The owner came over in a quick, shuffling walk, his sandaled feet making a hissing noise as they slid over the floor tiles.

'Two house specials,' Beaky-nose said.

The man raised his eyebrows. 'Sorry, Ma'am, we don't have a house special. I can offer noodles with shrimp, pork, chicken, squid, duck, whatever you like.'

'Bring me whatever you serve to the staff. Big bowls. And jasmine tea.'

He nodded and walked away, pushing through a curtain of dangling multicoloured plastic strips that clattered quietly. Mei heard him shouting the order.

'Who are you, please?' Mei asked again.

She chose to be more polite this time. That business with the knife hadn't scared her, not exactly. But she'd formed a more respectful opinion of Beaky-nose, who had, after all, saved her from being raped and kicked to death in the cop shop.

Beaky-nose smiled.

'I bet you've got a nickname for me already. What is it? Long-nose? Egret?'

Mei shook her head. She was about to lie and say that she hadn't, then she caught the look behind the woman's eyes. A sharp look that suggested to Mei that lying would be unwise at this point.

Keeping her eyes down, and picking at a loose bit of skin on the side of her middle finger, she told her.

'Beaky-nose,' she mumbled.

The woman laughed. A rough-edged caw that made Mei think of birds all over again.

'Well, you are an honest girl, that's good. And it's far from the worst I've been called,' she said. 'My students call me the Crane.'

Mei nodded. It was a good nickname. Better than hers. She glanced up at the woman. She supposed she *could* be a teacher. But did teachers really watch cops beat up girls and then tell them to attack the police chief? On the whole, she thought not.

'But what's your *real* name, Ma'am?' she asked.

'What's yours?'

'Wei Mei.'

'Very well, Mei,' she extended her hand. 'I am Du Minxia. But you will call me Ma'am, as you have been doing.'

Mei frowned. Was she supposed to shake hands like she saw the business types do? Beaky-nose waggled her fingers. Mei gave a sort of mental shrug. *OK, then.* She took the woman's hand and they shook like two suits doing a deal.

The cafe owner reappeared and placed two steaming bowls of noodles heaped with fried chicken feet and soft, see-through greens before them.

Mei's stomach growled so loudly the two adults both heard. Cafe-man laughed as she blushed and clapped a hand to her stomach.

'Eat it all up, girl. Sounds like you need it.'

She took up her chopsticks and started eating, pausing only to wipe her chin clear of drops of the delicious broth in which bits of scarlet chilli, onion and coriander floated.

Du Minxia picked a chicken foot up and neatly scissored off a toe with her front teeth. She chewed and swallowed, all the time looking at Mei as if she were still a beast she was considering buying.

'Are your parents alive?'

'My mum is. I don't know about my dad,' Mei said after swallowing a spoonful of the richly-flavoured broth. 'Mummy Rita said he stayed behind.'

'In Hong Kong? Rita's an Islander's name.'

'I don't know, Ma'am. I think so.'

Du Minxia stretched out a finger and put her nail under the point of Mei's chin to tilt it up a little towards the overhead light. Then she stretched the skin at the inner corner of Mei's eye.

Mei tried not to flinch, remembering the threat about taking her eye out with the knife. Du Minxia tipped her own head on one side. It made her look even more like a crane. Whoever the kids were at her school, they'd got that name just right.

'Mummy Rita's full Chinese, yes?'

'Yes, Ma'am.'

'Did she tell you anything about your dad?'

'No, Ma'am.'

'Was he a Westerner? British? American, maybe?'

'I'm sorry, Ma'am, I don't know.'

But she knew what the lady with the bony hands was on about.

Her eyes.

Some of the other kids had asked her about her looks. Meaner ones called her a half-breed on account of how Mei's eyes looked almost like a *gweilo*'s. Rounder than their own.

Mind you, they only asked once. After their noses had stopped bleeding, or their balls had returned to their normal position, they didn't ask her again.

'It doesn't matter,' the lady said. 'In fact, it could be useful. Ah, tea!'

The cafe owner placed a dark-green china pot with a bamboo handle on the table between them and a tiny white cup before each

45

of them. He poured, keeping his head bowed. Then left them to their strange conversation.

'Ma'am?'

'Yes, Mei?'

'This school you teach at. Is it for normal kids?'

'Why do you ask?'

Mei shrugged. 'I'm not a normal kid. I haven't been to school since even before I left the village. Now I live out there,' she said, pointing at the door of the cafe.

The lady smiled. 'That's why I want you.'

'But what *kind* of school is it?'

'It's a school where very special children, very talented children, go to learn how they can help our country,' she said. 'They learn how to protect our country from its enemies. Do you know much about how the world works, Mei?'

Mei shook her head. 'I'm sorry, Ma'am. Not really. I know how Shenzhen works, and how the village worked, but nothing else.'

'Don't worry. We'll teach you. But what you must understand, my little fighter, is that China has many enemies, both within and without its borders. Bad people who want to change her, weaken her, make her citizens poorer and take away all that we have striven for.'

It all sounded terrible to Mei. Enemies? She pictured dragons like in the village storyteller's tales, roaring and breathing fire and snarling with yellow fangs dripping with strings of poison and eating children who didn't go to bed on time.

Then she pictured a building, like the little village school only a thousand times bigger; like everything else in Shenzhen.

A massive concrete block with tiny little windows and the faces of all the children held prisoner inside, forced to learn sums and history and writing and play sports and sing songs while the teachers stalked up and down between the rows of desks, whacking slow learners with a cane or a leather strap.

Enemies, or not, that sounded worse than being eaten by a dragon.

'What if I don't want to go to the school?' she asked. Then hastily added, 'Ma'am.'

Du Minxia smiled as she laid her chopsticks and bamboo spoon in her empty noodle bowl.

'Then I will take you back to the police station and hand you over personally to the police captain. I'm sure he'll be pleased to see you again. You see, Mei. Life is full of choices. You chose to leave your little village. You chose to leave Mummy Rita and all your friends there,' she said, counting off all the choices Mei had made on the tips of her bony fingers. 'And the animals, and the fields where you used to play when you should have been in school. You chose to come to Shenzhen and make your living on the streets. You chose to rob the son of a very important man. You chose to fight back. You chose to kill the policeman who wanted to abuse you. Now you have another choice. You can choose to come with me to the school where I work. Or you can choose to stand trial for your crimes, if you last that long. It's up to you.'

Mei looked down at her bowl. It was nearly all gone. Her belly was full, properly full, for the first time in days. She imagined they probably fed the kids at this school.

Then she thought about the men coming to the village, threatening Ping. Getting her to tell them where Mei had gone.

She looked up at Du Minxia.

And she chose.

9

Mei opened her eyes. Sunlight was streaming through the window.

No curtains, not that it bothered her. Back when she was living at the carpark with Spark, Tina, Panda and the rest, they didn't have curtains there, either. They woke up at dawn, scrounged breakfast and went to bed whenever they felt like it. If someone had had a good day and bought some speed, they might stay up all night.

She looked around without raising her head. Because that was another thing. She had a proper bed, with sheets, and a soft pillow under her head. If this was what school was like, she reckoned she could handle it.

A clock on the wall ticked away the seconds, like at the railway station in Shenzhen: 6.30 a.m. – a good hour to be up. She climbed out of bed and gasped as her bare feet hit the floor. Cold ceramic tiles, a sort of clay-red colour.

The dark-blue pyjama trousers they'd given her were tight round her waist. She stuck her thumb inside the band and pulled it away from her belly. She looked down. The elastic had left marks in a circle, uneven strips of red and pale skin. She rubbed the tip of her forefinger along the bumpy surface.

She'd never slept in her own room before. This was a first. There wasn't much to look at. Apart from the bed, it contained a chair and a desk and a plain wooden bookshelf: two upright planks and three shelves running between them.

Mei crossed the room to the window. She pressed her nose against the glass and stared down into a courtyard. A group of people, children, she realised, marched across from right to left, swinging their arms as if they were soldiers. They were all dressed alike, in green tunics and wide, flapping trousers. Black shoes, plimsolls, maybe.

Marching off to one side was an adult. A man. He was carrying a long black stick and he was conducting them with it, swinging it, twirling around his head, sometimes thrusting out in front of him.

They wheeled left, then right, then came to a halt. Even through the glass, Mei heard the thump as their feet all slapped down onto the concrete in time.

Were they the other students? If they were, it must be some kind of military school. Which made sense. The Crane had told her it was a school for special children who learned how to fight China's enemies. What was that phrase she used? 'Within and without?' Something like that.

Mei didn't really fancy being a soldier. All that marching about looked pretty dumb. As she watched, one of the kids in the front row swayed, then fell forwards into the grit.

The kids either side stepped forwards to help, but before they could do anything, the man stepped forward and slashed his stick backwards and forwards, catching each one a solid whack round the bottom with it. They leaped back into line.

He walked up to the fallen kid and toed their side, prodding like you would if you found a dog lying at the side of the road. Just checking it was really dead.

Then he squatted down and rolled the kid over and Mei saw it was a boy. At this distance she could make out his short haircut and the general shape of his features, but that was about all.

The man stood. Mei was relieved. She thought he'd been going to slap the kid, or punch him in the face. Then she realised he was

50

going to get a couple of the others to carry him to the sick bay or the infirmary, or whatever military types called it.

A gun appeared in his hand. He pointed it down at the boy's head and pulled the trigger. Through the glass, the noise was a pop. All the other kids stood completely still. Mei recoiled from the window, hand clamped to her face.

He'd killed him! Just for fainting. Shit! She had to get out of here. Then she realised the awful truth.

The Crane had gone to the trouble of springing Mei from the cell at the cop shop. Then feeding her up till she could hardly walk. Driving her out of the city, blindfolding her for the last hour. Then leading her to a clean, secure room with a real bed.

They'd hardly let her just walk out the front gates with a cheerful, 'See you all later!' would they?

Still shocked by what she'd just witnessed, she wandered over to the bookshelf. Three books stood side-by-side on the middle shelf, leaning against the plank. She pulled out the first one: small, bound in red plastic with a face on it everyone in China recognised, even though he'd been dead for years. *Quotations From Chairman Mao Tse-Tung*. Boring! She tossed it onto the bed.

The next book looked just as dull. Brown paper cover, pretty battered. Plain black writing. *The Art of War*. By some guy she'd never heard of. Sun Tzu. She tossed it aside.

The third looked more interesting. The cover depicted a girl of about Mei's age, maybe a little younger. She was standing over a guy who was either dead or not far off it to judge from the blood spreading out under his chest. The girl was looking down at the man and holding a...Mei squinted. Was that a pencil in her hand?

She read the title. *Weaponless Killing: Tools, Tactics and Techniques*. As she took in the author's name, her eyes widened. Du Minxia. She backed up until her calves hit the edge of the bed. She sat and opened the book.

The first page was headed, *Introduction: A Note From the Author*. And below it, looking sternly out from the grainy printed surface of the cheap paper, was the woman who had bought Mei chicken and noodles.

Mei read the first sentence, grateful once more that Mummy Rita had forced her, sometimes at the point of a knife, to sit with her books and, 'Learn, girl, learn! It might save your life one day'. As she did, the room faded, along with the sounds leaking into the room from beyond the glass.

* * *

There is nothing clever or remarkable about shooting someone dead.

Any fool can kill with a gun.

One round, a close-range shot, a rudimentary knowledge of anatomy, and the job is done.

Knives are no better.

A child can take a life, given a narrow enough point or a sharp enough edge.

Bows. Axes. Swords.

All excellent killing weapons. All with their advantages. All with their uses.

All with the same limitation.

They look like weapons. An enemy sees you carrying one and is instantly on their guard.

If captured, you will be relieved of your weapons. And if you rely on such weapons, you will be denied your goals.

But there are other ways of killing. Ways just as effective, just as quick, just as deadly. Ways that are also silent or undetectable or natural.

Best of all, ways that are available everywhere. Freely. In places where you may be confined. In your enemy's own stronghold. On their body. Or yours.

This manual explains them all.

How to find them. How to use them. How to disguise them. How to get rid of them.

Study the text and the diagrams. But, most importantly, study the photographs. THEY ARE NOT STAGED.

And remember this.

Your enemy may be bigger than you. More powerful than you. Better armed than you.

None of this matters as long as you are better at killing than they are.

The lion has an impressive mane, a loud roar, frightening fangs and claws. But, worldwide, more people are killed by the mosquito.

Du Minxia
Instructor
School for Technical Studies, 2nd Intelligence Bureau, People's Liberation Army

* * *

Mei closed the book and studied the cover photograph. Closer, this time. Yes, it was a pencil gripped in the girl's fist. The dead man's eyes were open, but blank. Staring sightlessly at the ceiling.

Mei nodded, impressed. The girl, maybe fifteen or so, had killed the man with a pencil. Maybe he'd been going to rape her like those Party kids at the building site. Or beat her to death, like the cop at the station.

Or, that phrase again, 'enemies within and without' came to mind, in Du Minxia's quiet, insistent voice. He was an enemy of China. Probably a Russian, or maybe an American.

Everybody knew about the Americans. They hated China because it had grown rich and found a way to feed its people without capitalism.

Mei hadn't even heard that word until she came to the city. But one of the kids, who they called Brains, used to sit them down after they'd eaten, maybe a bit high on stolen liquor or some weed if someone had scored. And he'd tell them stories about what he called 'the big wide world'.

Brains knew about everything. But his favourite topic was what he called politics. He told them how China was different from the other big countries. He said they were like beasts fighting over territory or food, or mates – *Ugh! Disgusting!*

The main ones were China, obviously. Also America. Japan. And Russia.

Europe was another one, but it wasn't much to worry about because it wasn't really a beast at all. More like a colony of birds. Lots of separate little countries banded together. Dangerous, but easy to defeat because they were always squabbling among themselves.

Brains explained patiently how different beasts had different ways of seeing the world. China's was best. But the other ways kind of worked. The one he talked about most was capitalism. That was what America and Japan had. He said it made them dangerous.

Mei always thought it sounded cool. She kept her thoughts to herself. Unlike the others, she'd come from Hong Kong. Mummy Rita told her stories about the place she called 'our true home'.

How you could buy this drink called Ko Kakola that prickled your tongue and tasted sweeter than lychees? A black liquid with little bubbles that hissed like a snake when you opened it.

They had tons of different chocolate bars, too. Fancy cars from America and Japan. And you were free to do what you liked. No secret police. No Party to tell you how to think.

Mei thought some of Mummy Rita's stories sounded a bit far-fetched, like she was just making stuff up to make Mei go to sleep. But, on the whole, Mei believed her. There were just too many details that stayed the same whatever story she was telling.

The ones Mei liked the best weren't about Ko Kakola or candy bars or Japanese cars. They were about the triads.

10

Mummy Rita had explained that she used to work for a triad, along with her husband, whose name was Dennis. Triads were gangs: that was easy enough to understand. Mei had been the leader of a gang in the village. Half the time when she was skipping school, she was off in the forest or the paddy fields with the gang.

Mei's gang was called The Blue Tigers. She'd thought it up herself. But Mummy Rita's gang, her triad, was called The Four-Point Star.

According to Mummy Rita, triads helped their local communities. They protected them from other gangs and also sorted out neighbourhood disputes. They ran laundries and restaurants and shops and places where people went to enjoy themselves after work. Once, Mei asked how they got enough money to do all that and Mummy Rita just tapped the side of her nose and winked at Mei.

'Business,' was her cryptic reply.

Probably she thought Mei didn't know what *business* meant. But Mummy Rita didn't know everything. Business was when you bought stuff off someone else and then sold it to another someone else for more yuan than you paid for it. Funnily enough, Brains said that was also how capitalism worked.

It sounded like a great idea, although Mei wasn't entirely sure how you made something worth more than it was when you bought it.

Since moving to Shenzhen, Mei's understanding of the world had skyrocketed. You couldn't stay a country bumpkin for long in the city or you'd die like a rat under someone's boot. Now she knew all about how adult gangs worked.

She knew they were into big-time crime. Serious stuff. Sometimes they had the cops in their pockets, despite all the official bullshit about being true to Mao Thought and the purity of the Chinese Communist system.

She knew that the places adults went after work for fun were the bars, gambling dens, drug hangouts and brothels.

The last were the worst. Disgusting men *doing it* with women, and sometimes girls, girls as young as Mei, even. Paying for it, too, although that didn't bother her as much as the raw facts of what they got up to.

Mei closed the book and replaced it on the shelf. She turned at the sound of a key turning in the lock. The Crane stood there, dressed as the day before in a simple two piece outfit of faded blue cotton, with black plimsolls on her feet.

'Get dressed,' she said, dropping some folded clothes onto the bed.

Mei wondered if she was going to leave her alone to change, but when the Crane made no move to go, she slipped out of the pyjamas and dressed in the clothes the Crane had arrived with.

Come with me,' the Crane said, 'there's someone I want you to meet.'

Mei's stomach was growling, but she ignored it. Going without breakfast was pretty much her standard start to the day, and she assumed there'd be food later.

Mei followed the Crane out of the room and down a narrow corridor. The walls were bare, painted a shiny green like apples.

Halfway down, they passed a boy swabbing the floor with a dirty mop that he kept sploshing into a tin bucket.

She tried to catch his eye, but he kept his head down and waited for them to pass before starting up again, the mop making a quiet swishing sound as he swung it back and forth.

Mei wondered whether he was a cleaner. Or was he a student at the school? They did chores as well as lessons: seemed fair enough. Unless he was being punished somehow.

She didn't have time to wonder anymore. The Crane turned to her.

'Hurry up!'

Mei quickened her pace obediently, though they were already marching along at a fair clip. Must be someone important they were going to see. The head teacher, most likely. It was interesting to Mei that the Crane seemed nervous, to judge from her tightened lips and the almost-trot she'd broken into.

Maybe she was frightened of the head teacher. It would make sense. Probably a Party official as well as a school-boss. That's how it worked: everybody knew. Even back in the village. All the good jobs went to people with Party connections.

The Crane led her through a door and into an echoey concrete stairwell. She took the stairs two at a time, in a flowing movement that was fast and silent at the same time.

Mei followed, and in this way they ascended four flights, their plimsolls slapping lightly on the smooth concrete steps until they reached a landing where the Crane, instead of turning anticlockwise again, pushed through a plain wooden door and led Mei into another corridor.

On the walls, pictures hung. Chairman Mao. Smiling workers, pausing from their jobs in a factory to point to the sun shining just at the edge of the painting. A photo of some kind of military parade, with several long, green trucks, each with a rocket on its back.

The Crane stopped outside a door on which was printed a single word:

Director

Mei supposed a director was like a head teacher. Perhaps they did things differently in the city.

The Crane looked Mei up and down, stretching out a slender hand to pick a piece of fluff off the front of her tunic. Then she did a funny sort of jerky thing with her neck, stretching and straightening it, that made Mei want to laugh. Finally, she turned to the door and knocked three times in a sharp, *rat-tat-tat* pattern.

'Come!'

The voice that pierced the wood like an arrow was male. Plenty of authority in it, too. He was used to giving orders and having them obeyed. Mei corrected herself. Obeyed *immediately*.

11

The Crane twisted the door knob, then ushered Mei inside by placing her hand in the small of her back and giving her a gentle, but insistent shove.

Facing the door was a simple wooden desk. The man behind it had a full head of thick, dark hair. Black-framed glasses magnified his eyes. A bulbous nose sat over a wide, fat-lipped mouth.

Another animal nickname leaped into Mei's head. The Frog. She knew she would never be able to think of him as anything else. A smile threatened to worm its way onto her lips. Somehow, she knew that would be a very bad idea and bit the inside of her cheek to stifle it.

The man wore a dark tunic over a white shirt. No tie, although the top button was done up. She tried to read his expression, but gave up. His face was like a pond that didn't offer a reflection back: just dark, murky depths.

'This is the final recruit for this year's intake, Director,' the Crane said, from a position just behind Mei's left shoulder. 'A street child.'

The director stood, walked round the desk and stood to one side so that Mei had to turn to face him.

'What is your name?' he asked.

His voice was warm. She wouldn't say kind, not exactly, but it was OK.

'Wei Mei, Sir.'

'Pretty,' he said, nodding. 'From now on, you are Twelve.'

'Actually, I'm sixteen, Sir,' she said.

The slap was so fast she didn't realise he'd hit her until after his hand had returned to his side. Not hard, though. She clutched her left cheek, which was burning.

'Your *name* is Twelve,' he said, calmly, as if nothing had happened. 'After this, Miss Du will take you to meet the other students in your cohort. There are eleven of them. Understand?'

Keeping her head bowed, she murmured, 'Yes, Sir.'

'Good. We're making progress already. And progress is good, yes? Progress defines China.'

'Yes, Sir.'

So this was how he liked to play it. Dumb little power games to show everyone who was in charge. That was fine. She could play those sorts of games in her sleep.

'What did you do to earn your place at the School for Technical Studies?'

Mei didn't know what he wanted to hear, and braced for another blow. The Crane saved her, though.

'Tell Director Gao why you were arrested.'

Mei nodded. Now she understood. They'd picked her because of what she'd done to those Party kids, maybe the cops, too. What the hell kind of school was this? And the answer presented itself just as quickly. A school for delinquents.

Her heart sank. Whatever ideas she'd been entertaining about having some fun vanished like morning mist off the village carp pond. This was nothing more than a punishment place. Where they sent kids who didn't fit in at regular schools.

That didn't fit in with Mei's plans *at all*. She resolved to escape the first chance she got. But first she had to say the right thing. Something told her lying would be the wrong course of action.

'Three boys were going to rape me, Sir. I fought them off. Then

I was arrested. A policeman was also going to rape me and I defended myself.'

'Twelve is being modest,' the Crane said from behind her. 'The boys were older and bigger than her. Two are being treated at Shenzhen Hospital Number Six.'

'And the third?' the director asked, one eyebrow raised.

'At the morgue, Sir. She delivered a perfect temple strike with a brick.'

'The cop?'

'Dead. She relieved him of the cell door key and put it through his eye.'

Mei hadn't realised the boy she'd smacked in the head was dead. Sure, there was a lot of blood, but everyone knew head wounds bled like anything.

She wasn't sure how she felt about it. Not good. Not exactly. But not bad, either. If she hadn't, he *would* have raped her. And the others, too. No. She was right to hit him. He brought it on himself. As for the cop, he'd definitely asked for it.

'What is that, Twelve?' the director asked.

'Sir?'

'You frowned. What were you thinking? That they deserved their fate?'

That was spooky. How the hell did he know what she'd been thinking? More honesty was called for.

'Yes, Sir.'

'Yet you stole the boy's wallet. Or that of his friend, at any rate. That makes you a criminal, does it not?' he asked. 'Do Mao and his successors not exhort us to punish those who seek to enrich themselves without contributing work to society?'

Mei wasn't sure about all the words the director was using. Especially 'exhort', but she caught the gist.

'Yes, Sir. But...' She hesitated. Arguing with the Frog seemed like a really bad idea.

'But what, Twelve?'

Mei could feel her stomach knotting, as she anticipated another slap – or worse. She felt hot. The man standing slightly too close to her was looking down at her as if she were some kind of interesting specimen he'd pulled out of a ditch or a drainage pond.

'Answer the director!' the Crane snapped.

Inspiration struck. Brains had told them all kinds of stuff about Chairman Mao during their rooftop drinking sessions. And the Crane had spoken of China's enemies.

'Chairman Mao was a soldier, Sir. He fought against China's enemies,' she said, hoping she could cobble something together that might please the director. 'For progress. Like you said. Those boys said their fathers were Party officials, but they were going to do bad things in its name. To rape me. A young girl. So was the cop. They left me no choice. I had to fight my enemies, like Chairman Mao did.'

It was the longest speech she'd uttered since being arrested. She could feel her heart hammering in her chest and was sure if she looked down, she'd see the thin cotton at the front of her tunic fluttering in time with its frantic beating.

She waited. Anticipating the air rushing past her cheek as his right hand swept across in another blow, harder, this time, she was sure of it.

So when he croaked out a laugh, she was momentarily puzzled. It wasn't supposed to be funny, what she'd said.

She risked a glance over her shoulder, at the Crane. She wasn't laughing, but her thin lips had curved upwards a little. Something in her eyes reassured Mei that she'd passed the test, whatever it was. A little crinkle at their outer corners. A spark that had ignited in their deep-brown depths.

She snapped her head round, eyes front again.

'Tough *and* quick-thinking,' the director said at last. 'And you know a little history. Yes, I think you will do very well here, Twelve. Very well indeed.' He pointed at a hard chair in front of the desk. 'Sit.'

'Do you need me, Director?' the Crane asked.

'No. You are dismissed.'

She nodded and left, turning smartly on her heel and closing the door quietly behind her.

Instead of returning to his side of the desk, the director pulled the chair round the desk and positioned it a foot or so away from Mei. Then he took hold of the back of her own chair and swivelled it around in a quarter-circle.

When he sat down, their knees were almost touching. This close, she could see two hairs growing in the crease between his thick black eyebrows, just above the greasy nosepiece of his glasses.

'Do you wonder what sort of work we do here, Twelve?' he asked.

'Miss Du said you fight China's enemies. But I don't understand how a school can do that. Sir,' she added quickly.

He pursed his thick lips. Then he stood, rounded the desk and opened a drawer. She couldn't see what he was doing, but she heard something heavy scrape along its wooden bottom.

He pulled out a black pistol and clunked it onto the desk by her right elbow, before coming back to sit opposite her. The gun drew her eye. She couldn't drag her gaze away from it. She'd never handled one before, but she'd seen plenty.

The cops all carried, obviously. Sometimes, if the street kids got tangled up with the wrong people, guns would be produced and threats made. Kids would run, screaming and laughing as warning shots were fired above their heads.

'Pick it up,' the director said, jerking Mei back to the present.

She stretched out a hand and curled her fingers around the handle. It was heavy when she lifted it off the desk. Not so heavy she couldn't hold it up, but it had a sort of *weightiness* to it, like it was pulling her hand closed around it. Like it wanted to be a part of her.

She curled her finger around the trigger. Maybe she should just shoot him now and make a run for it. She could get outside into the yard and then run for the gate. Nobody would stop her if she had a gun. Then she remembered the man who'd shot the kid outside her bedroom window. So she'd have to be quiet about it. Stealthy; like an alley-cat stalking a rat.

She turned to face the director. And dammit if he didn't have that weirdo mind-reading expression like before when he asked if she'd thought the Party kid deserved to be killed.

'Point it at me,' he said, in a mild voice, like he was asking her to pour him some jasmine tea.

'Sir?'

He smiled, revealing tobacco-stained teeth. 'Point it at my face.'

It was a trap. Had to be. Probably the gun didn't have any bullets. Or else it was rigged up to fire backwards or some other shit that would end up with her dead and him laughing that 'yuck-yuck' laugh of his.

She let the gun lie in her lap, though she didn't loosen her grip.

'Now!' he barked.

Startled, she held the gun up and pointed the muzzle at the spot between his eyebrows where the two hairs grew.

'Pull the trigger.'

Something made her bring her left hand up to steady her right, then, stomach flipping, she did as she was told. The trigger was quite hard to pull and she gritted her teeth with the effort. Then it sort of loosened up, and all at once her index finger jerked back.

The director screamed and jerked backwards in his chair.

12

Mei's mouth dropped open.

What the fuck? She'd just killed the director. No. Wait. How could she have? The gun hadn't gone off.

As she tried to match the information reaching her eyes – a dead man sprawled over the back of his chair – with that from her ears – no bang from the pistol – the director calmly straightened in his chair.

'That was good, Twelve,' he said, taking the pistol from her. 'Following orders is your number one duty as a student at the School for Technical Studies.'

Mei's hand was shaking as he took the gun from her unresisting fingers. She clamped her other around it to stop the trembling. The guy was a loony! Had to be. Even if it wasn't loaded, she could have smacked him in the face with it, or cracked his skull.

'You think I am mad to give you, a violent delinquent, a pistol?'

How was he doing it? Reading her mind as if all her thoughts were written in little bubbles over her head like in the comics the Party put out about brave communists fighting counter-revolutionaries.

'It was a test, Sir,' she answered. 'You were seeing if you could trust me to do what I am told.'

He nodded. 'A fast learner. Would you obey me if I told you to point a loaded pistol at someone else?'

This was easy. Mei felt the ground solidifying under her feet again. She hadn't spent a great deal of time with adults in her life, but she knew the kinds of games they liked to play. Cops were always doing it; expecting you to follow their stupid question-and-answer routines until they got bored, gave you a slap or a couple of kicks and then let you go.

'Yes, Sir, I would.'

'And pull the trigger.'

'Yes, Sir.'

'Why?'

'If you tell me to, they must be our enemy.'

'And we know you have no compunction about killing your enemies.'

Mei didn't know that word – 'compunction' – but she could figure it out from the context. Guilt, basically. Or maybe it meant fear. She'd do whatever it took to stay alive: that was the start and the end of it, whatever fancy words the director used to dress it up.

'No, Sir.'

'Over the next two years, you will be instructed in how to kill, Twelve. It is as simple as that,' he said, brushing at the top of his thigh. 'You will become a weapon in China's arsenal to defeat its enemies, just as you used that brick to kill the boy who intended to violate you, and the key on the corrupt police officer.'

Mei recalled the cover photograph of the book in her room. The one written by the Crane.

'Like in Miss Du's book, Sir?'

'Exactly. You will learn all about guns like my little Type 54, there,' he said. 'Knives, too. But also improvised weapons, and even your own body.'

Mei nodded. She'd had an idea. But then she thought about the Frog's eerie ability to read her mind, so she squashed it down, for now.

66

'When do I start, Sir?'

He rose to his feet. 'Now. Stand.'

She stood. Then drew in a sharp intake of breath as his hand snaked under her tunic and up, over her ribs and across her breasts. He spun her round with the other, so she was looking out of the window, with her back to him. She heard the quick rasp of a zip.

His breathing was hoarse. It quickened and then he squeezed her so tightly she gasped, before releasing her just as suddenly.

'Stand still,' he said. She heard the zip again. 'Leave. Miss Du will meet you outside.'

Cheeks aflame, Mei walked to the door, and was standing outside in the corridor a moment later, her back to the cool painted wall. So they were going to teach her how to kill, were they? Well, the Frog would regret *that* decision one day. She would make sure of it.

Unsure what to do, she waited until she heard the slap-slap-slap of plimsolls. She turned to her left to see the Crane striding down the corridor.

Stopping in front of Mei, she stared into her eyes. They were almost the same height, which made Mei feel oddly powerful. She stared back.

'Now you know why you are here,' the Crane said, 'it's time to meet the others.'

* * *

That first day taught Mei a great deal about the School for Technical Studies. Mostly, what she picked up was that the students, of whom there were six girls and six boys in her group – or, what had the director called it? Cohort, that was it – were totally at the mercy of the adults.

Over a midday meal of rice, vegetables and pork, the boy she found herself sitting beside whispered to her what he called 'The Golden Rule'.

'They say, we do. OK? Say it back to me.'

Smiling, she'd swallowed her mouthful of rice and dutifully repeated it.

'They say, we do.'

'Yeah. You'd better learn that good, my friend,' he said. 'They say, you *don't* do?' He drew a finger across his throat.

'I saw a kid get shot this morning,' she said. 'Did they disobey?'

He grinned and shook his head.

'It's a show they put on for new kids. To frighten them right from the start,' he said. 'We're not supposed to tell, but you look like you can keep a secret. Am I right?'

She smiled back at him. 'Yeah, you're right. What's your name?'

'Five.'

'Your *real* name.'

'Oh.' He glanced up from his almost-finished bowl of food, checking where the adults were in the canteen. 'Shudi, but everyone calls me Rats.'

'Rats? What kind of a nickname is that?'

'I used to have pet rats. Before I came here.'

'I'm Mei,' she said. 'But you can call me Juice.'

She learned that Rats had come from a village just like she had, two years before. He'd been living on the streets until he'd knifed a cop to death after being cornered on a rooftop.

Just like Mei, he'd been arrested, beaten and then rescued by Du Minxia.

She had so many questions to ask him, but one of the adults had banged a gong and all the children had immediately jumped to their feet like soldiers at attention.

At a barked order, they'd all filed outside and lined up in a row in the dusty quadrangle where Mei had seen the fake execution. They'd been sent on a run, accompanied by two instructors, out of the school gates along a red-dirt road and into a forest.

They'd run for hours, with only a short break for water. Everyone had managed to keep up. But by the end of it more than a few, including Mei, were puking at the side of the road while an armed guard unlocked the tall metal gates to readmit them back to the school's grounds.

Mei learned that the boys were numbered One through Six, and the girls, Seven through Twelve.

She learned that she would be instructed in Mao Thought and correct Communist belief alongside the tactical, technical and physical aspects of her new job. That sounded boring and she resolved to find a way to get out of all that political bullshit as often as she could.

There was no mixing between the years. Year Two students were studying overseas for much of their time, in any case. The rest of the time they were on assignments with graduates of the school, learning first-hand how to do the job for real.

The only time everyone was together was at passing-out ceremonies or addresses to the whole school from Director Gao or a visiting Party dignitary.

The sleeping arrangements came as a surprise. After waking up in the bare room that morning, she'd assumed that would be her accommodation for the rest of her stay. But no. The six Year One girls slept in a big room the Crane called a dormitory.

It was so weird. Back home, she had shared the one-room hut with Mummy Rita, sleeping in the same bed behind a thin hanging blanket dividing the sleeping area off from the rest of the interior. Here she had her own bed.

And it was big! Twice as wide as she was. Much more space than when she was squished in between the wall and Mummy Rita's fat, sweating body.

The sheets were soft against her skin, and cool to the touch. She pressed her nose against the material and breathed in its sharp scent. Soapy, but something else too, something that caught at the back of her throat. It made her sneeze. But she liked it all the same.

It smelled like someone had given it some sort of powerful cleaning. She doubted she'd find any bugs lurking beneath the folded-back top sheet and thin grey blanket. They'd all have run away to find somewhere nice and stinky. The thought made her giggle.

'Who's that?' the girl in the next bed whispered.

'Mei, I mean Twelve,' she replied.

'Why are you laughing?'

'I was thinking this place is really different to where I used to live.'

The girl, Ten, rolled onto her front and propped herself on her elbows. Mei could just make her out in the moonlight that was filtered down to a pale grey by the thin cotton curtains. Her hair was cut short, almost like a boy's.

'It's pretty much exactly like where *I* used to live,' Ten said.

'Where was that?'

'Juvenile Detention Centre Number 1073.'

'What were you in for?'

'I killed a shopkeeper. But it wasn't my fault,' she added quickly. 'He caught me stealing an apple and took me into this backroom. He was going to rape me so I hit him.'

'That's all?'

Ten shook her head. 'He got up and pulled a knife on me. He gave me this.' She pushed her pyjama sleeve up and twisted her arm round to reveal a scar that stretched from her wrist to her elbow. 'I got it off him and I stabbed him. Right between his legs. You should have heard him scream.'

Mei wished she had. What was it about men? Always trying to do it to you? Why couldn't they stick it in their wives? Or go to a brothel like Mummy Rita's triads used to run? The Party kids were just as bad. And as for the Frog, he was the worst by far.

'What happened next?' she asked, eager to hear how Ten had ended up at the school.

'I ran, but the dirty pig bled to death anyway. They picked me up the next day.'

'The cops?'

'Nu-uh. *They* picked me up. The Crane and the Bull.'

This was a new piece of information. The Bull? Must be another adult. But she hadn't met anyone else. Yet, she added mentally.

'Is the Bull another teacher?'

Ten rolled her eyes. 'He's the senior technical instructor. Everyone's frightened of him.'

Maybe this was the man who'd pretended to shoot the kid at the start of the day. He was tall, broad across the shoulders. Mei thought he'd make a good bull if every human being had to change into an animal.

'What does he do? I mean, what's a technical instructor?'

'I'm not exactly sure. I only got here two days ago,' Ten said. 'The Crane said the term starts as soon as they have twelve students, so I guess you were the one we've all been waiting for.'

'I'm Juice,' Mei said. 'What's your name?'

'Sisi.'

'Got a nickname?' Sisi shook her head. 'You have to have a nickname,' Mei said. 'I'm gonna call you Sis.'

'Hey!' another girl hissed across the narrow aisle between the two rows of three beds. 'Shut up! I'm trying to sleep.'

'Fuck off!' Mei hissed back.

'No, *you* fuck off!'

The door opened, letting yellow light from the corridor into the dormitory and making Mei squint.

'Quiet!' It was the Crane. 'Any more noise and all six of you will be on a midnight run in your underwear. Understood?'

'Yes, Ma'am,' the six girls chorused.

The door closed quietly. Somehow Mei found that more worrying than if the Crane had slammed it.

Most adults seemed to believe that the more noise they made, the more frightening they became. But they just came off as silly to Mei. Red-faced stallholders bellowing, cops yelling about discipline and how they were going to beat up any kid they caught in their patch again.

Even Mummy Rita, when Mei had tested her patience to its admittedly narrow limits, had been given to shouting and throwing pots and pans around.

But the Crane's 'Quiet' had been delivered in barely more than a normal voice. But they'd all obeyed her instantly. Mei had a feeling it would be a very bad idea to get on her wrong side. It wouldn't be long before she'd discover how right she was.

71

13

After a simple breakfast of fried noodles with chicken, the twelve new students were lined up outside, facing the school building. The Crane stood to attention in front of them, though Mei doubted her rigid pose was for their benefit.

The Crane looked nervous. Her eyes kept flicking to her left and Mei could see the cords of her scrawny neck standing out as though she was just dying to swivel her head round to look behind her.

Mei didn't have long to figure out why. The main door swung inwards and out stepped the Frog. He was wearing a fancy army uniform. Green the colour of pond-weed with red shoulder boards and collar flashes and a ton of medals. A peaked cap shaded his eyes.

He marched out and stood beside the Crane. She turned her head and nodded to him. He took a step forward and cleared his throat. Mei looked at his disgusting face. He'd probably been eating flies in his office, shooting out a long slimy tongue and picking them off the window pane or the ceiling.

He smiled so that his lips stretched wide. The resemblance to a frog got stronger. Mei fought down an urge to giggle. She felt nerves in the pit of her stomach and had to bite her lip to quell the laugh threatening to break free.

'Welcome, new students of the School for Technical Studies,' he said, sweeping them with his eyes. He lingered on Mei and she felt hot. 'You have been selected to perform a valuable service for China. Her enemies are many. They are devious. Ruthless. Aggressive. They will stop at nothing to destabilise us.'

As he droned on, Mei's attention wandered. She could smell the boy standing next to her. She didn't know his name. Only his number. Three. He had a large black mole on his top lip. Overhead, a dozen or more sparrows flittered over the roof of the school and swirled for a moment above the courtyard before heading towards the trees, filling the air with their cheeping.

She could see the Frog's lips moving, but in her head she had moved far beyond the gritty concrete square. Because she'd figured something out.

Training was all very well, and she didn't mind running, or doing gym work or whatever else they had planned for them. But how could you learn to kill people except by actually doing it?

And that was another thing. She would never kill innocent people. However much the Frog and the Crane kept on about China's enemies, Mei thought they'd be like the cops only with even more power. They'd pick on people they didn't like and get rid of them for causing trouble.

Mei had other plans. She decided she'd study as hard as she possibly could, eat their food, sleep in their bed, become as strong as tough as she could manage, and then, when the time was right, she'd leave. Simple as that.

She'd go back to her friends in Shenzhen and now, properly trained, she'd lead them like her own triad. She'd teach them how to look after themselves properly.

Then she remembered Ping's note at the *People's Daily* stall at the bus station. The men had come back and threatened Ping's mum and dad. So maybe what Mei really ought to do after escaping was head home and see if she could straighten things out.

The Frog stepped back. His mouth had closed and his lips had stopped flapping. That was something, at least. Mei refocused her attention on the adults. The Crane stepped forward.

'The last student standing will receive pudding after their evening meal.'

What the hell did that mean? Mei looked to her left. Rats was frowning. To his right, Sis made a 'search me' face. Then she screamed. The big kid on the other side of her had just punched her in the side of the head. He was smiling.

Another kid stumbled as his neighbour kicked him high on the inside of the leg. That's when it happened. Mei understood what the Crane meant.

The kids scattered into an untidy melee, fists flying, feet lashing out. The kid who'd hit Sis wasn't smiling anymore. He'd got another boy in a headlock and was methodically punching him in the face.

Someone grabbed Mei round the neck and started squeezing. She let herself go limp and as she fell to the ground, her attacker lost their grip. Mei whirled round and swept out a foot, catching the other girl, Eleven, on the side of the knee and felling her.

Mei danced away from an incoming punch and blocked another with a raised forearm. This was madness! Twelve kids intent on beating the crap out of each other, all for a bowl of ice cream or sweetened rice pudding?

She spun round. Four kids were already down, nursing split lips or bloody noses or, in the case of the two boys, cupping their groins. Three other pairs were tangled on the ground, thrashing about, teeth bared, arms locked around each other. However their individual battles were going to play out, they weren't standing.

The big kid, the smiler, advanced on her. His face was spattered with blood. Not his, she could see. No way was she letting him touch her, let alone put her on the ground. If anyone was getting the pudding, it was going to be Mei, not him.

She took a step towards him and then feigned a stumble, bending at the knee so her head was level with his belly. As he reached for her, she straightened like a rocket going up at New Year. She squeezed her eyes shut and tensed every muscle in her neck.

The crack as the top of her head connected with the point of his chin made her dizzy. She reared back in time to see his eyes rolling upwards in his head. He fell backwards like a tree being cut down and landed awkwardly across two of the fallen kids, eliciting yells of pain and outrage.

Mei turned, in case someone had won their fight and was planning a surprise attack from behind. No need. She alone was on her feet.

'Enough!' the Crane called out over groans, whimpers and panting.

She strode over to Mei.

'Twelve is the winner.'

* * *

That evening, when the rice and vegetables were finished, the cook came out from behind the stainless-steel serving counter and placed a plastic bowl of peach slices in a thick syrup in front of Mei.

'Well done,' he whispered, putting a spoon to the right of the bowl.

Rats and Sis were sitting to Mei's left and right. After sliding one of the deliciously sweet slices of peach into her mouth, she turned to Sis.

'Take one,' she said.

Sis didn't need to be told twice. Her hand darted out and she popped one of the slippery orange crescents into her mouth.

'Thanks,' she mumbled, letting a thin dribble of syrup run down her chin.

'You, too,' Mei said to Rats.

He pincered a peach slice between thumb and forefinger.

'Oh, man, that's good,' he groaned. 'Thanks, Juice. I owe you.'

'We look after each other, OK?' Mei said, turning her head left and right. 'Whatever shit they make us do, we've got each other's backs.'

Sis jerked her chin in the direction of the smiling kid Mei had knocked cold to win the tournament. He was staring over at them.

'What's up with him, do you think?'

Mei thought she knew. She'd met a kid like him once before. She and Spark had been scavenging at the city dump one day, rooting among the piles of old domestic appliances looking for copper wire they could strip out and sell to this dude on a back street who paid cash for decent metal he could reuse.

They'd heard a voice chanting some cracked line of poetry over and over again and scrambled over a hill of half-dismantled washing machines to see who was making the racket.

'Inside, outside, doggie tried to run; outside, inside, doggie's having fun.'

The scene before them made Mei want to be sick, but she kept her food down.

A teenage boy, skinny and gangly, was squatting in a greasy patch of bare ground with the body of a dead dog before him. He'd opened it up along its belly and was pulling stuff out of it.

'Fuck me, look at that!' Spark hissed.

He shifted his weight to get a better look and dislodged a stripped electric motor, which tumbled down from their hiding place and landed with a crash on the concrete.

The kid looked over his shoulder. Then went back to what he was doing.

'You can come and watch if you like,' he said.

'Fuck that!' Spark hissed. 'He's crazy. Come on, Juice, let's go.'

They slithered back the way they'd come and left with a couple of untidy coils of copper wire, already thinking of the snacks they'd buy with the money from the guy they called Mr Metal.

But when they reached ground level, the kid was waiting for them. He must have run round the pile of machines to intercept them. Horrid, clotted matter clung to his hands, which were almost black with blood. He smiled.

'Are you going to tell people about me?' he asked.

'Fuck you, weirdo!' Spark threw back.

The kid produced a knife from somewhere. Its long blade glistened red in the sunlight.

'Come here. I've got an idea,' he said.

They ran, not looking back, for at least three city blocks before they dared to slow up and check behind them. The kid was nowhere in sight.

That night Mei had woken from a nightmare, convinced the boy from the dump was slitting her open and pulling long bloody strands of copper wire from her belly.

She shuddered at the memory and turned to Sis.

'He's got something missing.' She tapped her temple. 'In here. Forget about pudding, I think he'd kill us all for fun. Just to see what it was like.'

A nickname for him popped into her head.

Psycho.

14

The next morning they were told to assemble in the gym.

'I bet it's going to be the Bull,' Rats said to her as they filed in to the huge hall that smelled of sweat.

Waiting for them in the echoing space was a man who looked like he had forgotten to stop growing. He was so much taller than the other adults, and broad, too. His forehead bulged above his eyes, the left of which was covered by a black eye-patch. Mei had no trouble imagining a pair of curving horns jutting forward from that bony ridge.

He wore grey tracksuit pants and a white T-shirt. His bare feet were lumpy and bony. A jagged scar ran down his left arm, curving around the ropy muscles. Mei tried to imagine what sort of weapon had caused such a wound.

Once they had all assembled in a line in front of him, their feet sinking into the red vinyl crash mats arranged in a large square in the centre of the gym, he folded his arms across his massive chest.

'My name is Long Yan,' he said. His voice echoed off the plain, white-painted walls. 'You will call me Sir or Master Long. I am sure you know that I have a nickname, too. You may be tempted to use it in my hearing.' He paused. 'That would be unwise. Now, if you have a question before we start, put your hand up.'

Mei thought asking a question would also be 'unwise' and kept her arms glued to her sides. But she caught a movement out of the corner of her eye.

'Master Long, how did you lose your eye?'

Everybody turned towards the speaker. It was Psycho. Of course it was.

The Bull smiled. 'That would have been at the Battle of Fakashan. Anyone know any history?' he asked in a loud voice.

Nobody answered at first, then One put his hand up.

'China was defending herself against the Vietnamese aggressors, Sir. In 1981.'

The Bull nodded and Mei saw One smirking. What the Bull said next wiped the expression clean off his smug face.

'You got the date right, One,' he said. 'But the rest is bullshit. *We* were the aggressors. China! We took territory off the Lettuce-Eaters and they wanted it back. That's all.'

'But your eye, Sir,' Psycho persisted. 'How did you lose it?'

'The Lettuce-Eaters had my platoon pinned down: a machine gun nest in a stand of palms,' he said, looking at the gym ceiling. 'We'd lost our corporal and two of us had bad bullet wounds. We were being cut to ribbons. I charged the nest with a grenade. Blew them to pieces. One of the pieces, a jawbone, I think, flew out and took my eye with it.'

Mei glanced sideways at Psycho. He had a faraway look on his face. She knew exactly where he'd gone. He was on that battlefield. Scratching around in the mud for the missing eyeball. He wanted to pick it up and play with it like a marble.

She looked back at the Bull, and the long, looping scar on his arm. She found she was holding her arm up.

'Yes, Twelve,' the Bull said.

'Sir, what sort of weapon did that to your arm?'

The Bull rubbed a hand over the ridge of puckered flesh stretching from the middle of his bicep to below his elbow.

'A reaping knife. They used them to harvest rice. Are you interested in knives, Twelve?'

'Yes, Sir.'

'Ever use one?'

'No, Sir.'

'No? You know, every student here earns their place with a kill. Most use knives.'

'Not me, Sir.'

'What, then?'

Mei thought he probably knew already. The Crane would have told him.

'A brick. And a key.'

The Bull nodded slowly. 'Very good.' He raised his voice and swept the line of students with his gaze. 'Weapons are all very well. Until they run out of ammunition, or are taken from you. Remember what Twelve just said. Always be ready to use whatever comes to hand.

'All right, listen to me carefully. During your time here, I am going to teach you how to fight. I am going to teach you how to hurt people. And I am going to teach you how to kill. You *will* pay attention. And you *will* excel. Nobody leaves this school except as a fully trained assassin. You fail, you're dust. Understand?' The twelve students gathered before him mumbled their assent.

'Understand?' he roared.

'We understand, Sir,' they yelled back, all finding, in their shock, the same words.

As she shouted her part of the chorus, Mei really meant it. With what she could learn from the Bull, she'd be invincible when she made it back to the streets. And it would come in handy when she came face-to-face with the fat man again.

'You,' the Bull said, pointing at Psycho, then at a spot in front of him on the mat. 'Out here.'

Psycho stepped out of line and sauntered over to the Bull. The difference in their size was comical. The top of Psycho's head only just came up to the Bull's collarbone.

'You like to hurt people?' the Bull asked.

Psycho grinned. 'Yes, Sir.'

Mei eyed him and shuddered. What was *wrong* with him? He made no attempt to hide it. She thought it would be a weakness in the outside world. He was greedy to cause pain. It would make him careless.

'OK, then. Hurt me,' the Bull said.

Any normal kid would have hesitated, Mei was sure of it. No way would the Bull just let someone hurt him.

It was a trap. And a pretty obvious one at that. But Psycho wasn't any normal kid, was he? He still managed to surprise Mei by producing a knife from the sleeve of his sweatshirt. He must have stolen it from the kitchen at breakfast.

He swept it across the Bull's chest. Mei expected to see a gout of blood wash down the Bull's white T-shirt, staining it scarlet. But nothing happened. Well, not precisely nothing. The thin cotton parted in a long curving gape. Something metallic and shiny glinted from within.

Before she could work out what it was, the Bull's left hand had shot out and disarmed Psycho. The knife now lay across his throat. He tried to jerk his head away, but the Bull's other hand had clamped around the back. Psycho went very still. Hurting people was fine when it was him doing the hurting, but he wasn't an idiot. He wouldn't fight the Bull only to get his throat opened, would he?

The Bull thrust Psycho away from him.

'Back in line, Three,' the Bull said.

He ripped the T-shirt open and threw the two pieces of fabric to the mats. Now Mei could see what he wore beneath it. It was some sort of metal mesh. Thousands of little circular chain links all joined together. Like one of Mummy Rita's cheap necklaces. She used to buy them from the pedlar who came through the village in spring with a wagon stuffed with trinkets.

The Bull tapped his chest, making the vest clink.

'Not everything from China's ancient history is bad,' he said. 'We have studied their methods, their tactics, and their equipment. Much can be adapted for our uses. For bladed weapon training, you will each be issued with a full suit: we call it fish-scales.'

* * *

A week later, Mei and the other eleven students stood in a line before the Bull. They were in the gym, as before. But this time, they were clad in the fish-scales: long-sleeved vests that came down to the groin, and shorts that reached mid-thigh. Mei felt the weight of it: comforting, but still restrictive.

The Bull had a long leather-bound case at his feet. When he had their attention, he gestured towards it.

'Knives,' he said, with a grin.

Mei's heart started beating faster. This was it. After seven days of physical training including long runs outside the fence, wrestling matches and free-for-all scraps where anything except biting was permitted, they were actually going to get their hands on weapons.

She was sure she'd be OK. Clearly the school didn't want them to get hurt, else why bother issuing the fish-scales? She guessed it was just to see who would strike without mercy and who'd hold back.

Over the previous week she'd learned that all twelve of them had killed at least once. Some, like her, had been picked up in the immediate aftermath. Others had been pulled in by the Crane days, or weeks, afterwards. The youngest, Two, was just twelve years old but with an old look in his eye Mei had seen only on the toughest street kids. Experience did that to you.

'Come and get 'em,' the Bull commanded.

As they had been taught, they marched over in numerical order, which meant Mei was last in line.

'Do you think we'll have to fight each other with them?' Eleven asked her, turning her head and whispering out of the corner of her mouth.

'Probably. That's what the fish-scales are for.'

'But what about Psycho? He'll go for the face.'

Mei had been thinking the same thing. 'If you get him, hurt him fast and hard,' she said. Show him it would be a bad idea to try anything.'

Eleven nodded. 'Thanks.'

'Quiet back there!' the Bull yelled. 'Unless you want to do this without the fish-scales.'

Mei had no doubt he meant it, and clamped her lips tight.

As each kid got their knife, they formed a new line down the side wall of the gym. Mei reached the front. She squatted in front of the open case. It was lined with grey foam. Eleven slots were empty, one contained a knife. *Her* knife.

Mei picked the knife up.

The handle was wrapped in leather. Maybe it had once been brown but all the hands that had held it before Mei had blackened it with sweat and grease.

The blade was half as long again as the handle and sharp on both sides. It came to a rounded tip. It didn't look like it would be much good for actually stabbing anybody. She liked the balance, though. And the handle felt snug in her palm.

'When you've finished admiring your new toy, get in line, Twelve,' the Bull said, not unkindly.

She nodded – 'Yes, Sir,' – and trotted over to complete the line against the wall.

The Bull marched over to join them.

'OK, this is how this goes,' he intoned.

Mei thought it sounded like the start of a speech he'd given many times before. She wondered how many young assassins the school had turned out. Hundreds? Thousands? She supposed if China had as many enemies as the Frog liked to make out, the more the merrier.

'I'm going to pair you up and you're going to practice one simple strike at a time. Follow my instructions and you won't get hurt.'

Five minutes later, six pairs of would-be assassins stood a metre apart from each other.

Mei looked down the line. Rats and Sis were paired off with regular kids. Or as regular as anyone could be in this fucked-up school. So was Eleven, who'd been worried about drawing Psycho. She caught Mei's eye and offered a quick smile-and-nod combo.

Mei looked straight ahead. Into Psycho's dull eyes.

15

Something about the way Psycho's eyes were set in his head meant they never reflected any light back like normal people's. There was just this blackness, like staring down an empty well.

She gripped her knife a little tighter and tested the edge with her left thumb. She only used a featherweight pressure, but it was enough to score a line through the tough skin. She made sure she had Psycho's attention.

'Just try it,' she mouthed.

He smiled back at her as if she'd just invited him to share a stolen melon.

'Twelve, out here, facing me,' the Bull said.

Relief washing through her, Mei stepped away from Psycho and went to join the Bull.

'Stab me over the heart,' he ordered. 'You do know where the heart is?'

Some of the other kids giggled. The Bull let it pass. She'd already learned something about him. He demanded strict discipline in his lessons, but reserved his anger for people who didn't follow instructions, not for titterers.

If you behaved well and respected him and the weapons and tactics he taught, he was pretty cool about the other stuff.

'Yes, Sir,' she said.

She pictured the cop back at Shenzhen Central Station. Imagined it was him she was knifing. Saw his blood spurting out all over the place.

Trying not to think, but only to *do*, she drew her arm back and struck the Bull fast. As hard as she could. Directly over where she imagined the heart to be. She tried to intensify the overhand blow by stepping into it.

The impact jarred her wrist and now she understood why the knives had rounded points. The fish-scales had stopped it dead. Too narrow a tip and it would slip between them, maybe even force one of them to open out.

The Bull didn't so much as grunt. He kept breathing evenly.

Mei stepped back.

'Not bad,' the Bull said. He turned to the line. 'What did Twelve do wrong? Anyone?'

Nobody said anything. Too frightened to get it wrong.

As Mei replayed the moment he'd given the order to attack, she saw it. The way she'd brought the knife over her shoulder in a big swoopy arc.

'The backswing, Sir. I showed you what I was going to do. I left myself exposed to a counterattack.'

The Bull nodded, focusing his single eye on her like a searchlight.

'Very good, Twelve. Do it again, slowly, exactly the same move. But this time, when I say "Stop", you freeze.'

Mei nodded, already understanding what he wanted her to do. He was going to show them the risk and then how to make it disappear.

Rotating her torso and sliding her left foot forwards, she brought the knife up and back, past her right shoulder and cocked her wrist, ready to swing the knife over and down towards his heart.

'Stop!'

Mei froze, her knife suspended above her head. She looked

down. The tip of a long, narrow-bladed knife was digging into her right armpit.

She recalled an anatomy class from earlier in the week. They'd studied the major blood vessels of the upper body. The Bull had the knifepoint right over the thickest part of the artery that ran from the neck all the way down the arm. Cut it and your target would bleed out.

It was an impossible wound to treat without immediate surgery and had the advantage of not instantly showing up the way a slit throat would. The instructor had explained how to fold down the target's arm after the strike so they would continue bleeding without turning into a human fountain.

'Where's my knife, Twelve?' the Bull asked.

'Over the axillary artery, Sir.'

'Over the axillary artery,' he repeated. 'Not smart. Try again, and this time protect yourself.'

He relaxed his arms and the knife vanished from view. Mei looked into his eyes. Unlike Psycho's, his were full of expression. She detected amusement, curiosity and a hawklike watchfulness. She wanted to please him.

Unlike some of the others, especially the Frog, he was fair with the kids. And so far hadn't tried it on with Mei or any of the other girls, as far as she could tell from their conversations at meal times or after lights-out.

She opened and closed her fingers on the knife, enjoying the way the handle's leather wrapping seemed to mould itself to her grip. But how to reach the heart without leaving herself open?

If the overarm strike was out, then she ought to hit him more in a straight line. That way, she could keep everything more compact and less vulnerable to his counterattack.

She switched her grip so the blade emerged, point uppermost, from between her thumb and index finger, instead of downwards from the fleshy part of her palm.

She drove it in towards the Bull's belly, keeping it low, and at the last moment swung upwards. The point connected with the fish-scales just below where she hoped his ribs ended.

The Bull gripped her wrist and squeezed tightly so she couldn't move. He was smiling.

'Very good,' he murmured. 'Very good indeed.' Then, louder, 'Gather round. I want you to see this.'

Once the other kids had formed a tight circle around them, the Bull used his free hand to indicate the blade still gripped in Mei's – and his – hand.

'See the angle? She's going to come in under the ribs and either hit the heart or damage the liver, stomach or lung. Not bad for a beginner.'

After that, they were back in their pairs, practising the upwards stab Mei had tried on the Bull.

Psycho still had that weird distant look in his eye, like he wasn't really there in the gym at all. But either Mei's murmured threat earlier, or his fear of what the Bull would do to him if he messed around, kept him honest.

After fifteen minutes, Mei's hand was aching and her right arm was tingling like someone had been jabbing it with an electric cattle-prod.

The Bull switched them around, and Mei found herself facing Rats. They nodded at each other. They were friends, but this was for real. No punches – stabs – pulled. This time they were to aim for the femoral artery, the big one inside the thigh.

Taking turns, Mei and Rats crouched and lunged, stabbed and withdrew. Even though the practice knives were blunt-ended, they still hurt. Rats was a big guy and he was putting everything into his strikes. Each time he struck, the nerves in the tender spot on Mei's inner thigh crackled with pain. She bit back the yells that threatened to burst free: nobody would hear *her* making a sound.

Then somebody else did scream. A thin, piercing cry that ascended in pitch like the beginning of a song. Everyone stopped what they were doing and turned to the source of the noise.

16

Nine was staggering backwards, away from her opponent – Psycho, who else? – clutching her right thigh. From between her fingers arterial blood streamed, bright with the oxygen the muscles needed for fighting. Nine's face was deathly pale as she collapsed backwards. Her hand fell away from the wound and blood spurted down her leg and onto the mat.

'Stand back!' the Bull shouted.

He knelt beside Nine, yanked her shorts down, then dug his right thumb deep into the soft flesh above the slash in her skin. Miraculously, the bleeding slowed to a trickle then stopped altogether.

Mei stepped forward, glaring at Psycho. He was inspecting the blade of his knife, which was smeared with Nine's blood.

'Where's the first aid kit, Sir?' she asked.

The Bull jerked his chin at a door on the far side of the gym.

'Kit room. Red nylon holdall. Quick about it!'

She sprinted across the gym, her bare feet light on the varnished floor and burst through the door into the room where the mats and other equipment were stored. At first she couldn't see any holdall and spun around, frantic to find it. There it was! On a shelf behind the door. Mei grabbed the looped tape handles and ran back to where the Bull was still kneeling beside Nine.

Nine's eyes were wide and she was breathing shallowly.

Mei unzipped the holdall.

'What do you need, Sir?'

'Anti-clot sponge and a number one field dressing. Look at the labels.'

Mei scrabbled through the brown paper packets until she found both items. She ripped open the white paper packet containing the sponge and handed it to the Bull. He pushed it hard against the wound with his left hand, still keeping his right thumb pushed deep into Nine's thigh.

Mei unwrapped the field dressing and knelt beside the Bull. She held it ready beside the edge of the sponge. The Bull took his hand away and Mei stuck the dressing straight over the sponge and pushed down with all her strength. With the bleeding controlled, the Bull reached for the holdall, withdrew a bandage and began winding it in tight coils around Nine's thigh.

Finally he stood. 'Maintain the pressure,' he said to Mei. He pointed at Sis. 'Ten, run to the medical officer. Tell him we need a stretcher and to prepare for surgery.'

Sis nodded and ran for the main door.

Mei looked into Nine's eyes. They were unfocused, the pupils wide.

'Hey, Nine,' she whispered. 'You're going to be OK. The doctor's coming. He'll patch you up.' She smiled. 'You're going to have a really cool scar, too.'

Nine looked up at Mei. Her eyes started working in unison again.

'Thanks,' she whispered. 'I owe you.'

The Bull stalked across to where Psycho was standing. His arm shot out and suddenly Psycho was on tiptoe, his eyes bugging out of his skull, as the Bull's fingers squeezed his windpipe.

Everybody turned and Mei thought she wasn't the only one hoping the Bull would choke the life out of the weirdo who'd nearly killed Nine.

'You disobeyed me, Three,' the Bull said, shaking Psycho like he was a rag doll.

'No, Sir,' Psycho gargled out.

'No?' the Bull roared. 'Now you contradict me as well? Why should I not kill you right now?'

He relaxed his grip on Psycho's throat. Mei watched the blood return to his knuckles, but saw he'd only left Psycho enough freedom to draw breath. If he tried anything, the Bull would probably go in for the kill: his thumb was right over Psycho's carotid artery.

'She flinched, Sir. My strike would have hit the target, but she moved and the point went under the edge of her shorts,' Psycho said, as calmly as if he'd been discussing the weather outside the dorm. 'It was an accident. I'm sorry, Sir. I'll try harder next time.'

Mei watched Psycho's face. Not a flicker of emotion. He was lying. Of course he was. He meant he'd try harder to kill one of them next time. That was all. Mei hoped the Bull could see that.

The Bull released Psycho, who reached up and rubbed his reddening throat gingerly.

'See that you do, Three, or I'll open one of *your* arteries for you. And maybe I won't send Twelve for the medical bag that time, eh?'

Mei swallowed down the bitter taste of disappointment. They'd have to put up with Psycho's weird antics for a while longer. He caught her eye as he rejoined the line, a smirk on his face.

Later, when they were eating their evening meal, Psycho went up to the serving counter for a second helping of rice and beef. On the way back he gave Mei a good hard bump with his elbow as he rounded her end of the table.

She shot to her feet. In seconds she had him in a headlock, the tip of a chopstick hovering just over his left eye. Psycho dropped his tray of food; the clatter brought one of the kitchen attendants running over. She delivered a swinging slap to the back of Mei's head.

Mei briefly considered feigning a stumble and accidentally ramming her chopstick all the way to the back of Psycho's skull – *the occipital bone*, an inner voice chanted – before the attendant's hand snaked out and relieved her of her weapon.

'Come with me!' the attendant said, 'Director Gao won't be happy to hear you've been fighting. It's bad for discipline.'

Actually, Mei thought he'd be delighted, but she held her tongue. She needed to find a way not to be left alone with the Frog.

What could she say that would get her out of this jam? Pleading wouldn't do any good. The kitchen staff might be happy dolloping out second helpings; no doubt they'd been told to let the kids build themselves up. But she had a shrewd idea they were equally happy dishing out punishments.

Then she realised. The attendant was wrong.

'You're making a big mistake,' she said, as the attendant dragged her out of the dining room and into the empty corridor.

'Oh, yeah? Don't tell me, your uncle's on the Politburo. No wait, your big sister's a general in the army.'

'No. That fight back there? It was on Director Gao's express orders.' Mei was pleased with that word 'express'. She'd heard the Crane using it. 'It's part of our training. He'll be really pissed off to find you interrupted it. Especially that you bothered him with your so-called discipline.'

The attendant's eyes flickered in the direction of the Frog's office. Mei could see she was in two minds. Was the kid telling the truth? Or was it just teenage bullshit?

'Seriously?' she asked, letting Mei go.

Mei nodded, all wide-eyed and serious, like a good schoolgirl should be.

'Oh, yes, Miss. It's called "readiness". We're supposed to attack each other out of the blue to check we're always able to deal with a surprise attack by one of China's enemies.'

The attendant nodded. She looked up the corridor a second time. Mei knew exactly what she was thinking. The director wouldn't be pleased to have his evening wank interrupted by some kitchen worker boasting of how she'd broken up *a training exercise*!

'How come I've never seen it happen before?'

This was too easy. Mei nodded as if the attendant had made a really good point.

'It's new, Miss. Tomorrow it might happen in the yard, or in the dormitory at three in the morning,' she said. 'We just never know when the attacks will come, Director Gao says.'

The attendant nodded thoughtfully. Then she nodded towards the door.

'Back you go, then. And work on your readiness. Remember, an attack could come at any time.'

Mei preceded the attendant back into the dining room. She couldn't help the smile that broke out on her face when she caught Sis's eye.

* * *

Over the few weeks, the students formed alliances, friendships and enemies.

Nobody liked Psycho. He didn't seem to mind. He paid attention in class, especially when they were learning about the human body and its internal workings. Other than that, he showed no interest in his fellow students at all, unless he'd caught a bird or a small rodent in the school grounds and invited them to join him in playing with it.

The Frog led them in daily study devoted to Marxism-Leninism. It was all bullshit as far as Mei was concerned. Who even *were* those guys? They weren't even Chinese!

She feigned interest, even putting her hand up from time to time to spout off about worker solidarity, false consciousness and capitalist running dogs, though she had zero idea what it all had to do with killing people.

It pleased the Frog, though. Thankfully, he hadn't asked to see her in his office again, although a couple of the other girls had shared stories about him that tallied with Mei's own.

Wouldn't it be fine to stick a knife right between his legs?

Mei thought she'd be pretty good at it: knife-fighting was the subject she enjoyed the most.

She was quicker than the others and when they had mock-fights with blunt blades, she was always the one who ended the bout crouched over her opponent, the blade to her throat, or poked into his belly just below the ribs.

The trouble was, every now and again her thoughts returned to Mummy Rita and the men with suits who'd pointed pistols at her, demanding to know where her daughter was. She wished she could escape and get back to the village, just to see her face and make sure she was OK.

17

Three more months passed. Mei and her eleven classmates became skilled in martial arts. Not the pure, rules-based styles China did so well in at the All-Asia Games. Those were, as the Crane and the Bull explained, for show.

'Zero use for attack, let alone defence,' the Bull told them.

Instead, the instructors schooled them in faster, dirtier forms of fighting in which, one way or another, they'd already developed some level of proficiency.

What mattered was hurting your enemy and not getting hurt yourself. To that end they'd studied human anatomy, from the skin inwards, through the muscles and fascia to the tendons, ligaments, internal organs and, finally, the bones.

Mei paid attention in every lecture and practical session. She learned of, and could accurately point out, the seventeen places on the human body where, with the correct application of force, she could either disable or kill her enemy without the need for a weapon.

One scorching morning, they gathered in the drill square and stood to attention before a row of tables on which sat human skulls. Each student had been issued with a long-bladed screwdriver.

Mei stared at the row of skulls and wondered where the school had got them.

The Crane picked up a thirteenth skull and held it aloft like some sort of trophy, gripping it by the lower jaw.

'The skull is strong, but it has weaknesses. Like China's enemies. Today you will learn where they lie,' she cawed.

Her voice carried far beyond their ears, to the back of the courtyard where it bounced off the high walls of the main school building.

She picked up a screwdriver and placed the tip against the side of the skull.

'One, the ear.'

A sudden jerk and the entire length of the screwdriver disappeared into the skull with a sharp crack as the bone splintered.

'Two, the temple.'

She withdrew the screwdriver and jammed it against a spot just forward of the ear opening. Again, it appeared as though she had performed a magic trick, as her fist jammed up against the cream-coloured bone curve.

'Where next?' she asked, raking the students with her sharp-eyed gaze.

'The eye, Ma'am,' Mei called out before anyone else could beat her to it.

The Crane nodded, though she did not permit a smile to cross her lips.

'Join me, Twelve,' the Crane said.

Mei stepped smartly out from behind her table and went to stand beside the Crane. She handed Mei the screwdriver and turned so they were standing face-to-face.

'Show the class,' the Crane said.

Mei switched her grip on the screwdriver so the blade was pointing down. She cocked her wrist.

For a split-second, a vivid image flashed before her eyes. She saw her arm flash forwards, burying the long black blade deep into the Crane's left eye socket.

She saw herself sprinting towards the gates. Leaping over the head of the guard. Vaulting off his shoulder to a spot halfway up the chain-link fencing before swinging her newly powerful body over the top. Then dropping onto the balls of her feet, dashing down the dirt road and losing herself in the forest.

'Try it,' the Crane murmured, so quietly Mei was sure only she could hear. 'You'll be dead before your brain has finished telling your right arm what to do.'

Mei looked into the Crane's eyes. They had narrowed a fraction, but it was the change to her thin lips that interested Mei. They had crept upwards, just a little. Was the Crane smiling?

She didn't have time to find out. The Crane's hand flicked out, so fast Mei only registered the movement after it had happened. She felt pain in her right hand as the Crane snatched away the screwdriver, then shock as the tip of it stopped just short of her left eye.

The Crane's hand snaked around the back of Mei's head and gripped her, hard. She started forcing Mei's head forward. Mei fought back, arching her back and straining to maintain the tiny gap between the delicate, moist membrane covering her eye and the sliver of steel the Crane was aiming at her brain.

Without easing off the pressure, the Crane addressed the other students.

'Twelve thought about killing me with my own screwdriver,' she said, in her infuriatingly calm voice. 'And that was her mistake. When you must kill someone, you do not *think* about doing it. You *do* it,' she said, tightening her grip on Mei's head.

Now the tip of the screwdriver was actually touching Mei's cornea. She squeezed her eyes shut but, sickeningly, the edge of the half-centimetre wide blade slipped between her eyelids.

Mei wanted desperately to fight back, to wriggle, buck and lash out, but she was frightened that either she might jab the screwdriver into her own eye, or the Crane would. Maybe this was one of the ways they taught the students how to kill. By using one of them as a demonstration model.

She ground her teeth together, fighting the nausea as the screwdriver rested on her lower eyelid. No way was she going down without a fight. If this was how it all ended, then she'd give the Crane a goodbye present to remember her by.

Stiffening her fingers into a blade, just like the Crane herself had shown them the previous month, Mei lashed out and upwards, beneath the arm holding the screwdriver, aiming for the soft spot beneath the Crane's jaw.

There was a thick bundle of nerves there that, if you hit it right, would knock your enemy out cold. Mei would lose an eye, but she could grab another screwdriver and do for the Crane at least.

Her left hand shot upwards into thin air. The space occupied by the Crane's jaw was empty. Instead of dropping to the ground, the Crane sort of floated sideways. She seized Mei's hand on its upwards trajectory and brought it over and down onto the tabletop with a loud, flat slap.

Mei heard another sound; a hard, crackling *chunk*. For a moment, she couldn't work out what had made it.

Pain erupted in her brain. Hot and loud and bright and shooting into her guts, blotting out conscious thought. She screamed as she took in the screwdriver pinning her hand to the table. Blood ran out from around the thin shaft, trickling over the straining tendons and onto the scarred and scrubbed wood.

She felt her legs going, but forced herself to stay upright. Partly from sheer bloody-minded pride and partly because she didn't want to imagine the screwdriver tearing her flesh if she let her weight drag on her pinioned hand.

The Crane stepped away from her and turned to face the remaining students.

'Leave the thinking to Party strategists, military commanders, engineers, scientists...intellectuals,' she said in crisp, sharp-edged language, making the last word sound like a profanity. 'We deal in action.'

Tears combined with agony to blur Mei's vision, as her legs shook violently, but she saw the expressions on the faces of her fellow students. Rats and Sis looked horrified. But there were a couple of others with sly smiles. Psycho seemed fascinated. He was running the tip of his tongue over his top lip.

The Crane stepped over to where Mei was crouched by the table, using it to support her bodyweight.

She placed her hand over Mei's, her index and middle fingers splayed around the shaft of the screwdriver. That only added to the pain, which was blotted out by a new level of agony so extreme Mei screamed as the Crane grasped the fat handle with her other hand and pulled it free.

Mei slumped to the ground, gasping, to find the Crane crouching over her, this time with the screwdriver tip in her left ear.

'Remember, Twelve,' she murmured, 'if you want to kill me, *kill* me. Otherwise, do what you're told and don't bother thinking about it. Understand?'

'Yes, Ma'am,' Mei panted, seeing multicoloured sparks and streamers chasing each other across the Crane's face.

'Good girl.' The Crane stood. 'One, Four: take her to the sick bay.'

The two others stepped out from behind their tables and took one of Mei's arms each. She shook them off angrily. No way was she going to let the Crane, or Psycho, or *anyone*, see her as weak.

Head held high, despite the black spots that swam across her vision, she walked, as steadily as she was able, in the direction of the sick bay.

Four grabbed her elbow. He jerked backwards as Mei's fist connected with a spot over his heart.

'Leave her,' the Crane commanded.

Mei continued her stiff-legged walk to the double doors. The pain in her hand was like a glowing poker from the fire, drilling through skin, tendons, muscle and bone, burning her flesh away from its red-hot surface. She didn't want to look down, but forced herself.

Blood was flowing freely from each side of the wound, but faster from the palm-side, where it ran down to her fingertips and dripped onto the concrete. She lifted her left arm and then, teeth clamped together so hard her jaws creaked, she squeezed her right thumb and middle finger against the holes.

She grunted with the effort of not screaming, as the agony

intensified. She shouldered her way through the doors and moved away from the glass so she could lean back against the wall.

It was cooler in here than out in the yard, but still warm. Black curtains swung across her vision and she slumped to the ground, her bottom hitting the floor and jolting her tailbone.

'Mei! What are you doing back here?' Mummy Rita asked her.

Two tawny-feathered chickens dangled from her right hand, wings flapping, emitting angry squawks.

'I miss you,' Mei said. 'I want to come home.'

Mummy Rita smiled. 'Help me with Mr Marx and Mr Lenin here, then we can have some tea. Chicken and rice, yes?'

Mei nodded, already salivating at the thought of her favourite of Mummy's home-cooked meals. A rich stew of chicken, wild radish, mushrooms and hot red chillis, scented with lots of fresh green coriander leaves, served on a pile of steaming white rice.

She strolled with Mummy to the shed and the squat cylinder of tree trunk that served as her chopping block, its surface scarred with many hundreds of cuts.

Mummy gave Mei one of the chickens.

'Here. Hold Mr Marx while I kill Mr Lenin.'

Mummy raised the cleaver and separated bird from head with a quick chop.

'Your turn,' she said, handing the cleaver to Mei.

Mei placed her bird down on the block and raised the cleaver.

'Don't kill me!' the bird shrieked. 'Workers should unite to fight the forces of capitalism.'

Left hand throbbing, as the blood started to flow out to coat the bird's glossy plumage, Mei shook her head.

'Bullshit!'

She swung the cleaver and the bird's head, with its human face and bushy grey beard, rolled off the chopping block and into the dirt.

The head came to a stop, eyes upwards, and it continued to speak.

'You'll kill for me. And one day, you'll die for me.'

'Never!' Mei screamed, as the head began growing until it had reached human size.

'Never! I hate you! I hate you!'

Marx got to his feet on his regrown body, dressed now in a rough brown suit. Blood coursed out from the sloppy join between his head and neck. He grabbed Mei by the shoulders.

'Come with me. I'll teach you the twelve laws of Marxism-Leninism. Let's start with twelve and work backwards. Twelve.'

Mei squeezed her eyes shut.

'No!'

'Twelve. Twelve. TWELVE!'

Mei looked around, hands clenched into fists as she prepared to fight off the grotesque, bloodied figure. But he'd gone.

The Bull was crouching over her.

'What the hell happened to your hand?' he asked.

She looked down, her left hand was resting in a pool of dark blood that had spread outwards towards her hip.

'Training accident,' she mumbled. 'I was on my way to the sick bay.'

He frowned. 'This wasn't anything to do with Three, was it? Has he been up to his usual tricks?'

Mei shook her head, then a wave of nausea washed through her. She turned away just in time to prevent the vomit that rushed from her mouth from splashing him.

Without saying another word, the Bull scooped her up and carried her down the corridor towards the sick bay.

'Orderly!' he bellowed.

A youngish man in a brown overall ran down to the corridor.

'Sir?'

'Clean up the mess back there.'

The Bull pushed through the doors into the sick bay. The swinging motion as he carried her did nothing to calm Mei's churning stomach and for a moment she feared she'd throw up again. She swallowed hard and the feeling passed.

The doctor, dressed as always in her knee-length white coat, rose from her chair.

'What happened?' she asked.

'I found her in the hallway,' the Bull said. 'She says it was a training accident.'

The doctor picked up Mei's dangling left hand and glanced at it. She nodded.

'Put her on the table.'

The Bull carried Mei over to a stainless-steel bed raised on concertinaed steel legs. The thin mattress was covered in a green cotton sheet. With a gentleness that belied his bulk, he lowered her and slid his hand free.

He leaned down. 'I have to go. The doc will fix you up.'

'Thank you, Sir.'

The Bull nodded, turned and left.

The doctor snapped on a pair of white rubber gloves. 'What do we have here? A nice neat hole. Weapon?'

Mei's hand was still throbbing, each beat of her heart sending a dirty purple bolt of pain up her arm and into her brain.

'A screwdriver, Ma'am.'

The doctor wrinkled her nose.

'It'll need stitching. Let's get a local anaesthetic in there and that will take away the pain.'

'I'd like that, Ma'am.'

The doctor smiled, briefly. 'I'm sure you would. It's going to hurt a little when I put it in because there are lots of nerves in there. But you lot have to learn how to take your hits, don't you?'

'Yes, Ma'*aaa*—'

The end of the word turned into a shriek as the doctor stuck the hypodermic into the tissue of Mei's injured left hand.

'Don't jump,' the doctor said. 'Or I'll have to redo it.'

Mei nodded, grateful that it was over.

'Yes, Ma'am. Sorry. Are you going to stitch it now?'

'Three more to go and then we need to wait for the anaesthetic to take effect.'

Three? Mei thought on balance she'd rather deal with the pain of the stitching.

'I don't want any more, Ma'am. I'm ready to start now.'

The doctor looked at her.

'Tough little bird, aren't you? The others won't hurt so much. Now, hold still.'

The doctor was sort of right, Mei thought. The rest of the injections, one more to the back of her hand and two in her palm, weren't *as* bad. But that was a bit like saying the second time you hit your head against a brick wall wasn't as bad as the first.

The doctor turned away, explaining that she'd need to wait for five minutes until the anaesthetic had done its work. She sat at her desk and commenced fiddling on a computer.

Mei lay back and stared at the ceiling. Little by little, the throbbing in her hand faded to a dull ache then ceased altogether. Her senses clearing, she took in the clinical smell of the sick bay: disinfectant and a faint odour of vomit. She raised herself on her left elbow and leaned over to look at her hand.

Now that it wasn't hurting, she found the hole fascinating. She touched the spongy surface with the tip of her little finger. She felt nothing from her hand except a soft pressure. The blood had stopped flowing out and was just pooled there.

She turned her hand over. The hole in her palm was messier. Maybe wood from the tabletop had got into it when the blade of the screwdriver punched through the skin.

The Crane had shown no emotion. That was impressive. When Mei got into fights, she knew that she was at the mercy of her own emotions.

She could remember vividly fights with bigger kids, or against worse odds. Her jaw clenched involuntarily as she recalled the sudden brief flares of violence. Knives, half-bricks, bits of broken crockery: you used whatever came to hand.

Was that it, then? The key to being an assassin? You had to be in control of your emotions as well as your muscles? Psycho would be brilliant at it then: the kid barely even seemed to *have* any emotions, let alone be ruled by them.

Mei decided something. Right there, in the sick-smelling medical room, surrounded by posters charting acupuncture points and the circulation of the blood. Emotions would make her weak. She'd push them right down where they couldn't hurt her or slow her down. And if they fought back, bubbling up and making her want to cry or laugh or cower, she'd beat them, like she'd beat her enemies.

Nobody was going to make her suffer again.

18

That night, as Mei and the other five girls prepared for bed, the door to their dormitory opened and the doctor came in, accompanied by the Crane. The doctor was carrying a metal tray.

As they'd been taught, the girls all stood up straight at the ends of their beds, hands flat against their sides, thumbs pointing straight down at the ground. Mei's left hand was throbbing beneath the dressing.

'There is a new school policy,' the Crane intoned. 'All students will now take a vitamin tablet at bedtime to aid mental development and physical fitness.'

The doctor approach Seven's bed.

'Take one,' she said.

Seven picked up the tiny paper cup and tipped it to her mouth. Mei watched as she swallowed.

It was probably some kind of mind-control pill. That's what Brains always used to say. The Party kept everybody tame and not wanting a new government by putting drugs in the water.

There wasn't much Mei could do about the water. But she was as sure as hell not going to help them rot *her* mind by swallowing whatever shit they were handing out in the little paper cups.

'Open,' the Crane said.

Seven dutifully gaped like a baby bird waiting for its mother to drop in a nice juicy bug. The Crane stuck a pen in her mouth – *ugh!* – and used it to move her tongue around, pull her cheeks out, even poke under her upper lip.

Satisfied, she nodded. They moved onto Eight's bed.

Mei saw what she had to do and thanked those older city kids who'd trained her to have a sneak-thief's quick hands. The Crane checked her watch as they arrived in front of her. Good. She was impatient to get away. Probably had a bottle of rice wine or whisky she wanted to drink.

Mei looked down. The tray now held five empty cups and one containing a tiny white tablet.

She picked it up, nodded to the doctor, then tipped it into her mouth, made a face and swallowed. She placed the cup back on the tray.

The Crane repeated her one-word instruction and poked around in Mei's mouth with the pen. Being last had given her time to think, but it also meant the pen had been in five mouths before hers. She hoped none of the others had a stomach bug.

The Crane nodded for the sixth and final time. All the girls had taken their vitamins.

'How is your hand, Twelve?' she asked quietly.

Mei nodded, keeping her eyes down.

'It's fine, Ma'am. The doctor is very skilled. It doesn't hurt anymore.'

A lie, but Mei didn't want to give the Crane the satisfaction.

The Crane pursed her thin lips.

'Doesn't hurt, eh? They must breed them tough where you come from.'

She whispered something to the doctor and then both women left, closing the door behind them.

Once the door was closed, they all climbed into bed.

'Night night,' Sis whispered.

'Night,' Mei whispered back.

She lay on her back and, keeping her movements as small and

quiet as possible, picked a hole in the stitching of her pillow until she could poke a finger in. Then she transferred the little white tablet from her palm to her thumb and forefinger and pushed it through the hole right into the centre of the filling. And there it would stay.

Keeping her breathing nice and easy, she listened for the others to start turning in their beds until they found a comfortable position to sleep in.

Every night was the same. The other girls had to spend ages wriggling and coughing until they were happy. Mei just lay on her back with her eyes closed and waited until she dropped off.

Maybe it was all those years of sleeping in the big bed with Mummy Rita that did it. Mei had learned to just…stop. To let the day go and fall asleep quickly so she could enter her dreamworld and escape the village and its restrictions, for a night, at least.

She frowned. That was strange. Nobody was making a sound. Not a peep.

Even Eight was silent. Despite being the oldest, she often had trouble getting to sleep and whined about the mattress, or the heat, or the mosquitoes, until someone's patience ran out and they threatened to give her a good hiding unless she quietened down.

A couple of the others were snoring. That was odd, too. If it happened at all, it was in the early morning, when Mei often woke for a while, missing the sounds of the city, before drifting off to sleep again for a few more hours.

Mei raised her head off the pillow and peered over the humped form of Eleven to look at Sis in the next bed over.

'Hey, Sis,' she hissed. 'You awake?'

Mei realised Sis was one of those snoring.

Was it the vitamin tablets after all?

She sat up in bed and scanned the room. It was like her and five corpses in there. Nobody was moving, apart from the soft rise and fall of the sheets covering their chests.

'Hey!' she said, louder, this time. 'Anyone awake? No? Just me? Hello? Hello!'

A snore broke the silence, which was otherwise total.

Shit! It *was* the tablets. They weren't vitamins at all. But they weren't mind-control pills like Brains was always banging on about either. They were sleepers. Powerful ones, too.

They sold them on the street in Shenzhen. Twenty yuan would get you an official one. But if you didn't mind one without a label, maybe made in some dodgy lab out in the boonies, you could get them for as little as seven.

But those just gave you a mild high or helped you block out the traffic and building site noise if you actually needed help sleeping.

The little white pills were proper knockout drops. She'd been thinking she might sneak out and flush the tablet in her pillow down the toilet, but now she thought she'd hold onto it.

She fished it out from the pillow and posted it through a hole in the upright of her metal bedstead. She listened to it rattle its way to the bottom where it came to rest on the rubber bung that stoppered the steel tube.

That night, as the other girls slept their chemically induced sleep, Mei lay awake. The anaesthetic in her hand had worn off and the pain had come back. Not the white-hot lancing agony, but a dull, unpleasant burning that swelled and faded like the distant sound of a tractor engine in the fields back home, rising and falling as the farmer dipped behind a low-lying hill.

The vision she'd had of Mummy Rita when she'd fainted was troubling her. She wished she had a way of getting her a message. And more than that, she felt guilty for just running off three years earlier without telling her.

Was this guilty feeling an emotion? She wasn't sure. But she didn't like it and tried to force it back into the dark place where it had come from.

The trouble was, it didn't want to be quiet.

How could she have done that to Mummy Rita? Just left without even saying goodbye?

Mummy had raised her. Clothed her. Kept her warm. She'd bound her wounds when she'd cut her foot on broken glass lying in the road or broken her finger falling out of a walnut tree.

Mei remembered with a sad smile the last time Mummy had scolded her. It had been at the end of a massive row.

'Oh, you ungrateful, girl! After all I've done for you. I put food in your belly and a shirt on your back and look how you repay me! I wish I'd never taken you.'

At the time, Mei had been blinded by her own anger to pay much attention to Mummy Rita's torrent of complaints, accusations and abuse.

She'd flung a few choice swear-words of her own over her shoulder and run off down to play by the bank of the Little Mekong.

'I wish I'd never taken you.'

That was a funny word to use. Why 'taken'? Why not 'had'?

Mei shook her head. Her memory must be playing up. It was a long time ago. She'd probably got it wrong. All the same, she wished she could ask Mummy to her face.

They'd be shelling peas together outside the little house they shared. A big tin bowl for the empty pods and a smaller one for the peas, so sweet, like little explosions of freshness in your mouth.

The sun would be out. Mei would feel it warming her back as she squatted beside Mummy. She'd pick pod after pod, squeezing them gently to split them down the seam then running her thumbnail along the peas to send them tumbling and flipping into the bowl.

From nowhere, she felt a surge of homesickness. *I want to see you again, Mummy Rita. I miss you.*

This was *definitely* an emotion. She cursed it. But gave in all the same. Tears welled in her eyes and overspilled to run down her cheeks. She swiped them away with the palm of her undamaged hand.

19

The weeks passed in an endless rotation of instruction in Communist thought from the Frog and increasingly brutal training exercises from the Crane and the Bull.

Every day, they worked until they were so tired they could barely keep their eyes open as they shovelled their food down at dinnertime. Every night, the doctor dispensed the little white tablets. And every time, Mei palmed hers then posted it into the little screw-hole in her bed frame.

The kids kept asking about when they'd be learning to shoot guns, but every time they got a knock-back, sometimes literally. One was the first. He pushed his luck too far, piping up at the end of a demonstration on the use of pressure points to immobilise an opponent before disarming them.

'This is all very well, Master Long,' he said. 'But we need to learn to shoot, too, don't we? Else how are we going to defeat China's enemies?'

The Bull nodded, stroking his chin as if One had asked a really sensible question. Mei was already flinching internally.

'That's a good question, One,' the Bull said eventually. 'I tell you what. Come and take the pistol off my belt and we'll see how good a shot you are with it.'

One's face lit up. 'Really?'

'Sure,' the Bull said, a broad smile on his face. 'After all, you can't expect to be an assassin with what I've been teaching you, can you?'

Mei wanted to scream at One. To tell him to get back in line and apologise to the Bull. On his knees, preferably. But the boy was a lost cause. No doubt he was already imagining himself killing some CIA agent with a well-aimed shot to the back of the head.

Shaking his head, then turning to wink at Rats, One left the line and strode up to the Bull. Mei even detected a hint of a swagger. All she could do was watch and wait. Saying anything now would earn her twice whatever was about to befall One.

One came to a stop about a metre in front of the Bull. Hands dangling by his sides but unable to keep his eyes off the butt of the Type 54 on the Bull's waist.

'What now?' he asked.

'Like I said. Take it.'

Mei watched One stretch out his right hand and close his fingers around the pistol's grip.

There was a loud crack. Then a louder scream.

One's mouth was stretched wide and his eyes were wider. He was looking down at the spot where the Bull's massive hands were clamped around his wrist.

Something bad had happened to his arm. Halfway between his elbow and his wrist, it took a sharp downwards direction. The Bull's hands were clamped around it; One's own right hand swung uselessly, the index finger pointing at the ground.

A couple of the kids had gasped. Mei kept her lips buttoned. She'd known what was going to happen, or at least the flavour of it.

And it served One right. Who in their right mind would dare challenge any of the instructors, let alone the Bull? Even when One had the chance to back off, he hadn't taken it.

After his first involuntary scream, at least One had realised he needed to be silent. Despite the obvious agony he was in, his mouth was a grim line in a white face. Tears streamed from his eyes.

Mei noticed that the fingers of his left hand were sticking out straight like a little bundle of bamboo sticks, twitching as their five friends dangled limply just half a metre away.

The Bull didn't release One. But he turned to the others, speaking over One's drooping head.

'Anyone else fancy some firearms training?'

Nobody replied. In this, at least, they were smarter than One.

The Bull unclamped his vice-like grip. One staggered backwards, finally able to cradle his broken arm.

'I, I'm sorry, Master Long,' he said in a low voice. 'It won't happen again.'

'You're correct, One, it won't. Now, off to the sick bay with you.'

Once One had stumbled off and entered the school building, the Bull resumed where he had left off, as if the intervening five minutes hadn't happened.

'Your enemy has a pistol pointed at your head. He is feeling confident. Correct?'

Nobody answered.

'Correct?' he asked again, louder.

It was a trick question. Mei could see that. It wasn't hard. All the Bull's questions were like this. An obvious answer dangled in front of them like a ripe peach in a basket offered to a monkey. Stick your hand in to grab the peach and you were trapped.

They'd been learning about disarming opponents. So she went for the *un*obvious answer.

'No, Master Long.'

He raised his eyebrows.

'Really, Twelve. Then perhaps you can enlighten us. If he is not feeling confident, what *is* he feeling?'

'*Over*-confident, master. He has a gun: I am unarmed. He thinks he has nothing to fear. His guard is down even while his gun is up.'

The Bull grinned.

'Tactical awareness *and* poetry in one answer,' he said. 'Maybe you should be teaching me and not the other way around, eh?'

Another trick question, though sprinkled with sugar this time.

Mei bowed her head.

'I am here only to learn, Master.'

'Then come up here, Twelve.'

She stepped out of line, just as One had done, and closed the distance between them to the same one-metre space.

Her heart was thumping in her chest. Maybe he wasn't going to break her wrist, but the Bull was quite capable of administering a beating if you didn't follow his instructions. Or even if you just didn't appear to be listening.

So fast she could have sworn she must have dropped off to sleep for a split-second, the Bull's Type 54 was pointing at her face.

The muzzle looked huge as she squinted at it, holding her head steady, though every muscle and nerve was screaming at her to jerk it backwards.

She adjusted her focus and saw that the pressed-steel safety catch was in the Off position. And she was more than sure the Bull had chambered a round before beginning the exercise that day.

She imagined the bullet nestled in the chamber whistling out and smashing her skull like a ripe melon. Oddly, it calmed her. All she had to do was listen and follow the Bull's orders and everything would be OK.

20

The Bull straightened his arm until the bend at his elbow disappeared and it was extended in a straight line from his shoulder. The Type 54's muzzle was so close Mei could feel it brushing the fine hairs that grew in the cleft between her eyebrows.

Her heart was tripping along like a deer running through the forest, a light skipping beat that would come on when she was running from the cops back in Shenzhen.

Then, her mind would come free of her body. She'd be hardly aware of running, of dodging down alleys or vaulting high chain-link fences, jumping for the lowest ladder of a fire escape or darting in and out of market stalls.

Instead, she'd be planning her route, counting the cops from their shouts or the thumping of their boots on the tarmac.

Or even just thinking about totally random things like the pretty shade of blue of a baby's shawl as she sprinted past the open door of an apartment building, or the delicious smell of frying onions from a street vendor's cart.

What would it feel like to be shot in the head? Would it hurt?

On the whole, she thought not. It would be far too quick.

There'd be a flash of blinding white light and then nothing. Blackness.

She doubted you'd even hear the gun firing. Brains said light travelled a thousand times fast than sound which was why you saw the explosion of distant fireworks before you heard the bang of the gunpowder.

No! Focus, Mei!

Was this the time for daydreams? Idiot! If she wanted a thrashing from the Bull, this was *exactly* the right way to earn one. She looked into his eyes. However far she'd travelled in her mind, clearly only a second had passed in the real world.

The Bull met her stare in a way that felt almost friendly, but pitched his voice for the others.

'As Twelve says, your opponent is over-confident. Of course, *he* doesn't think that,' he said, extending his arm fractionally, but enough that the cold steel of the muzzle now pressed against the crinkled ridge of skin between Mei's eyebrows. '*He* thinks he's in control of the situation. After all, what could *possibly* go wrong when he has a gun aimed between your eyes?'

Mei waited. She knew what she wanted to do, but getting ahead of yourself with the Bull was as bad as falling behind.

He nodded at her. A tiny movement she was sure only she could see.

No time for thinking. Only for acting.

She fell to her right, twisting clockwise to bring her right arm up and across her body. As her movements sped up, time slowed down. *Ha! More poetry for you, Master Long.*

The Type 54's muzzle was no longer touching the bridge of her nose. It was moving sideways, relative to her head, sliding over her left eye, the bony rim of her eye socket, the edge of her skull and then into empty air. A real opponent, even one with sharp reflexes, would still be way off pulling the trigger.

Mei's hand rotated between their bodies, fingers bunched into a fist. Her target was a point midway along the Bull's upper arm. His biceps were big and bulgy, like grapefruits sewn under his skin. But that didn't matter. What mattered was the bundle of nerves that ran between the muscles and the bone.

They'd studied them in the classroom. Even been taken to an autopsy at the local hospital to see how everything fitted together in real life – well, death.

The ulnar and median nerves were Mei's targets. Strike correctly and the Bull's arm would become as powerful as a dead fish. She didn't bother thinking about what an incorrect strike would mean. Would he pull the trigger? It would be a good lesson for the others, at least.

At the last moment, she rotated her fist so that the knuckles struck deep into the tissue below the Bull's biceps and jumped back.

With a grunt of pain, but no more than that, he dropped the pistol to the ground. His arm swung down like a pendulum and he, too, stepped back, out of range of any follow-up Mei might have been planning.

But she was too cunning to try. He'd no doubt be ready with a kick or a left-handed strike of his own to send her hobbling off to join One in the sick bay.

The Bull nodded to her a second time. It was all the praise she'd get, and more than she needed. The fact she'd disarmed him, twice her size and an experienced PLA commando, was enough for her.

She rejoined the line as the Bull retrieved his pistol with his left hand and replaced it in his holster. Rubbing his right arm, he addressed them.

'Being captured is not failure. Sometimes being captured is part of the plan. The only way you can get close to your target,' he said. 'What is failure?'

Sis stuck up her hand.

'Being killed, Sir?'

'No. Anybody?'

Psycho, who had been silent throughout, raised his hand.

'I fail only if I don't kill my target,' he said in that curiously flat voice of his.

The Bull nodded.

'Three is correct. Once it has been determined by your

commander that a target must be eliminated, that is your only consideration. Hear me? Your *only* consideration.' The Bull raised his voice. 'It does not matter if you die. It does not matter if your support team dies. It does not matter if your *commander* dies. Once the mission is set, the target must die. Repeat it.'

Keeping time by thumping his right boot down onto the concrete, the Bull led them in five minutes of chanting this simple, deadly mantra. He brought the chorus to a stop by slicing his hand through the air like a blade.

* * *

'Would you kill the target's wife if she was between you and the target?' Rats asked Mei at lunchtime.

Slurping some more of the chicken noodle soup into her mouth, Mei nodded. She doubted they ever had privacy, and especially not indoors. No way was she going to risk her life by coming out with anything against the school's teaching. Even a gesture might be enough to land her in front of the Frog, and that was *absolutely* not going to happen.

'How about his children?' Sis asked from her other side.

Mei swallowed.

'You heard what the Bull said.' She used his nickname on purpose. If the Frog *was* eavesdropping, calling the teacher Master Long when they were supposed to be relaxing would ring a warning bell for sure. 'Once the mission is set, the target must die.'

'Oh, yeah, I would, too,' Sis said. 'Kill 'em all. You have to.'

Mei could see her friend wasn't convinced. But across the table and two seats further down, Psycho was leaning towards them and nodding, catching every word they said.

'How about you, Three?' Mei asked, knowing what his answer would be.

He smiled. It made her flesh crawl, the way he could make his mouth curve upwards without it ever reaching his eyes. Like he was performing some kind of act.

'I'd kill his wife, his kids, his old granny and every last koi carp in his ornamental fucking fishpond,' he said.

The others gasped. However hard the authorities at the school tried to lecture, harangue and beat it out of them, their respect for old people was twined around their souls like vines around one of the old temples that still dotted the countryside. Even though Mei was more than capable of hurling insults, that's all they were. But Psycho was doing something simpler and scarier. Telling the truth.

She eyed Psycho warily. She had no doubt he couldn't care less whether he was being bugged or not. He meant every word of it. He'd take pleasure in it, too.

'What are you looking at, freak?'

Psycho was glaring at her.

'Don't call me a freak,' Mei said quietly.

He grinned. That horrible eel-like expression, showing a few teeth this time but still no change in this dead eyes.

'Why? What are you going to do about it?' A beat. 'You round-eyed freak.'

'She could teach you a lesson, that's for sure,' Rats said.

Mei turned to him. Great. That was all she needed. A cheerleader goading the most dangerous kid in their class to ratchet things up a level or two.

'Ooh, a lesson from the freak! What're you going to teach me? Stuff you learned off the Bull? I'm not surprised the way you suck up to him. Probably suck his dick at night, too, don't you? Freak.'

Throughout this whole speech, Psycho's expression never wavered. Despite the hostility that from another kid would come across loud and clear in his tone of voice, he sounded as if he were reading out the instructions for what to do if the fire alarm went off.

Under the table, Mei's left knee had started bobbing up and down. She knew Psycho was itching for her to start a fight. Probably thought he could wipe the floor with her.

Well, he wasn't the only one who could keep their emotions under control. But she still knew she'd have to do something to put him back in his box. It was either that or let him get bolder until he put one of his grotesque suggestions into action.

She stood, slowly. Psycho watched her as she rounded the table and came to stand behind him. He pushed his bowl away and stood, making sure to jam his chair back hard into her thighs.

Mei's fingertips were tingling and she could hear a high-pitched whine between her ears.

Psycho grinned at her, that cold smile like someone had painted it on.

'Any time, freak,' he murmured.

Mei glanced past him at the table. She feinted left and as he matched her movement, she twisted over and down to the right, darted out her hand and snatched up one of the chopsticks he'd discarded.

By the time he'd realised his error and swivelled round to pin her against the edge of the table, she had the chopstick in her fist, the pointed end jabbed into the soft place to the side of his windpipe.

She could feel the throb of the fat artery beneath the wooden stick pulsing into her hand.

'I just need to push a little harder and you're history,' she said, staring into those unreadable eyes of his.

Then she dropped the chopstick and stood to attention.

Psycho grabbed her around the neck and started squeezing, his face impassive. Mei simply let him. She wouldn't have to suffer it for long. Because the Bull was standing right behind him. He dealt Psycho a crushing blow to the right shoulder, right over the brachial plexus, where all the thick white bundles of nerves ran close to the surface. With a high-pitched scream, Psycho let Mei go and fell to the ground, clutching his injured joint.

Their punishment for fighting was brutal. Twenty laps of the running track in bare feet while carrying a brick in each hand. By the end, Mei's arms felt like someone had doused them in petrol and set them ablaze. She dropped the bricks to the ground and staggered away, back to the dormitory. She didn't even bother looking to see where Psycho was.

The Bull's shout followed her inside:

'Next time it'll be fifty laps. And four bricks.'

21

As the weeks and months went by, Mei made several attempts to escape.

Initially by simply hiding in the back of a laundry truck just before the driver climbed into the cab and started the clattery old engine. *That* beating had meant standing up at mealtimes for a week and sleeping on her belly.

After that, she'd become smarter. She tried to use the training she was receiving to her own advantage.

One night, after the others were asleep, she crept from her bed, dressed silently and slipped out of the dormitory door. She wondered, briefly, why they never locked it. The answer presented itself just as quickly. *Because they don't need to, dummy.*

And if anyone did manage to leave, where were they going to go? The whole place was surrounded by a tall fence topped with coils of scary-looking barbed wire. The main gate was flanked by a guard tower.

You could look up there at any time of the day and see a soldier with a machine gun. Maybe he was there to keep people out. Mei had a shrewd idea his orders were mainly focused in the other direction.

The school grounds were spacious, though. Mei was relying on the fact that there had to be *one* weak spot. There always was.

Hotels had kitchen doors left propped open with a brick so the staff could sneak a crafty smoke when they should be working. Building sites had sections of fencing distorted by the weight of steel girders propped against them by lazy contractors. Apartment blocks had front entrances whose wheezy closers took so long to shut the doors, you could slip in behind a resident without even being seen.

Beyond the dormitory was unknown territory for Mei after lights-out. She imagined the guards playing cards in the office, or maybe snoozing with their peaked caps pulled down over their eyes.

She waited until her eyes adjusted to the dim light in the hallway, her back pressed against the door. When she could see well enough to make out the shapes of things, she ran down the hallway on the balls of her feet, grateful for the concrete floor that wouldn't creak and betray her.

Halfway to the stairwell, she spotted a soft yellow light seeping out from under the office door. From inside she heard a sudden shout and froze. If they opened the office door and saw her here it would be a one-way trip to Director Gao's office. Her stomach clenched as she waited.

A laugh followed the shout. Then good-natured banter about cheating at cards. Mei heard the scrape of chairs, footsteps and the plink and hiss of a beer bottle being opened.

Good. Keep drinking. It'll make you slow.

She reached the stairwell and took the steps carefully, holding onto the sticky, plastic-covered handrail. The light darkened further until she was descending in total darkness.

On the ground floor, she felt her way along the wall, using her memory alone. The main door was closer, but more likely to be locked, she thought. The wall was rough beneath her fingertips as she trailed her hand along its plastered surface towards the kitchen.

She knew her way, but in any case, the smell of much-used grease and the sharp aroma of spices would have led her there like a bright-red neon trail floating in the air.

Crouching below the level of the circular windows in the double doors, she pressed her ear against the door. Trying to ignore her thumping heartbeat, she strained to catch a sound, *any* sound, from the room beyond the plywood panel.

She heard nothing.

Placing the palm of her left hand against the door, she pushed. For a moment, when it refused to move, she feared it was locked. Then it gave and she realised it was just the angle she was pushing from causing the trouble.

Inside the kitchen, she stood, relaxed just a fraction, and skirted the big stove with its blackened iron burners. She was heading for the back room. The stores.

She'd watched a delivery van pull up from time to time, dropping off vegetables, tinned goods and sometimes sides of meat, reddish-purple and mottled with creamy stripes of fat.

The kitchen porter would slide open a steel shutter that rolled up inside the opening with a clanging rattle. Then he and the van driver would unload the supplies straight into the store room.

Mei had no intention of exiting via the shutter. That racket would have the whole school rushing down to the kitchen to kill the intruders come to steal the food. But next to the roller shutter was a normal-sized door. A door with a cheap-looking metal handle. The weak spot.

Inside, the store room was chilly, raising goose bumps on her arms, She shouldered her way between sides of beef hanging from hooks, wooden bins piled high with vegetables, and metal racks groaning with tinned water chestnuts and bamboo shoots and bottles of soy sauce.

There was the shutter, padlocked to a steel ring-bolt in the floor. And, beside it, the access door.

She crossed the remaining two metres of floorspace, stood in front of the door and grasped the handle. If the door was locked, she'd have to go back the way she'd come, trying to avoid being spotted. If they did catch her, she had a story ready. Not great, but probably enough to earn her a beating instead of expulsion.

Expulsion? Ha! That was a joke. Who was she kidding? If they caught her, they'd kill her.

'I was hungry, Ma'am,' she'd say. 'I know stealing food is wrong, but I didn't want to disappoint Master Long in tomorrow's training exercises.'

She could picture the expression on the Crane's face. Equal parts disgust and doubt. Maybe just a smidgen of understanding. She must've undergone something similar, surely? In her own training? Maybe she'd just give Mei a cuff round the ear and send her back to bed with a warning not to try it again.

Mei actually snorted at the thought of it – *How ridiculous!* – then covered her mouth with her hand. She pushed down on the aluminium handle and the door opened, just like that. She was outside.

Mei caught the acrid tang of the cheap cigarettes the guards all smoked. She flattened herself against the wall and inched her way along until she reached the corner.

Peeping round, she saw one of them slouched against a piece of training equipment, the red end of his cigarette glowing in the darkness. He had his back to her and was humming a song off the radio.

Mei slid round the corner and, keeping her eye on him, moved away, into the shadow of the dormitory block. When she was sure she was out of his eyeline, she turned and continued along the wall, listening out for any sound that might come from a human source.

Plenty of *non*-human sources were contributing to the nighttime entertainment. An owl hooted somewhere in the trees beyond the fence. Crickets and cicadas kept up a ceaseless buzz and chitter. She heard a bullfrog croaking away merrily from the big pond over near the eastern end of the compound.

A human cry of pain brought Mei to a sudden stop. It sounded like someone being tortured. Her mind flew to the threats the Crane made if she detected any of what she termed 'disorderly thinking' among the students.

She took a slow, deep breath. Panic was her enemy. She'd known that long before fetching up at the school for Technical Studies. But it was a lesson they had drummed into them time and time again by the instructors. She exhaled. Repeated it. And again. Felt the fear leaving her.

The agonised cry pierced the night a second time. This time, calmed by her breathing exercise, Mei smiled. That was no human. Just a pair of foxes mating in the underbrush.

The thought of what they were doing reminded her of the Party boys on the building site. Of the cop in the cell just before she'd stabbed him through the eye with his own door key. Of the Frog and his disgusting, groping hands and rasping breath. She was never going to let any man do that to her again. Not ever.

Most of the activity at the school took place towards the front half of the grounds. The square where they practised martial arts. The main gate with its guard tower. The gravel track they ran on as they left the complex of buildings.

Back here, the scrubby trees, flowering shrubs and low-growing vegetation had been allowed to run wild. Something was giving off a delicious scent, like the peaches Mei had been awarded on that early day of training. For being the last one standing.

Would they run the exercise again? Only with knives this time? Or guns? Surely not. It would waste all the money and time they'd spent training the twelve of them.

But maybe they needed to be sure the students wouldn't bottle it when the time came. It was one thing to stab training dummies, or slash at each other while protected by the fish-scales. But sticking a knife into a real person? Or shooting them in the head with a sniper rifle?

Mei shook her head. She wouldn't flinch. But the others? She didn't know.

Like Sis. She said all the right things in class. But there was a softness to her. She flinched when the adults demonstrated new attack methods or killing strikes.

Sis cried in her sleep sometimes. Not loud enough to wake the others, deep in their drugged slumber. But Mei was a light sleeper. She heard the sniffs and the thin sounds of her weeping, face buried in the pillow.

She'd climb out of bed, placing her toes down on the cold lino first. Then walk on what Mummy Rita used to call 'cat's feet' over to Sis's bed. There, she'd lay a comforting hand on her friend's exposed shoulder until the noises stopped, replaced after a few minutes by quiet snoring.

Mei heard Mummy Rita's voice in her head, as clear as if she'd been standing right beside her. 'Wool-gathering again, Mei?' She frowned. Back home, daydreaming might earn her a clip round the ear for neglecting her chores. Out here it could get her killed.

As she pushed deeper into the scrub, her nerves settled further. She looked over her shoulder. The school buildings were mostly dark. Just a couple of lights on. Out here, it was just her and the animals. The bullfrog was still belching away like a fat man after a big meal. Mei grinned at the image.

She crouched in a patch of tall, reed-like grasses and rubbed a hand over her eyes. How had this happened? How had she gone from a little village where everybody knew everybody's business to the megacity of Shenzhen and her gang of street kid friends and then the school, where grown-ups taught kids how to kill people?

22

The answer came to her at once.

She'd run to escape the men who'd come to the village with their guns and their threats. At first she'd thought they were from the Party. But now she was living in a Party school. Training to be a Party assassin!

The Party, as the Frog loved to remind them, put food in their mouths, clothes on their backs, education into their heads and a roof over their head.

Well, the Party could go fuck itself. She just needed to find that weak point in the perimeter and she could escape. But where was it? And how, exactly, was she going to get past the guards and random patrols by the Crane or one of the other instructors?

She had no time to think of an answer. Something, no, someone, was coming her way. Crackles and swishes of vegetation as they swiped them aside with a stick. And voices.

Shit! Not one person. Two. A man and a woman. And not just any man and woman, either. The Bull and the Crane were out here. Why? Why couldn't they stay indoors with their whisky and cigarettes like normal people?

The breeze had gone, and their voices carried in the still night air. Mei felt panic rising and this time no amount of breathing exercises would slow it. She wanted to stand up and sprint into the darkness towards the perimeter fence. But they'd hear her. They'd see her! And then that would be it.

Instead of running, Mei dropped to her belly and pressed herself down into the soft earth, sliding her narrow frame between the clumps of reed stems and hoping it was enough to keep her hidden. But the footsteps were getting closer and now she could make out every word.

'...still say he's trouble, that one,' the Bull was saying.

'Maybe. But he could be our best-ever trainee. He has the look.'

'Yeah, I've seen it. Like you're not a real person to him.'

'So much the better for an assassin. No troublesome emotions getting in the way of the operation.'

Mei desperately wanted to listen in, but if they didn't stop walking, they were going to trip over her. Every muscle was quivering as she readied herself to run. Then the footsteps halted. Had they found enough privacy? She hoped so.

'He's unreliable. I wouldn't trust him with my life,' the Bull said.

The Crane laughed. 'Luckily for you, you don't have to.'

'But one of the others might.'

'They're solo operators. They shouldn't be relying on anyone.'

'I disagree. Maybe for the final stages they're on their own,' the Bull said. 'But you know as well as I do, they have to be able to work in teams.'

This was interesting. They were arguing. And it was obvious about who. Psycho. Mei flattened herself still further and turned her head a fraction, the better to catch their conversation.

'He'll be fine.'

'He's a psychopath.'

'So?'

'So? What do you mean, so?'

'He enjoys killing, that much is obvious,' the Crane said in a patient voice like a teacher bashing times tables into some dim kid's brain. 'But that's to our advantage. We're going to give him a job where he gets to do just that. No repercussions. No blame. Just a pat on the back and another target.'

'Listen, you've been in the intelligence corps your whole life. Spying, covert shit, I get that,' the Bull said. 'Me, I was just a humble soldier. I—'

'Hardly humble. You are a highly decorated veteran of many patriotic conflicts. A commando.'

The Bull continued as if the Crane hadn't interrupted him. It wasn't fair. If she'd been one of the students, he would have busted her jaw for that level of insolence.

'I learned how to kill. But I also learned how to follow orders. And, yes, give them. My people obeyed me because they trusted me. Nobody trusts Three. He's a liability. I want him gone.'

Mei wanted to shout out, 'Me, too!' Psycho *was* a liability. If he felt like it, he'd kill one of his own instead of the target. She could picture him doing it, too, with that creepy smile on his face. Sliding a knife in under their ribs or putting a small-calibre bullet into the roof of their mouth.

You'd ask him, *What the hell did you do that for?*

And he'd just shrug. *I felt like it.*

'You want him gone?' the Crane repeated, amusement in her voice like the Bull had said something funny. 'Then it's simple. Just go to Gao and tell him. I'm sure he'd kick Three out of the programme immediately.'

'Funny.'

'Well, really, what do you expect me to say? You know how things work around here. And anyway, the Frog chose him specially.'

Mei had to stifle a sudden giggle that threatened to burst from her throat. They called him that, too? Oh, that was too good. Wait till she told the others.

The Bull made a sort of harrumphing cough in the back of his throat. Like a dog trying to dislodge a wad of half-chewed meat it had bolted to keep it from the others in its pack.

'He's trouble, Minxia. I'm telling you. And you know who'll catch it in the neck when he does screw up. Clue: not the Frog.'

'Then we'd better make sure he doesn't.'

Mei nodded in agreement, vowing to keep an even closer eye on Psycho from now on. Then her left leg cramped violently. The pain twisted the muscle like wringing out a wet wash-cloth. She bit down hard to stop herself screaming out and tasted blood in her mouth.

Trying to stay quiet, she stretched the leg out behind her. But the pain was too strong. If she didn't relieve it, she knew she'd not be able to hold the scream back.

She rolled onto her back, reaching for her toes, but all she did was brush against some of the tall reeds giving her cover. They rattled together. In the quiet it sounded as loud as mah-jongg tiles being shuffled on a cafe table.

'Someone's out here,' the Bull said.

'Come out. Now!' the Crane commanded.

Mei heard the catch being unsnapped on a holster. The whisper of metal against leather as one of them drew their Type 54.

The bang was deafening. They'd fired into the grasses. Above her head a reed toppled lazily sideways, its stem severed by the bullet. If she'd even been kneeling, it would have smashed her brains into pulp.

For once she didn't know what to do. All her street smarts had deserted her. Her leg was still cramping and the ringing in her ears wasn't helping, either. It clouded her brain like the early morning mist that rolled out of the forest and through the school grounds.

She could run. Yeah, and get shot down before she'd made ten metres. Or stay down. And then what? Let them grab her and take her back inside for the biggest beating of her life? No thanks!

Run it was, then. She readied herself. At least moving would relieve the pain in her leg. On three, she told herself.

One.

Two.

'Idiot!' the Crane said. 'It was just a rat or a lizard or something.'

Mei squashed herself even lower until she could feel each grainy clod of earth through her thin pyjamas.

'Big fucking lizard,' the Bull snorted.

'Forget it. You almost deafened me. Anyway, who do you think would be out here at this time of night? A KGB agent?'

'Fair enough. I guess it was just my training kicking in.'

'Nothing more than I would expect. It's why you're such an asset to the school. Listen, it's the first field exercise tomorrow,' the Crane said. 'I've thought of a new twist we can add.'

The two adults moved away. The sound of their feet swishing through the undergrowth and the ringing in Mei's ears combined to block out whatever the Crane said next.

Mei hated missing out on whatever secret the Crane was sharing. But on the positive side she could finally stretch out her leg and massage the cramp away.

When she was sure the two instructors had reached the main block, Mei raised herself into a crouch and peered through the feathery reeds. She was just in time to see the door closing.

23

Mei spent another two hours making a slow circuit of the perimeter, looking for a weak spot. Looking for anything she could exploit to get over the fence. But the authorities who'd built the school had been thorough.

All the way round, coils of the vicious-looking barbed wire topped the chain-link. Mei tried to figure out a way she could get over them, but the only images that came to mind involved her stranded on their razor-sharp points while a guard cut her free, a gun aimed at her temple.

It was just before sunrise – the sky lightening from an inky blue to a pale, washed-out turquoise – when she regained the safety of the accommodation block. Keeping to the shadows, she made her way back to the girls' dormitory and slid into bed.

Unable to sleep, she lay there until the morning bell clanged in the corridor and the others raised their heads from their pillows, bleary-eyed and ghost-like as they rolled or, in one case, fell, out of bed and began preparing for another day.

Mei knew something was up as soon as she reached the front of the breakfast queue.

There was sweet porridge. Plus rice and chicken. And bananas and sticky cakes that smelled deliciously of toasted coconut. Even bars of gritty, super-sweet chocolate, their red paper wrappers decorated with a picture of a heroic peasant, scythe raised above her head and smiling like she'd just been given a new cow.

She was just wondering what to choose when the kitchen assistant, a man they all called Bun, on account of his pockmarked, doughy round face, said irritably, 'You get it all today, just hold out your tray.'

Mei did as she was told. He ladled a dollop of the thick porridge into one depression in the pressed aluminium tray, followed by everything else. She walked away to a table goggling at the sheer amount of food she was carrying.

'What's going on?' Sis asked, pointing at her own heaped tray. 'Chocolate for breakfast?'

Mei looked towards the far end of the dining room where an instructor was leaning against the wall, smoking a cigarette. It had to be for the exercise. But surely this couldn't have been the twist the Crane was bragging about to the Bull. Could it?

The door from the corridor opened, banging loudly on the wall as it swung back on its hinges. Everyone turned to look, some still chewing.

The Frog entered the dining room, flanked by the Crane and the Bull. They were grim-faced, but Mei read nothing into it. Neither of them ever seemed that sparky first thing in the morning. If she had to guess, she'd say they probably stayed up late drinking whisky in the Crane's room.

The Frog waited until the room was silent. From the kitchen came a crash as someone dropped one of the heavy steel cooking pots. An oath in the local dialect followed. A couple of the students smirked. Someone giggled, then abruptly cut it off.

Mei kept her eyes on the Frog. His wide mouth crimped at the sounds from the kitchen. He was good at keeping a straight face, though. In his boring lectures she could never tell what he was thinking. Well, until he turned that bulgy-eyed gaze on her. Then she could. Could, and didn't like it.

She started counting. Reached nine before the Frog opened his mouth.

'Students of the School for Technical Studies, you have made excellent progress,' he said. 'I receive glowing reports from all of your instructors, but especially from Miss Du and Mr Long.

'But your work – your real work – will not take place in the classroom, the gymnasium or the grounds of this fine institution.'

Mei had long ago grown used to the Frog's particular brand of bullshit. But he seemed to be making a special effort today. 'Fine institution'? He made it sound like it was one of those posh universities in Beijing, when in reality he was the boss of a school for killers.

She caught the Crane looking at her. The woman's lips tightened into a thin line. Not for the first time, Mei wondered if she was a mind-reader like the ones in the travelling fairs that used to trail around the countryside stopping at each village and town for a day or two.

She looked down then up, refocusing on the Frog and trying for a facial expression that would give the right impression of unthinking loyalty. The Crane took no further action, so Mei guessed she'd got away with it.

The Frog was still droning on. She tuned back in.

'...practical exploration of your newfound skills. That is why we have granted you additional food privileges this morning. Straight after breakfast you will report to the front yard in your training outfits.'

He turned and left, the Crane and the Bull following him. As soon as the door closed behind them, the room erupted into excited chatter. What was that all about? What was he going on about? What did he mean, 'practical exploration'?

'We're going outside the wire,' Mei said loudly, stilling the chatter.

'What do you mean?' Psycho asked, his lip curling.

Mei glared at him. 'Sorry, Three, I forgot how stupid you were.' Titters. 'I said we're going outside the wire. That means *we*,' Mei swept her arm around in a half-circle, encompassing all the students, 'are *going*,' she tapped the tips of her first two fingers on the tabletop and scissored them along like a stick girl walking, '*outside the wire*'!

She concluded her little dumbshow by sending her pointing index finger in a curving, up-and-over arc.

'You don't know that,' he said.

'Want to bet?'

'You have nothing to bet with.'

She turned to Sis and winked the eye hidden from Psycho.

'That's where you're wrong. If I'm right you have to talk back to the Crane next time she's in here with us. If I'm wrong, I'll do it.'

She stared at him. There. Let him have a little think about that. Those were high stakes.

Maybe Psycho was the Crane's favourite, but giving an instructor lip was unthinkable. The Bull would probably damage you permanently. The Crane, now, she'd probably have some really seriously weird torture she'd inflict on you.

She could see it in Psycho's eyes. He loved the thought of watching her be hauled off in a headlock and beaten senseless. But he was cunning enough to realise that Mei would never risk that unless she was completely sure it would never happen.

What would he do? She smiled at him. Mei was happy to wait. All around them, the other students were leaning in, waiting to hear what he'd say.

Psycho opened his mouth.

'Actually, I think you're probably right. It's about time we got to play outside, don't you think?'

Very quietly, so low that none of the kitchen staff would hear, Rats made a low noise in his throat. It sounded exactly like a broody hen getting ready to lay. The kids burst out laughing, earning a shouted rebuke from the other side of the serving counter.

* * *

Lined up under a sky the colour of old bruises, pregnant with rain, the students listened as the Crane and the Bull filled them in on what was going to happen.

'You will spend the next thirty hours in the wild. No food or water but what you can find for yourselves. No weapons but what you can fashion for yourselves,' the Crane said with what looked to Mei like a smile of pleasure.

'The exercise will end at,' the Bull consulted his wristwatch, 'eighteen hundred hours tomorrow. Airhorns will sound – three short blasts, followed by two long – every minute for ten minutes across the entire training area. On hearing the signal, students will make their way due north until they hit the highway, where they will be collected.'

The Crane took over.

'Your objective is to survive, pure and simple,' she said, raising her voice as a low rumble of thunder rolled across the land. 'In case you think that is too easy, we are sending the guards out four hours after you leave. Their orders are to track and capture you. Each student captured earns the guard a bonus.' She paused. 'The reward for the student brought back before the exercise ends will be less welcome. Any questions?'

She surveyed the group. Nobody raised their hand. Mei thought that was wise.

You were supposed to listen when the instructors were talking. They told you everything you needed to know. Asking questions was for idiots and suck-ups. Idiots got punished by the staff, suck-ups by the other students.

The only question Mei had was for herself. Was this her chance to escape? On the whole, she rated her chances no better than fifty-fifty.

None of them knew where the school was located. So getting to Shenzhen would be a matter of guesswork. Plus the guards would be after them, hungry for a bit of extra pay that week.

She had a sneaking suspicion that the Frog and his lieutenants would have considered the problem of escaping students long ago. She doubted she was the first to rebel against the school and its brutal regime.

But what would they do with anyone caught on the run? Send

them to bed without any tea? Of course! Because that was how they treated all kinds of disobedience.

She thought a bullet to the back of the head was more likely than a slap on the wrist. After all, they were training to be protectors of China and her economic development. The mother country could hardly trust her future to cowards and runaways, now could she?

Lightning flashed, and thunder rolled overhead. The temperature began dropping from the heat that brought sweat to the forehead even first thing in the morning.

A green military truck with its red star on the cab doors pulled off the road passing the school and turned down the red-dirt track that led up to the main gates. It rolled to a stop and sounded its horn. A guard opened the heavy gates, swinging them back and securing them with long bolts to the concrete pads. The truck roared through and into the main compound, coming to a stop with a hiss of air brakes and a clatter from its engine.

'In!' the Crane shouted as lightning struck a tree on the far side of the gate, setting it ablaze.

Mei exchanged looks with Sis and Rats. Looks that said, *They picked a nice day for it, didn't they?*

They clambered into the back and snagged seats on the welded metal benches next to each other.

Once all twelve students were on board, a guard slammed the tailgate back into position. She pulled down the canvas and laced it. Visibility dropped to a few millimetres where the drab green canvas stretched between the brass eyelets.

The truck lurched forwards, throwing everyone against their neighbour. Mei heard the gates clang closed behind them and the shouted farewells between driver and gate guards.

Mei worked her way to the back. Kneeling in the narrow space between the benches, she forced the taut canvas apart a little at the centre spot and peered out. All she could see was the school growing smaller as the truck left the place that she'd learned to call home.

'What can you see?' Sis asked.

Mei shrugged. 'Just the school.'

All around them the students were starting to chat. The tone was one of excitement. Whatever lay ahead, they all felt ready for it.

This was an adventure. The task didn't sound all that difficult and evading a bunch of blockheads with Kalashnikovs should be easy. They were trained for it, after all.

As the journey lengthened, the storm intensified. A couple of the bangs of thunder overhead were so loud everyone flinched. Mei imagined being a soldier in the PLA. They were under attack from enemy forces. Counter-revolutionary insurgents from Taiwan or Japan. Or maybe the Americans were invading, intent on bombing China back to the Stone Age.

The Frog had delivered a whole series of lectures about the war in Vietnam. He'd told them how the imperialist forces of the USA had tried to destabilise the legitimate Communist government as it strove to achieve its goal of political unification of the whole country. To her, it sounded like more of his Party BS but there was one film he'd shown them that stuck in her memory like a burr.

Huge American planes – B52s – were dropping sticks of bombs over thickly-forested countryside that reminded her of the outskirts of the village back home. The Frog strode back and forth in front of the screen so the bombers and their deadly freight rippled over his fat face, turning it a deathly greenish-yellow.

'Carpet-bombing!' he screeched. 'Kissinger stated publicly that he intended to bomb Vietnam and its peace-loving citizens back to the Stone Age.'

Mei wasn't altogether sure what 'the Stone Age' actually was, but she could see the pictures of the devastation wreaked by the bombs and she imagined life afterwards, for those who survived, would have been pretty shit.

Then again, she'd seen close up what the Communist Party did to people in China whose only crime was not to smile at a poster of Chairman Mao. Maybe the Americans had a point if they were trying to stop them from taking over another country.

And overhead, as the truck rumbled and jounced along the crappy road, the skies continued their civil war.

After a while, the truck came to a sudden stop, throwing

everyone forwards. As they righted themselves, cursing the idiot-driver for his crap driving skills, the canvas was unlaced. A guy with a Kalashnikov pointed at One, who was sitting nearest the back of the truck.

'You. Out!'

One obeyed without question, jumping down into the squishy red mud. Mei caught a glimpse of dark-green forest just like the one in the movie the Frog had shown them. The door was laced up again. She heard the door slam and then they were off again.

Ten more times the routine was repeated. Until Mei was left alone in the back of the truck.

24

The truck rumbled along for another half hour or so, then, with a hiss from its wheezy old air brakes, it slowed to a stop. Mei checked the time on the little steel watch they'd all been issued with before leaving the school. It was a little after eleven.

Mei waited patiently. The back of the truck felt so empty now everyone else had gone. She ran through her priorities. One, find water. Two, food. Three shelter. No. Start again. Shelter would be first. She needed to hide from the soldiers hunting her, eager for a bonus to supplement their meagre pay. Once she had a base, she could start looking for water. As for food, she'd find roots, berries or mushrooms, or maybe set out to trap some small game. A rabbit, if she was lucky.

The canvas flaps were jerked apart and the same armed guard as before jerked his chin at Mei.

'Out.'

She dropped down from the load space onto the red-dirt road.

Without another word, the guard sauntered back to the cab and hoisted himself in through the open door. He slammed it with a loud clang.

The truck executed a swerving circle, coming all the way onto the gravelly, gritty margin then swung back onto the road and headed back the way it had come.

Mei watched it, until all that was left was the drifting smoke from the exhaust. Then even that was gone, dispersed by a sudden squally wind into the thick trees lining the road.

She shivered. The temperature had dropped still further and she was glad of the jacket that she'd slung over her shoulders. She took it off and poked her arms down the sleeves, then zipped it up properly. She still felt full after the huge breakfast, but wondered how long the feeling would last.

With her fists shoved down into the pockets, she turned a full circle. Now what?

Their instructions were clear. Stay unseen until thirty-six hours were up. Until then? Survive. Shouldn't be that hard. True, she'd never gone that long without a home-cooked meal when she'd been living with Mummy Rita. But she'd spent the night in the forest loads of times without coming to any harm.

In Mei's experience, the worst threats were the ones in the village, not out there, in the swamps, forests, streams and hills surrounding it. She headed into the forest that thickened into a solid green wall maybe half a kilometre further on.

As she walked among the trees, she felt the tightness that had encircled her chest ever since she'd arrived at the school start to ease. It was so much a part of her life now that she hardly noticed it. But now that she was outdoors again, with the Crane, the Bull, the Frog and all their BS way behind her – at least – for now, she felt she might be able to relax. Just a little.

An old song Mummy Rita used to sing in her garden came back to Mei and she began, tentatively at first, then in a high, strong voice, to sing it.

Come, come down, O ancestors!
    My garden needs your tenderness.
    Smile upon my little crops
    And bless them with your love.

Will you find the rain and sing to her?
Ask her to fall and fatten my vegetables.
Will you find the sun and sing to him?
Ask him to shine and ripen them.

She liked the chorus the most. Remembered joining in with her reedy little girl's voice when she'd trail behind Mummy Rita as she worked in her garden. Pinching out pea shoots. Smearing blackflies between thumb and forefinger. Thinning carrot seedlings.

Thank you, loving ancestors!
I grow these fruits for you.
Thank you, kindly ancestors!
These fat vegetables, too.

Smiling, she worked her way deeper into the forest. It smelled so lovely out here. No stink from the school kitchen. No smell of fuel from the trucks that smoked and clattered in and out of the yard at all hours of the day and night. Just sweet sappy trees, and the spicy scent from the vegetation that crunched and crackled underfoot.

After an hour's walking, she emerged into a small clearing, maybe just a little bigger than the dormitory back at school. She walked into the centre and spun round in a slow circle. Yes. This might do very nicely.

Despite the cold that had descended, she'd worked up a sweat pushing through the thick undergrowth. She wiped her forehead with her forearm.

She strode to the edge of the clearing. Among the thick-trunked mature trees were younger saplings that had sprouted up from the seeds and never been cleared. In a way that was a good thing. It meant nobody lived out here, clearing trees for construction timber or firewood.

Mei wished she'd been given a knife. But maybe she could find a piece of stone she could knap to a sharp edge. They used to do it at home, she and Ping. Maybe a boy, too, if he wasn't being too annoying.

She scrabbled the dead leaves away from the base of a tree until the soft red earth beneath came into view. The ground was studded with small white stones but nothing big enough to make a knife. She swept her hands left and right, scraping the soil away, hoping she might find a big one deeper down.

Her fingers scuffed against something. She hooked it out: a nice round stone that sat in the palm of her hand quite comfortably. It would do fine, *if* she could find a second to hit it with.

It took her another ten minutes, during which time she'd scraped out an area as big as her bed, before she found a suitable hammer stone. She pushed deeper into the forest until she found what she was looking for next. A second fallen tree.

She ran her hands over its smooth bark, feeling for the depression in the surface she needed. She found it about a third of the way along from the flattened root ball.

With the knife-stone nestled in the little basin and secured with her left palm, she started knocking the hammer stone against its tip in slanting blows. The work wasn't hard, not physically, anyway. What mattered was the angle of your strike and the force you applied. A bit like fighting, really. Too steep and angle with too much force and you just smashed the end off the stone. Too shallow, or too little force, and you just scratched the surface without removing any chips. But get it right and you removed circular flakes of stone from the tip, creating a nice sharp edge.

As she worked, her mind wandered away from the stones and the wooden anvil. This was like being back home again. Clean air to breathe. Open space. No skyscrapers hemming her in. No garish neon signs and brightly-printed posters telling citizens to work hard for progress and maintain purity of Mao Thought.

Years of city living had hardened her. She was so much tougher than when she'd fled the village. And she was a woman now, whereas when she'd left, she'd been just a kid. But as she worked the stone into a blade, she realised how much she'd missed just…

…she struggled to put the thought into words. Missed just… what, exactly?

Just being alone. That was it. Being alone, and outdoors. Free to come and go when she wanted. In Shenzhen, she could do what she liked, but there were always the cops to worry about. The cops and rival gangs. And getting enough to eat. And not getting robbed or beaten up in your sleep. Or worse.

Mummy Rita did used to nag her, that was true. But there'd always been good food to eat. And even if she was fat and snored at night, she always made sure Mei was OK.

Mei sighed. One day, soon, she'd leave the school and all its BS behind and find her way back to the village.

She looked down. Somehow, while her mind had been back home, her hands had shaped the rock resting in the hollow of the tree bark into a serviceable knife. Maybe an axe. A knifeaxe. An axeknife. She smiled.

She found a suitable sapling, its bendy trunk a little thicker than her thumb, and cut it down with quick chopping motions. She stripped off the branchlets with their vivid green leaves until all that was left was a straight length of bendy wood a bit like the fishing poles she used to make.

When she had fourteen, all about three metres from end to end, she carried them back to the edge of the clearing.

Using the axeknife, she carved out a hole in the soft red earth until it was elbow deep. She took the first sapling and pushed its thick end down into the hole, twisting it like a drill to drive it as deep as she could.

She reached up and grasped the sapling as high as she could manage and brought it down so it was bending in a graceful curve. She marked a spot in the earth with its tip then released it to spring back. Once she'd excavated a socket, she pulled it down again, only this time she stuck the end of the sapling down into the earth.

She pushed the loose soil back into the hole around the green-barked sapling and stamped it down with her heel. Now for the moment of truth. She held her breath and let go, leaning back so if it sprang free of the ground its speeding tip wouldn't slash her across the face.

It held.

She used the axeknife to mark out, then dig, twenty-six more sockets in the ground. In went the saplings, one by one; thick end first, whip end second.

When she'd finished, she had a domed structure like an upturned bowl. OK, a bowl that would let all the hot soup through and burn your thighs, but the outline of her shelter was there. She nodded to herself.

After two more hours, during which she'd stripped down to her vest, she'd woven thinner saplings in and out of the framework so the bowl looked a bit more leak-proof. She'd left their branchlets on, too, and tucked them into the holes left between the framework and the covering.

The final stage was to gather great armfuls of ferns and pile them up, starting around the bottom of the bowl – the lip – and working upwards until they all met at the crown. The result was a weatherproof shelter with a rough and untidy outer surface that would fool anyone who wasn't looking too closely.

She thought she'd be quite comfortable in there for a couple of weeks, never mind less than two days.

'Let's see then, shall we?'

She crawled inside, pushing between two saplings set wider apart than the others. Sitting cross-legged in the centre of the soup bowl, she nodded to herself in satisfaction. At a rustle from outside, every nerve in her body started singing at once.

Her pulse hammered in her throat. Surely she hadn't been discovered already! She'd barely got started. Never mind the beating when she was unloaded back to school: the shame of it was somehow worse. Knowing that everybody else, even the hated Psycho, had beaten her.

The rustling grew louder. Whoever it was, he or she had almost mastered the art of walking on dried leaf litter without making a noise. Almost. Despite wearing army boots, their tread was pretty light.

Mei readied herself. She was still holding the axeknife. She gripped it tighter and got ready to attack. Some words of the Crane's words came back to her: '*Do not* think *of killing me.* Kill *me!*'

Silently, Mei uncrossed her legs and manoeuvred herself into a crouch. She moved to the doorway.

The soldier was almost outside now. Another crunch of dried leaves sounded as if he were right on the other side of the soup bowl's leafy surface. She pictured him holding his rifle, ready to poke the barrel through the saplings and order her to come with her hands in the air.

Yeah, well, he had a surprise coming, didn't he?

With a yell, she launched herself at the opening and barrelled through, scratching her face in the process but not noticing. She tripped on the way out and tucked instinctively into a roll. She sprang to her feet, axeknife raised, ready to bring it down on the soldier's skull and put his lights out.

Then she burst out laughing.

25

Facing her, or, she supposed she should say, *arse*-ing her, was a big, fat porcupine.

Its black and white quills were erected into a sort of rosette around its tail-end. A few were much longer than the others and stuck out towards her like white-tipped spears.

It shook its hindquarters at her, while emitting a noise like a woodpecker as it clacked its teeth together. Mei tried to circle around it, but each time she moved the little creature swivelled his bottom around so the protective shield of needle-pointed quills was aimed straight up at her face.

There used to be a yellow dog that hung around the village, looking for scraps and the odd pat from one of the children who didn't see it as a pest the way the adults did.

One day it loped into the centre of the village looking very sorry for itself. The reason was plain to see. Dangling from its greying muzzle were three quills that it must have picked up in an ill-judged attempt to eat a porcupine.

Mei had crooned to it, squatting down and extending her hand until the poor mutt had given in and sidled up to her. Holding its head steady with one hand, Mei had plucked the quills out of its face, eliciting little yelps each time. But the dog must have known she was helping it because it made no move to escape. Just wriggled a little in her grip.

After that it adopted her, trotting around the village after her and growling if anyone came too close. But as the weeks passed, it became as much of a pest as the adults claimed. In the end, Mei had resorted to driving it off with pebbles flung in its direction, though she'd been careful always to miss.

The porcupine rattling its spiny arse at her now wasn't going to get the chance to embed any of its weaponry in her face, but she thought a couple of them might come in useful over the next day or so.

She grabbed a stick from the ground and tossed it at the chattering creature's rump. With an angry little squeal it shuffled off towards the trees, but not before leaving a handful of quills on the ground.

She stooped to collect them, being careful to avoid letting the wickedly sharp tips stick into her skin. The last thing she wanted right now was an infection.

Carefully, she slid them into her daysack. The Crane would be impressed with her improvised weapons. She'd only been out here for a few hours and already she had the axeknife and some deadly stabbing weapons – or maybe they were arrows. It didn't matter. Anyone who tried to mess with her was going to get one right in the eye.

The physical work in building her soup bowl shelter had made her thirsty. Maybe Mr Pointy Arse would know the location of some water. All animals needed to drink, so if she followed his trail it might lead to a stream or even a hollow log filled with rainwater.

Picking her way between the trees, Mei took the same route as the porcupine. His tracks were easy to follow in the soft leaf litter.

It took her almost half an hour to locate the porcupine's drinking source: a narrow winding stream running through a steep-sided gorge carving its way east to west through the forest.

She clambered down over mossy rocks until she reached the floor of the gorge. She scooped up water in her cupped hands and drank thirstily. The water was deliciously cool. After drinking her fill, she splashed it over her arms and chest then bent almost double and dunked the top of her head into the stream.

Sitting on a rock, she turned her face up to the sky and let the water stream down her face. If this was how she had to sit out the exercise, she thought she could probably manage just fine. The rushing sound as the stream coursed over rocks and fallen tree branches was soothing after the search for water and she closed her eyes, bathing in the white noise.

Should she try to escape? It seemed like she might never have such a good chance again. Alone out here with her improvised weapons and nobody within sight or hearing. She could strike out and …

… *yes, Mei*, she thought, *strike out to where, exactly? The nearest taxi stand?* She shook her head. Face it, she was in the middle of nowhere with armed guards already hunting her. This was like one of the Crane's tricks. It looked like a chance to escape, but in reality, it was the total opposite. No, she'd complete the exercise and return to the school, equipped with new skills. And when the right opportunity came along, oh, believe her, she'd take it.

It felt like the correct decision, and she smiled to herself. But beyond the sliver of sky visible above the gorge, dark, bruised-looking thunderheads were massing high above the forest. If Mei had been able to see them she might not have remained so optimistic.

26

A sharp crack from high overhead brought her out of her daydream and back to full alertness. Someone else had found the river gorge.

She looked around for cover. Behind her, a patch of huge ferns beckoned. Their deeply serrated leaves arched up, over and down like a bird spreading massive green wings.

Beneath the fern-leaf shelter she peered up at the sides of the gorge. At first she saw nothing. Heard nothing. Then she caught a movement, so brief had she blinked she might have missed it. A slender-stemmed plant had flipped forwards then back. Someone, or something, was on the move.

She kept her gaze fixed on that part of the gorge wall. A few seconds later, another tree branch moved forwards, then sprang back.

This time she did see what, or rather who, was coming. Not an animal, but one of the school guards.

His uniform blended in with the vegetation growing on the rocky sides of the gorge. But it wasn't perfect camouflage. Where the leaves were vibrant greens, as if lit from within by the energy they captured from the sun or the earth, he was dull and drab. Sucking the light in but not sending it back out again.

He emerged from a patch of ferns just like those giving Mei shelter. He had a rifle, but it was slung over his shoulder. She marked him down for that. What use was it on his back? If an enemy – if *she* – mounted a surprise attack, he'd be dead before he'd shrugged the sling off his shoulder.

Something tickled her ankle and she brushed at it, irritated with whatever insect or small furry creature had chosen that exact moment to distract her.

But it wasn't an insect. Or a rodent. Then it hissed.

She looked down and froze as she took in the sinuous, lime-green body and blood-red eyes of a bamboo viper. They'd learned about venomous creatures at the school. If it bit her, she could die out here.

The viper locked eyes with her. It raised its flattened head and swayed back and forth and side to side. As its mouth opened, revealing two needle-pointed fangs, Mei moved.

She shot backwards, backpedalling herself out of the ferns and rolling onto her back as she emerged into the light. The snake retreated, startled by the shower of dead vegetation Mei had kicked up.

From above her, she heard a shout.

'Got you!'

She glanced up to see the guard, who now *did* have his rifle in position and was aiming it straight at her.

She didn't *think*. She *acted*.

Darting sideways, she pushed her way back into the ferns, hoping the viper had really gone. A shot rang out, echoing off the rock walls of the gorge. Chips of stone rained down on her. Whatever else he was, he was a lousy shot.

She pushed deeper into the undergrowth. Behind her she could hear the guard splashing through the stream.

Something the Bull liked to say came back to her. *Nobody won a fight by retreating.* Then the Crane replied, a second disembodied voice inside Mei's own head. *Only fight when you are ready to win.*

Mei wasn't ready. But she would be. No way was she going to be captured and taken back to school in shame while the others were all out there, hunkered down somewhere cooking trapped game over a nice little fire. And, after all, she'd hardly even got started.

Somehow, she knew the guard would be expecting her to flee downstream. It was obvious, really. The ground fell away in that direction. And he'd come from upstream. So she doubled back through a stand of bamboo, cutting a wide circle that entailed half-scrambling, half-climbing to skirt her original fern shelter.

'Come out, little kitten!' he called. 'Game's over. Bonus for me, beating for you.'

He loosed off a burst of shots. Mei could tell he had no idea where she was: the bullets shredded vegetation fifty metres downstream from her position.

What a fool! Wasting ammunition like that. She didn't know if he had a spare magazine: probably he did. But it didn't matter. There'd come a point where his rifle would dry-fire. Then he'd have to stop to swap out the magazine. That's when she'd strike.

Careful to avoid the sharp points of the porcupine quills, she reached into her daysack and lifted out the axeknife. She hefted it in her right hand. Excellent for cutting saplings for her shelter. Not bad for stunning a pursuing guard, either.

Would that be all right, though? Knocking a guard cold? Nobody had said anything about defending themselves against capture. Mei took that as a sign that she and the other eleven students could do whatever it took to stay free until the end of the exercise.

And if she was wrong? She decided to worry about that when – and if – the time came. For now, she had a man on her tail and she wanted him gone.

She emerged from the bamboo onto the pebbly stream bed. The cold water soaked through her shoes instantly. That didn't matter. Nothing mattered right now except evading capture.

About a hundred metres downstream, she could see the guard. He was picking his way along the stream bed, pausing to reshoulder his rifle when he needed both hands to clamber over one of the larger boulders.

Maybe she should just let him go. If he kept on that track he'd disappear around the next bend in the stream. The gorge was narrower there and lush vegetation grew out from its rocky sides. She'd be invisible to him and could just wait it out or creep back to her improvised camp.

Then the unthinkable happened. He turned all the way around. It was as if someone had just whispered in his ear, 'She's behind you!' Even at this distance, she saw the whites of his eyes as they widened in surprise.

She had time to think he must be feeling embarrassed at being outflanked by a girl. Then he fired another burst from his Type 56.

This time, the bullets were coming straight at her. But at this range, with the fire select switch on auto, any shots that hit her would be the result of dumb luck, not the guard's marksmanship.

She ducked anyway and ran upstream, vaulting the smaller boulders, heedless of the noise she was making. The time for stealth was past.

Behind her, she could hear his boots splashing and crunching in the gravel streambed as he chased her. She was younger and fitter than him. Of that she was sure. Nor was she wearing heavy boots and carrying a rifle and a bigger pack.

Thanking the Crane, the Bull and the other instructors, she put on a burst of speed and rounded a slight curve in the stream.

A cave appeared as a thin black ellipse in the side wall of the gorge. As she neared it, the angle changed and the slit widened into the shape of the flower they used to call candle-flames.

Should she hide there? She'd be concealed, but also trapped. She hesitated for a second. And in that moment of indecision, another burst came from the guard's Type 56.

Mei screamed and toppled sideways into the stream. She looked down. Her left trouser leg below the knee was torn and bloody. And the pain! It was as if a thousand hornets had stung her in one spot.

She tried to stand. Found that she could, although as she got to her feet the whole world swayed crazily. It felt like when she'd drunk too much back in Shenzhen on those wild nights on top of the carpark when one of the gang had scored some rice wine or whisky.

The slab of rock to her right rushed at her and slammed into her shoulder. No. That wasn't it at all, was it? Rock walls didn't move. She'd stumbled. She felt dizzy. Looked down again. Blood was running down her leg, into her shoe and then streaming free into the stream, swirling away in little eddies and snake patterns, turning the water pink.

Mei staggered and sat heavily, banging her tailbone on a submerged stone. She didn't feel it, not really. The pain from her leg was screaming so loudly it blotted out everything else.

Then the world swung wildly and everything turned black.

27

Why was the ox that used to pull farmer Tan's plough kicking her in the ribs? She'd never done anything to him, had she? If anything, she was *kind*. Bringing handfuls of sweet grass from the other side of the fence so he could take it from her fingers. Ungrateful beast!

Talking of beasts, that fish was back. Standing on its tail fin and laughing at her.

'You tried to catch me, but I caught *you*, Twelve,' it said through those bony lips. Its sharp teeth glinted in the sunlight. 'Now you're going back to school.'

The ox gave her another kick in her ribs.

'Get up you little bitch! Let's go!'

His face wasn't an ox face anymore. He had human features. And how could she see them with her eyes closed anyway? She opened them and found herself still lying on her back in the stream, water burbling right in her ear.

Above her, the guard was standing with the muzzle of his rifle describing little circles over her face. She pushed herself up onto her elbows, wincing as a sharp stone on the stream bed dug into the spot between the bones where the nerves ran.

'I said, get up, bitch,' the guard said, sneering down at her. 'Or do I have to put another bullet in you?'

Mei stared up at him. Surely this wasn't allowed? He was a guard, sure. But she was a student. Training to fight China's enemies, within and without.

'You shot me. I can't walk.'

'Yes you can. I checked while you were out. It's just a flesh wound. It's hardly bleeding.'

Mei hoisted herself into a sitting position, heedless of the water soaking through her clothes.

She peeled back the ripped fabric of her trousers. The bullet had carved an ugly red trough through her skin, ripping down into the fascia holding the muscle in place, but that was all. No broken bones. No major arteries hit.

'Help me up, then,' she said, holding up her right hand.

He scowled down at her. 'Help yourself up. I'm not your servant.'

Trying to keep the weight off her left leg, Mei managed to boost herself off the stream bed and into a standing position. On the way up she snagged her daysack and thrust her arms through the straps.

She'd lost the axeknife somewhere in the chase but that didn't matter. Her shelter was already built and there were plenty of other rocks lying submerged in the crystal-clear water running over her feet.

'At least get me a stick so I can walk,' she said. 'Unless you want to carry me. Because the first step I take on the leg you shot, I'm going over.'

He glanced down at her bloody trouser leg, then back at her. She could see the response he wanted to give struggling to break free of his ugly mouth.

Find one yourself.

But he had enough smarts to realise that his own life would be easier if he got her a crutch of some kind. He jerked his chin at the rock wall to the right of the cave mouth.

'Wait there. If you move, I'll put a bullet where it'll really do some damage.'

Mei complied. Not because she believed his threat – if he shot her again, he'd have to carry her all the way. He wasn't that stupid. But because she needed him concentrating on something other than her. Even just for a minute or two.

Back at school, the Crane had made them all read and memorise *The Art of War*, the slim little brown-paper-bound book Mei had seen on her first morning. One of Sun Tzu's sayings had inspired her little bit of playacting.

'Appear weak when you are strong, and strong when you are weak.'

So she cried out as she hobbled out of the stream and over to the rock wall. In fact, the pain had subsided to a dull ache. Maybe being submerged in icy stream water had numbed the nerves. But it had the desired effect. The guard nodded, smirking, probably enjoying the thought he'd caused her pain.

He thought she was weak, and that was *his* weakness.

Turning his back and shouldering his rifle, he strode off, head moving from left to right, as he searched for something that might make a suitable crutch.

'I saw some bamboo back there,' Mei called out in what she hoped would sound like a fearful voice.

'Quiet, you!' he retorted. 'If I need your help, I'll ask for it.'

Nevertheless, he strode off in the direction she'd pointed and was soon bending at the foot of a tall stem of mature bamboo, hacking at it with a broad-bladed knife.

He broke it off at one of the bulging joints and returned to Mei.

'Here,' he said, thrusting the length of bamboo at her.

'It needs something to pad it at the top,' Mei said, looking him straight in the eye, daring him to argue.

Maybe she'd found another weak point. He might have the gun and the knife, and both legs working properly, but Mei was the one the school authorities cared for.

Deep down, she thought he knew that. Maybe hated it. But hate was close to fear: the Crane had told them, and Mei knew the truth of it from her own experience at home and in Shenzhen.

He tightened his lips and Mei could see the muscles at the sides of his jaw bunching. Finally he reached into his own daysack and withdrew a length of dark-green, loosely woven material like a fishing net. A scarf, she thought.

'Give it to me, then,' he snapped, holding out his hand and clicking his fingers.

Mei passed him the bamboo and he wound the scarf around one end until he'd created a soft, rounded top so the whole thing resembled a giant matchstick.

She stuck the pad into her armpit and nodded at him.

'Thank you.'

He swung his rifle off his back and jabbed her in the belly with the muzzle.

'Get going. And don't try anything.'

'How can I, with one leg wounded?'

'Don't give me that,' he said. 'We all know the stuff they teach you. Fucking little shits.'

And with that, it seemed he'd exhausted his appetite for conversation. Pushing and prodding her with the rifle barrel, he took Mei downstream for about three hundred metres before moving her off to the right into a clearing like the one where she'd pitched camp.

'OK, stop,' he said.

Mei stopped, glad of the chance to rest. Her leg was throbbing and the walking had started the bleeding again, although it was only a trickle. She dropped the crutch to one side and folded herself into a sitting position, with her bad leg stretched out in front of her.

The guard squatted, facing her. His eyes seemed restless, roving over her body, lingering on her chest then moving down. He licked his lips. Now his gaze flicked up to the sides of the gorge, left, right. Straight up, at the sliver of sky, which had turned the colour of lead while they'd been walking.

He looked back at her.

'They'll pay me a nice fat bonus for picking you up,' he said, picking at something between his teeth. 'You know that, right?'

He inspected the tip of his finger and flicked off whatever he'd caught on the nail.

Mei shrugged. 'We're not back, yet.'

He grinned. 'You think you're going to take me out, is that it? Try one of your Special Forces moves on me, maybe?'

'I just said we're not back yet, that's all.'

He looked at her chest again. He adjusted his position a little, so that his knees swung apart. He let his left hand drop from the rifle to dangle at his groin.

'The bonus is good, but I don't need it,' he said, in a voice that sounded thicker, somehow. 'The money they pay me is fine for my needs. Well, most of them. Trouble is, the nearest whorehouse is a hundred miles away.'

Mei had already figured out what he wanted. This just confirmed it.

'There are deer in the woods. Have you tried fucking one of them?'

Irritation flashed across his face. Mei saw the conscious effort he made to chase it away, replacing it with an expression he probably thought looked friendly.

'Funny girl. Listen, maybe you don't have to fail the assignment after all. May-be,' he stretched the word out into a sing-song sound, 'you can persuade me to let you go.'

'Oh yeah? How would I do that?' Mei asked.

She knew exactly what he wanted her to say. To *offer*. She'd rather die than do that. And it wasn't going to happen, anyway. But she was happy to let him think it might.

'You just have to be nice to me. We have a little fun out here and then I let you go, simple as that.'

'How do I explain the bullet wound you gave me?'

He frowned. 'Say you fell. Tore it open on a sharp rock.'

She paused as if giving his suggestion serious thought.

'And when you say be nice…'

He leered at her. Licked his lips again.

'I don't see any deer around, if you get my meaning.'

'You mean you want to fuck me, is that it?'

'Hey! No need for the coarse language, my little Red Lotus.'

'I can't get pregnant. They'll find out, and then before they give me an abortion, they'll force me to tell them who I've been with. You'll get into trouble.'

'I'll pull out. I've done it loads of times before.'

She shook her head.

'I've got a better idea. Come and see what I've got in my pack.'

His forehead crinkled with suspicion.

'Why? What've you got in there?'

'Condoms,' she said, with a wink. 'They're for making water containers. Come and see.'

Grinning widely now, he shuffled across the gap between them. Mei unbuckled the canvas flap and reached inside the pack with her right hand.

28

The guard moved up close to her on her left side.

This close she could smell his body odour; a sour smell with lots of garlic sweat mixed in.

'Show me, then,' he said, shucking off his rifle, which he lay on the leaf mould to his right.

Mei opened the daysack wide.

'See for yourself,' she said with a smile.

He leaned forwards. Striking fast, like a snake, Mei grabbed the back of his head with her left hand. At the same time, her right hand came out of the sack, gripping the bundle of porcupine quills.

She drove them into his right eye. He screamed; a high-pitched, animal sound that bounced off the gorge's high walls. Mei let go and, momentarily disgusted, watched the quills' free ends describe circles as his punctured eye swivelled in its socket.

The guard's hands flailed as he tried to get the quills out of his eye without hurting himself. Mei didn't give him a chance. She reared back and kicked down at them, pushing them deeper and breaking off the long ends. His cries deepened into a weird, off-key groaning. His mouth went slack and drool slimed out from between his lips.

As he writhed around, still emitting that horrid animal sound, Mei took the knife out of its sheath on his belt. She switched her grip so that it was point uppermost. Then she drove it up and under his ribs, hard, until the brass crossguard jammed against his stomach muscles.

Bright-red blood rushed out of his mouth in a torrent, soaking the front of his tunic and draining away into the ground on either side of his neck. Mei rolled away from him and watched as his jerky movements grew less violent.

After a final coughing spasm that sent a fine spray of scarlet droplets into the air above his face, he died.

Mei sat beside the body for a while. She felt no regrets for what she'd done. If he'd just tried to take her back to school, she would have fought to escape. Knocked him unconscious without a second thought. But kill him? No. There wouldn't have been any need. He was doing what he was told, so was she.

But then he'd crossed over. He went from being a person doing a job to one of *them*: the men who'd always tried to take advantage of her. Just because she was younger than them. Just because she was a girl. Just because they could.

Except they couldn't. Not the older boys back at her village. Not the Party boy she'd killed at the building site. Not the policeman. Director Gao had done that disgusting thing, sure, and one day she'd make sure he paid for it.

And now the latest man to try lay dead before her, a broken-off bundle of porcupine quills sticking out of his eye socket like a monk's pot of brushes.

She needed to hide the body. If the school authorities sent out more soldiers to look for him, they'd find him for sure. And then what? Would they know who'd killed him? Mei was the last student to be dropped off, so maybe they'd have a good idea it was her.

If the cave she'd discovered was closer, she'd have dragged him back there and hidden him in the dark. But it was at least three hundred metres upstream, over a rocky streambed. No way could she move him that far, even without a bullet wound in her leg.

She stared at the dead guard. Nodded as a story began to unfold in her head.

'Maybe you saw me from up there,' she said, pointing to the lip of the gorge. 'You shouted, I ran. So you scrambled down the sides to catch me. But you lost your footing and you fell. You knocked yourself out on a stone in the stream and you drowned.'

Except that wouldn't work, would it? Because they'd do an autopsy on him like the one they'd taken all the students to watch at the hospital. And they'd see that his lungs weren't full of water. Not to mention the eyeful of broken-off porcupine quills.

She saw what needed to be done.

It took Mei almost an hour to drag the dead guard from the centre of the clearing to the stream. By the time he was lying with his head and shoulders in the water, she was gasping for breath and had to sit for a few minutes to dispel the little white stars twinkling and spinning around the edge of her vision.

Moving upstream a little, she scooped up some water and drank. Lying half-submerged in the water, she saw what she needed. The rock had a sharp point. It was about the same size as a human head.

She worked it loose, then got to her feet before picking it up in both hands and hobbling back to the body. She placed it by the head, then rolled the body onto its back.

The eye socket was blackened with clotted blood. Mei placed her left hand over the mess so that the broken-off quills stuck up between her fingers. She gripped them with her other hand and pulled them free with a sticky squelch. She tossed them into the stream and watched as they separated before floating off in the current.

Mei stood over the dead guard with the rock cradled against her chest. She looked down at him.

'You didn't knock yourself out when you fell,' she said. 'You killed yourself. That's why your lungs are clear.'

She lifted the rock overhead, grunting with the effort, then, aiming for the ruined eye, brought it down on the dead guard's skull. It cracked with a noise like a branch breaking. Brains spilled out into the water: greyish-pink blobs of porridge that bobbed and eddied before swirling away to join the quills.

She replaced the rock in the water, then rolled the body over and on top of it. Maybe she'd get lucky and a wild animal would sniff it out and come to feed. Anything to disturb the scene would be helpful.

Mei returned to the clearing. She really wanted to keep the knife. The rifle she didn't need, but a good sharp blade would help her survive until the end of the exercise. It could have fallen out of its sheath as he fell. But suppose they went looking for it? Reluctantly, she realised it would have to stay with the body.

She retreated to the stream, using the rifle's muzzle to sweep away the footprints and scrapes in the leaf litter as she went.

Holding the rifle by the barrel, she brought it back behind her then swung with all her strength and hurled it towards the rock wall, where it came to rest with a crash amongst the ferns and bamboo.

The knife she cleaned, then replaced in the sheath at the dead guard's waist.

Before leaving, Mei lowered herself to the water and took another long drink. She kept her face turned upstream. A little way further up, she spotted moss growing in the crevices of a pair of large grey boulders. It was the medicinal kind they'd learned about on the survival course.

She splashed over and grabbed a double handful, which she pushed against the gouged flesh of her left leg. It felt wonderfully cool and she wondered if it could be working already. She shook her head. *Don't be silly, Mei. It's just because you know it will.*

She ripped away the lower part of her trouser leg and split the piece of fabric in two to form a rudimentary bandage. With the moss secured against the wound, she made her way back to her shelter in the clearing.

Once she reached the shelter, she crawled inside and collapsed onto her back. She checked the time. Had she really been out here for four hours already? Only another thirty-two to go.

She closed her eyes. Fatigue stole over her like the fog that used to roll in off the mountains and shroud the village with its ghostly white fingers. As she gave in to the exhaustion, she felt herself sinking down into the leaf litter beneath her.

Wei Mei tumbled into sleep. A deep, dark, dreamless sleep. A traveller, stumbling across her supine form inside its soup bowl of bent branches and fern covering, might have assumed she was dead.

* * *

A bomb detonated right above the clearing. The explosion brought Mei into full wakefulness and she was up and on her feet.

It was grey outside. No shadows. She didn't know how long she'd been asleep. She poked her head out through the gap in the saplings. The sky was a mass of boiling thunder clouds.

Lightning flashed, turning the clearing into a black and white photograph. Mei flinched. Seconds later, thunder boomed again. Then the rain came. Fat droplets that hammered through the trees with a sound like mah-jongg tiles being shuffled: what the old people called 'twittering the sparrows'.

From somewhere towards the gorge, Mei heard a sound she'd never heard before. A roaring, rushing noise, as if giants were dragging great rasping breaths into their lungs then heaving them out again in deafening sighs.

Mei looked down at her leg. Some time while she slept, the medicine moss had worked its magic. Her leg didn't hurt anymore.

She eased the makeshift bandage away from her skin to see that the skin around the wound was back to its normal colour: no longer red and sensitive to the lightest touch.

Grabbing her daysack, she pushed her way out of the shelter into a monstrous rainstorm. It was like nothing she'd ever experienced.

Lightning crackled every few seconds or so, lighting up the charcoal grey and purple sky like a photographer's flashgun. The air smelled of electricity and it made the hairs on the back of Mei's neck stand erect.

And the thunder. Like one of the Vietnamese artillery barrages the Bull had told them about, so loud it seemed the very air around her was being split in half. She could hardly think, but that rushing, roaring sound from the gorge was calling to her.

Half-blind from the thrashing rain that soaked her clothes in seconds, she stumbled across the clearing and through the trees towards the water. The stream, which a few hours earlier had been fordable on foot, was now a raging torrent. The water boiled over the rocks, mostly white now as it foamed and frothed.

Mei looked upstream, shading her eyes, not from sun but from the splattering raindrops that stung her eyes. The roaring noise intensified.

And then she screamed.

A wall of water was surging towards her from the head of the valley. It seemed impossibly high, many times taller than Mei herself was.

Branches, ferns torn out by their roots, smaller rocks and long, snaky vines: all roiled and tumbled at the front edge of the boiling flash flood. And then it was upon her.

She had time just to draw in a huge breath and then clamp her mouth tight shut before the flood waters caught her and whirled her backwards. It felt like being hit by a car: a sudden acceleration as tonnes of turbulent water lifted her bodily and flung her down the gorge.

Buffeted by the debris being swept along with her, Mei struggled to swim round and reach the surface of the floodwater. Her head broke free and she snatched another breath with a great whooping sigh. Then she was tumbled over and over again.

She flailed her arms and kicked in the direction she hoped was up, then saw a tree trunk coming towards her, rolling over and over. She tried frantically to escape it but it seemed hellbent on reaching her, as if it had a mind, a will, of its own.

The gnarled bark struck the back of her head. Everything turned white, then black.

29

Someone screamed.

Mei opened her eyes.

Every part of her hurt. Worse than in the fight training sessions. Worse than when she fell from the high net on the assault course. Worse than she'd ever been hurt before.

Above her, the sky was the pure blue of Mummy Rita's best porcelain tea cups. It seemed to sparkle. No, that was the sun glinting in the droplets of water suspended on her eyelashes.

The someone screamed again.

'Help me!'

She pushed herself up onto her elbows and looked around.

She was lying at the edge of a vast pool, a kind of swimming hole. Deep from the colour of it: a dark green fading to black at the centre.

'Help!'

Then a coughing, spluttering noise and a loud *gloop*.

Over on the far side of the pool, the water was white. Big ripples were spreading out from a point several metres from the far bank.

A hand shot out of the water. Then a second. Then a head.

It was Rats! Ignoring the pain from her bruised and battered muscles, Mei got to her feet and dived into the water. She struck out for the far side where her friend had just disappeared beneath the water again.

She reached the spot where she'd seen Rats go under, took a deep breath and upended herself. Kicking strongly, she swam down into the murk. Something bumped against her right shoulder. Then she was being pulled down. Rats had a hold of her forearm.

He had to let go. Or this was it for them both. She jerked her arm free, then closed with Rats. His eyes were wide open. So was his mouth. Bubbles blurted out as he screamed at her.

She swam around behind him and hooked an arm under his armpits, then kicked upwards.

He was struggling, which didn't make it any easier, but Mei was a strong swimmer, thanks to all those summer days spent mucking around in the Little Mekong.

As their heads broke the surface, they both coughed out mouthfuls of water and drew in huge breaths.

'I've got you, Rats,' she said, 'but stop fighting me. Unless you want to drown us both.'

He stopped wriggling in her grasp and, swimming on her back, with Rats floating above her, she hauled him all the way to the gravelly bank.

'Well, help me, then!' she said.

Rats was just lying there, gasping like a landed fish with half his body still in the shallows, trapping Mei beneath him. He rolled away and crawled out of the water.

'Thank you,' he croaked, then coughed out a spray of watery breath. 'You saved my life.'

'Yeah, well, I was getting lonely out here. I fancied the company.'

Despite everything, Rats found the energy to laugh. It was infectious and Mei found herself joining him, laughing harder and harder until her sides hurt and she slapped his arm to make him stop.

'Don't suppose you've got anything to eat, have you?' Rats asked, once they'd both sighed out the last of their giggles.

Mei shook her head.

'I was about to go looking when one of the guards caught me.'

Rats spun round to face her.

'What happened?'

'He's gone.'

'Did you kill him?'

'Yes.'

'Where's the body?'

Mei looked round to where the swollen river now surged along one side of the swimming hole.

'Probably ten kilometres downstream. They'll never trace him back to me now. And anyway, I made it look like he fell.'

Rats nodded. 'Smart move.'

'Where were you, then?'

'What?'

'When the storm hit. I thought they were dropping us off into our own bit of the forest.'

'They were. But I decided to try and track the road. See if I could find someone else. I thought I saw Sis, then it got really dark,' he said. 'I knew a storm was coming and I was trying to find shelter. Then I got hit by the flash flood. After that I don't remember anything until I was in the pool over there.'

'I hope she's OK,' Mei said.

'Yeah, me too. But right now we need to find somewhere safe. In case there's more flooding coming.'

'We should get out of this gorge.'

'Higher ground.'

'Yeah. Come on, I can see a path over there.' Mei pointed to a gap in the trees. 'Maybe animals made it. I bet it'll take us out of here.'

The climb out of the gorge took an hour. Rats tried to repay Mei for saving his life by constantly offering to help her up the steeper parts of the path, but she refused every time. He'd been the one who'd nearly drowned, and besides, this was excellent training.

The path meandered along through light scrub for a few hundred metres before emerging into a field left fallow. Tall grass that reached their waists grew everywhere, punctuated by yellow wildflowers whose thick, hairy stalks irritated Mei's bare leg.

She saw a roof off to their left and turned towards it, reaching forwards to tug on the back of Rats's jacket.

'Hey! Look over there,' she said. 'It's a barn, I think.'

He followed the direction of her extended finger.

'Yeah. Good spot.'

When they reached the building, it turned out to be a sorry excuse for a farm building of any kind. The planking sides had almost completely collapsed, revealing a basic steel structure supporting the wood. The roof was of corrugated iron, scabbed with rust and pierced by holes where the corrosion had eaten right through the metal.

The floor was covered in bales of hay, though, and when they climbed up onto them, they were more or less dry.

Rats turned to Mei.

'We should be able to last out here until the end of the exercise, don't you think?'

She nodded. 'Should be.'

'I'm starving,' he said.

'Have a look around. Maybe there're some dried apples or something.'

He slid forwards off his bale and began a methodical search, starting in the far corner and working his way around the edge of the structure.

While Rats looked for something to eat, Mei lay back on the hay bale and closed her eyes. Her stomach emitted a loud rumble. She doubted Rats would find anything, which was a shame, but what she wanted more than anything else was sleep.

The hay beneath her felt so nice. It was warm, and soft against her cheek. It smelled so nice, too. It smelled like...like...

(Her. It smells like Her.)

. . .

Wei Mei dreams. It is the same dream she always has when she is bone-tired, unable to keep her eyes open a moment longer.

Not a dream with a story to it, of chases where she and Spark sprint away from the cops, or share a companionable joint on a rooftop.

This dream is all sensation. Colours, sounds, smells, feelings.

A soft, fuzzy feeling against her cheek. Whatever this thing is, it smells special. Comforting, tender, nurturing. It smells of the one called, in the dream, simply *Her*.

It is *Her* milk that nourishes Mei. *Her* arms that rock Mei to sleep when she wakens, crying, in the depths of the night. *Her* voice that permeates Mei's waking and sleeping hours.

Somehow, Mei knows that *She* is not Mummy Rita. This is someone else. Someone…unknown.

Then Mei is lifting, rising up. There is a smell of cigarette smoke. Pressure around her sides. She is flying – no, not flying, falling.

The falling stops and instead she is rocking. The back-and-forth motion is reassuring. A harsh buzzing fills her ears.

She dozes.

Time passes.

The colours in her brain shift from reds and blues to the darkest of blacks. There is no more *Her*. All those sensations that speak together of *Her* presence in Mei's world have vanished. No more touch. No more smell. No more sound. *She* has left. *She* is gone.

30

Mei woke, salty tear-tracks dry and crusty on her eyelids and her cheeks. Rats was sitting with his back to her, staring out at the darkness beyond the barn's dilapidated walls.

Now that the storm had passed and the thick cloud cover had dissipated, a weak moon illuminated the countryside outside the barn, spearing through the holes in the roof in pale-silver beams.

She raised herself up onto her elbows and then swung her legs down over the side of the hay bale into a seated position next to her friend.

'Hi, Juice,' he said. 'You were asleep for hours.'

'What time is it?'

He glanced at his watch. The exact same model as that on Mei's left wrist. Then he frowned.

'I don't know why I even looked. This piece of shit stopped when I got caught in the flash flood. What's yours say?'

Mei looked down at her own watch. In the moonlight, she could see a bubble of air inside the glass. She tipped her wrist and the bubble flipped around the dial.

'I think it's saying, "Help! I'm drowning"!'

Rats looked up at the roof. 'Must be super-early in the morning. Two, maybe? Three?'

Mei's stomach growled. 'Did you find anything to eat?'

'Sorry, nothing. Not even a dead mouse.'

Mei thought she would have to be a lot hungrier than she was now to even consider eating a dead mouse.

She hugged her knees up to her chest, wincing as she caught the edge of her leg wound with her fingers. But the pain was so much better. It had almost completely gone. Whatever was in that moss, someone should turn to into medicine for real. It was amazing.

'Cold?'

She turned to Rats.

'Yeah.'

He shuffled closer until they were sitting hip to hip and put his arm around her shoulders. Mei leaned into him. With Rats there was none of that fear that she felt when men came near her. He was just her friend, like Sis was. Like Brains, and Panda and Spark. At the thought of her old friend, she gulped down a sob that suddenly threatened to burst free of her throat.

'What's up?' Rats asked, turning to look at her.

'I was thinking about a friend of mine, from back in Shenzhen.'

'He's dead, right?'

'How did you know?'

'Everyone dies, don't they? The people we care about, I mean.'

'Not everyone. My mum's still alive, and—'

Was Mummy Rita alive? Or had the triad guy come back and carried out his threat like Ping said he would? Now, more than ever, Mei wanted to be free of the school and its training, its stupid rules and the director's froggy face blah-blahing on about the glories of Chinese Communism and purity of Mao Thought.

'What?'

'Nothing.'

'Come on. We might as well talk,' Rats said. 'There's nothing else to do out here.'

'Do you think they'll make us actually kill people?'

'You already did, remember? The guard?'

'I know. But I mean, targets?'

Rats snorted, as if she'd asked the dumbest question in the whole world. Mei felt a sudden, unreasoning urge to hit him.

'Well, that's kind of the job, isn't it? To destroy China's enemies, within and without,' he said, parroting one of the director's favourite lines.

'No, dummy! I mean, do you think they'll make us do it as part of the training?'

It was a question that had been bothering Mei for a month or two. They'd practised on anatomical models; lifelike human dummies that split apart so you could assess wound tracks and organ damage after making your thrust. From there, they'd progressed to dead pigs.

They'd even been taken to a remote woodland firing range where, the Bull told them, the targets were the bodies of executed criminals. Mei had been revolted at the time, as she pulled the trigger and sent bullets flying down the range into chests and skulls, which burst apart in a spray of pink.

But, in the end, what were the pigs and the dead criminals but empty husks? They weren't living people. People who might have husbands and wives, friends, jobs, children, ancestors. They didn't scream as they died, spurting blood every which way.

But Mei knew, at some point, she would have to convert her training into action. And the only action Director Gao was interested in was killing. Could she do it? *You already have*, a quiet voice said in her head. *That Party kid. The cop. Like Rats said, the guard who tried to rape you yesterday*. They're all dead. And you killed them.

But that was different! she almost said aloud. *I had no choice.*

Rats was regarding her with a quizzical look, eyebrows raised, fingertip at the point of his chin.

'You still with me, Juice, or did you go somewhere far away?'

She smiled. 'Sorry. Wool-gathering.'

'In answer to your question, I don't think they will. Not yet, anyway. I reckon we'll be paired up with the ones who've already finished their training,' he said. 'You know, go on missions with them. I'm looking forward to it.'

'Really? You want to kill people?'

He wrinkled his nose. 'It's not that. But think about it. We'll get to travel. Maybe even outside China. I've never even been to Beijing. Anyway, if you're so against killing people, why'd you sign up?'

She snorted. 'Really? That's your question? It's not like I had a choice,' she said, crossly. 'The Crane basically said it was come with her or she'd march me back to the cop shop to be beaten to a pulp and dumped in a back-alley somewhere for the rats.' She caught his wince. 'Sorry. No offence.'

'Man, this is some fucked-up trip, don't you think? Training kids to be killers like in one of those movies.'

'I've never seen a movie.'

His eyes widened. 'Seriously?'

She felt ashamed in the face of his disbelief. Then irritated.

'Yes, seriously! We didn't have a lot of spare cash to go to the cinema where I was living in Shenzhen. And I suppose you were always in there, were you? Probably in a special row reserved for Party officials, eating chocolate and drinking Ko Kakola.'

Rats smirked. 'Sorry, what did you just say? Koe-what? Kakka-what?'

Mei felt the heat of a blush creeping up her face. Suddenly she wanted to hit Rats, to make him stop teasing her. It wasn't rational – to use one of the Crane's favourite words – but she couldn't help it.

'The drink, arsehole. You know what I mean.'

'Ohhh,' Rats said, rolling his eyes. 'You mean Coca-Cola!' He chuckled, then mimicked her bad pronunciation. 'Erm, excuse me, Mr Shopkeeper, I'd like one of your finest bottles of Koe Kakkolaaah, please.' Mei's blush grew hotter. How was she supposed to know how to say it anyway? It wasn't even a Chinese brand of pop. But Rats wasn't finished. He was laughing now. 'In fact, make it two bottles of—'

Her punch landed dead-centre on the tip of Rats's nose. Not hard enough to break it, although that would have been easy. She just wanted to shut him up. She failed. He yelled out as her fist crashed into the bulb of flesh so rich in nerves and blood vessels that a child could disable a grown man if she placed the blow correctly.

His hands flew to his damaged nose, but not before blood spurted out of his nostrils and ran down over his lips as he looked at her, eyes popping comically.

'You broke my nose!' *Brogue by doze.*

'Yeah? Well you shouldn't have teased me, then, should you? Anyway, I didn't. Here.' She grabbed a handful of the soft, dry hay and fashioned two little balls. 'Lean back.'

Perhaps still too shocked to do anything but comply, Rats leaned his head back. Mei gently removed his hands and plugged his bleeding nose with the hay.

'There,' she said, in the tone Mummy Rita used whenever Mei had gone running to her with a cut foot or a scraped elbow.

'Thanks,' he said. *Thags.* 'Sorry.'

'That's OK,' Mei said, already regretting punching her friend. After all, it wasn't as if she had all that many she could afford to piss one off.

After sitting in companionable silence for a while, Rats announced he was going to try to sleep. Mei sat on, watching the stars through the holes in the roof until she, too, could stay awake no longer. She lay down where she was and only woke when sunlight shone directly into her eyes.

She unwound the bandage around her leg and gingerly picked off the moss. A few strands were stuck to the dried blood where the guard's bullet had creased her, but they came away easily enough. Beneath, it had started to scab over.

She prodded the skin around the wound. It was soft, cool to the touch, and the right colour. Not hot, tight or red, like they'd been shown in the lessons on infection. She retied the bandage leaving the moss aside: it had done its job and she could always get more if she needed to.

'Morning.'

Rats was sitting up and stretching. He farted loudly, making Mei giggle.

'Morning. Good job this barn has open sides, otherwise you'd've gassed me.'

He grinned. 'It's my secret weapon. I'll kill China's enemies within and without with my amazing poisoned farts.'

'And anyone else with a five-K radius of the detonation site.'

He shrugged. 'Collateral damage.'

Shaking her head, Mei slid down off the hay bale.

She went over to him, and inspected his nose. The hay plugs were still in place. 'How's it feel?'

He reached up and pulled the plugs out, then touched each blood-crusted nostril in turn.

'Fine, I think.'

She nodded, feeling better about punching him the previous night. Her mouth was dry, and the dust from the hay hadn't made things any better.

'I need a drink,' she said. 'And you need to get that cleaned up. Let's go back down to the river.'

Rats nodded and soon they were walking down the path, which seemed a lot easier to navigate in daylight, back to the bottom of the gorge. The water had returned to its previous state; a gently meandering stream burbling over smoothed-off rocks that looked like they'd been there since the olden days.

They lay on their bellies side-by-side and lowered their heads to the cool water to drink. Mei imagined they looked like deer drinking. The thought raised another immediately. One of them should be keeping watch. She raised her head and looked left and right, behind them and upstream.

But they were alone.

'I really need to eat something,' Rats said. 'My belly thinks my throat's been cut.'

Mei's stomach gave an answering growl. 'Mine, too.'

They scavenged around the stream for an hour, finding nothing but some toadstools with evil-smelling blue-black caps.

'We could go back to the swimming hole where you found me,' Rats said. 'There might be fish in it.'

Mei was about to say that without a net or a rod and some bait they'd be better off conserving their energy, but then she saw the hopeful expression on Rats's face.

'Good idea,' she said.

They reached the bend in the stream just before the pool and Rats was about to run forwards when Mei stuck out a hand to stop him.

'Wait!' she hissed. 'There's somebody there already. Listen.'

At first there was nothing, and Mei wondered whether she'd been mistaken. She thought she'd heard the *ker-sploosh* of a heavy stone being lobbed into deep water.

'I can't hear anything,' Rats whispered. 'It's just your imagin—'

The splash changed his mind. It was followed by another.

Mei turned to face him. 'Wait here,' she whispered. 'I'll see who it is.'

'It might be a peasant. They might have food.'

'Yeah, and it might be a guard. And he might have a rifle.'

Rats nodded and retreated a few metres, hiding behind a knobbly boulder that looked like a giant warty-skinned toad.

Keeping to the soft greyish-brown mud at the edge of the stream, which muffled her footsteps, Mei crept towards the pool. She reached an overhanging tree and found a spot where she could peer between the rock wall and its trunk to spy on whoever was lobbing rocks into the water.

31

The girl had her back to Mei, but she recognised her all the same. A smile broke out on her face.

'Sis!' she shouted, stepping out from cover and walking over to her friend.

Sis turned in the act of throwing another stone, arm upraised. She beamed back at Mei and came over to hug her. Then she looked down at her leg.

'You're hurt.'

Mei explained about the guard. Then she called out. 'Rats! Come and see who I've found!'

Rats came jogging up the stream bed, splashing in the shallow water. He grinned when he saw Sis and the three embraced in an untidy tangle of arms and heads. Sis bumped Rats's nose with her chin and he yelped.

'Careful!'

'What happened?' she asked.

Rats glanced at Mei and she felt a pang of guilt.

'Hit my face on a rock in the flash flood. Juice saved me. I was sure I was going to drown,' he added, jerking his chin towards the pool. 'In there.'

Mei's feelings of guilt intensified as Sis turned an admiring gaze on her.

'Hero of the hour!' Sis said.

Mei shrugged. 'He'd have done the same for me.' Then, wanting to change the subject, 'Where did you end up?'

'A few kilometres southwest of here. I needed water and I followed the stream.'

'Did the flash flood get you, too?' Rats asked.

Sis shook her head. 'I was higher up. I saw it though. Really scary. You must have been right below me.'

'Does your watch work?' Mei asked.

'Yeah.' Sis looked down. 'It's oh-eight-thirty.'

'We've got nine and a half hours to go. Think we can make it?'

Sis smiled and nodded. 'We've got water, so yes. But I'm so hungry. That breakfast feels like a year ago instead of just yesterday.'

'We're going to try to catch some fish in the pool,' Rats said.

'What with?'

He opened his mouth, then shut it again with a *clop*.

'A spear,' Mei said.

'What?' Sis looked at her as if she'd suggested using an RPG or maybe a nuclear weapon.

'The men in my village used them to catch eels in the river.'

'Can you make one?' Rats asked.

'I think so. I just need a knife, or a sharp stone, at least.' Sis's answering grin was so wide, Mei wanted to laugh. 'What is it?'

Sis swung her pack off her shoulders and reached inside. When her hand emerged, it was wrapped around a dagger like the one Mei had almost taken off the guard she'd killed.

'Where did you get that?'

'You'll never believe it.'

'It's from a guard, isn't it?' Rats asked.

Sis nodded. 'Yup. Stupid fool was too lazy to even hunt. I found him with his back to a big old tree, fast asleep and smelling of beer. So I took his knife.' She turned to Mei. 'You're not the only one with pickpocketing skills.'

'I'd love to be there when he has to explain how he lost it,' Mei said.

Sis handed the dagger over. 'Come on, then. Show us how to make a fish-spear.'

Fifteen minutes later, Mei brandished a three-metre length of bamboo, one end split into four sharpened prongs separated by shorter pieces held in place with vines. She spent a few more minutes cutting simple barbs into the tips before declaring herself ready to hunt.

She led the other two over to the pool and squatted on a broad, flat-topped rock about a third of the way towards the centre.

While Sis and Rats searched for dry wood to make a fire, Mei focused on the water, which had begun to clear after the torrential rains of the previous night. It was still murky, though, and she thought the odds of her spotting a fish were slim. But better this than giving up. She had to do something.

Ignoring the hunger pangs cramping her belly, she squinted at the water, willing herself to spot a fish in the upper half-metre of water that was clear enough to see through.

Something flashed: she tensed her right arm, but it was just a long-bladed leaf turning over and over as it spun downstream. Maybe there weren't even any fish in this river. The whole exercise could be a complete waste of time.

A second flash – of silver, this time. Was it? She peered down into the pale-green water. There! A silvery-grey back, a blood-coloured tail fin. One of the fish they used to call 'Fat-boys' at the village.

Mei manoeuvred herself into a crouch and raised her right arm overhead, careful to keep the spear's shadow away from the fish.

The fish was drifting, just flicking its tail occasionally to hold itself steady in the current. Mei watched an iridescent blue fly with two pairs of transparent wings land on the surface. The fish darted upwards and with a *plop* from its wide-open mouth, snatched the fly before it had a chance to take off.

Mei hurled the spear, letting the smooth bamboo sections run through her loosened fist, catching it before it left her grasp altogether.

She missed the Fat-boy, which darted downwards into the murk with a strong swish of its tail.

'Damn! Almost got you,' she said.

She readjusted her grip on the spear and went back to waiting. Behind her, she heard the crackle of tinder as Rats and Sis got the fire going. Soon, the smell of woodsmoke permeated the still air, which turned a pale, silver-grey, the sun filtering through the trees creating lighter and darker bands.

It took another fifteen minutes before a second fish emerged, snout-first, out of the green depths of the pool. It was larger than the first fish, but like its predecessor, hunting for the pretty blue flies that were now swarming all over the surface.

Mei watched it, getting a feel for its rhythm. It would rise, sway just below and behind a fly, then surge upwards to gulp the insect off the surface.

Here it came again. Up. Sway. Surge. Gulp.

And again. Up. Sway.

She launched the spear. And missed again. The fish arched itself almost double in its haste to escape this swooping attack from above. She wondered as she retrieved the spear whether the fish thought this was a new type of predator. A hawk with ridiculously long talons. Or a heron with four beaks. The thought made her smile. She readied herself.

This Fat-boy seemed determined to earn its nickname. Within seconds it was back, hunting the flies from just a few centimetres below the surface.

Mei drew her arm back and launched her third attack.

'Yes!' she yelled in triumph.

She'd speared the fish through its back, between the head and the dark-red dorsal fin. Its thrashing sent the end of the spear swerving left and right in the water, but Mei had no intention of losing her prize. She pulled it out of the water before upending the spear so that the fish sat atop the spikes, showering her with pink droplets that glinted in the sunlight.

Mei carried the speared fish back to the fire. Rats and Sis clapped as she took a bow.

'It's a beauty,' Sis said. 'I'm so hungry I could eat it raw.'

'Me, too,' Rats said, 'but let's cook it anyway.'

Mei cleaned the fish, putting the guts to one side. She was thinking its liver might be good bait to catch another. Maybe a Snakehead or even a pike.

Soon the Fat-boy's silver-grey skin was turning a golden-brown and spitting over the fire as drips of fat fell into the flames. The smell was so good. Mei's mouth kept filling with saliva and she had to swallow to stop herself drooling.

'How long?' Sis asked, prodding the plump fish with a stick.

'Hey! Watch out!' Rats said, 'You'll knock it into the ash. You'll ruin the flavour.'

'Sor-ry, Mr Famous Chef! Didn't realise we had an expert doing the cooking.'

The fire crackled loudly. A double-snap like a branch breaking. Mei frowned. It was too loud a noise.

'Well hello, everyone.'

Mei whirled round. Beside her, Rats and Sis did the same.

Psycho was standing a few metres away, grinning down at them. His face was streaked with mud and he'd fashioned a makeshift camouflage suit of thin, leaf-covered branches, strands of water weed, vines and fern leaves.

He looked like a walking plant. But what held Mei's attention wasn't the vegetation. It was the Type 56 rifle he was pointing at them.

'What's that?' he asked, jerking the rifle barrel towards the fire. 'And if you say, "a fire" I'll shoot you. In the belly.'

Mei glared at him. 'What does it look like?'

He smiled again. 'Well, from here, it looks like my breakfast.'

'Where did you get that?' she asked him, pointing at the rifle.

He looked down as if noticing the Type 56 for the first time.

'This? From a guard, of course.'

'Sleeping?' Sis asked.

Psycho frowned. 'No. He was wide awake.'

'Then how——'

'I heard him coming from kilometres away. Crashing through the undergrowth like an elephant,' he said, still eyeing the fish. 'If that's the standard of training they're giving the PLA, it's a miracle we haven't been overrun by the Americans. I circled round behind him. When I was close enough, I took his knife and slit his throat. Just like the Crane taught us. Then I took his rifle. He had some rations, too. I ate them yesterday. Still hungry, though.'

Mei had time to wonder at Psycho's casual approach to killing the guard. Yes, she'd done it, too. But that was self-defence. She wouldn't have done it otherwise. But Psycho had just done it to get a rifle. In fact, she suspected he'd done it just because he could. Because he fancied it. Because he thought it would be *fun*.

What would the school authorities think of all this? Two guards down and one relieved of his knife. And that was just the ones she knew about. Was it all part of the plan? Was this how the school trained them to be killers? Guards were pretty easy to come by, after all.

She had no time to ponder this further. Psycho had advanced a couple of paces.

'I think I'll take my fish now,' he said. 'Throw it over here, Ten.'

Sis didn't move. 'Get it yourself.'

In response, Psycho raised the Type 56's barrel and squeezed the trigger. The burst of automatic fire was deafening in the silent glade. Somewhere overhead an excited squawking added to the noise as a flock of bright-yellow birds erupted out of the trees.

Psycho shook his head. 'Throw it here or I'll aim lower and cut you in half.'

'Do it,' Mei said, without turning away from Psycho.

'But——'

'Now!'

Sis lifted the fish by the stick they'd impaled it on as a spit and tossed it towards Psycho. It landed at his feet, bouncing once in the soft leaf litter.

Staring straight at Mei, and keeping the Type 56's muzzle on Sis, he bent and patted the ground until his fingers closed around the stick. He lifted the fish up and bit straight into its side, tearing away a chunk of the ivory flesh.

'Mm. Tha's good,' he mumbled, chewing with his mouth open. 'Got to go.'

He backed away from them, swinging the gun barrel left to right. Mei held up a warning hand as Rats started forwards. 'Don't.'

As if picking up her whispered command, Psycho fired another burst towards them. All three threw themselves down. Chips from a nearby tree trunk flew everywhere, pattering down into the leaves.

By the time they'd raised their heads, Psycho had disappeared, leaving a cloud of blue smoke floating a metre or two off the ground.

Mei shook her head and sighed, inhaling the acrid tang of burnt gunpowder along with the sweeter smell of the woodsmoke.

'Fuck it!'

Although Mei went back to hunting Fat-boys in the pool, she didn't even see another one, let alone spear it. Rats and Sis disappeared off, looking for anything edible. Roots, berries; even carrion, so long as it wasn't too far gone.

Sitting on her flat-topped rock, Mei kept a rough track of the time from the position of the sun.

As the hours crept onwards, the pain from her empty stomach faded from the sharp stabbing pangs into a dull ache. At one point she started feeling faint and had to sit back down on her bottom before she tumbled into the water.

Now, even that sensation had passed. The hunger just sat deep in her belly, gnawing away at her like a fox at a chicken carcass.

32

When the airhorns finally started up, Mei felt tears pricking her eyes. She looked around. Rats and Sis were already on their feet.

'Which way is north?' Rats asked.

Sis lifted her left wrist and pointed her arm towards the sun, angling it this way and that until she'd lined up the hour hand of her watch. Taking a bearing, as they'd been taught. She turned and pointed towards a stand of bamboo.

'That way.'

The journey up to the highway took two hours. By the time the trio emerged from the forest, they could barely walk, let alone talk. Mei's wounded leg had started hurting again and now she sat in the dirt by the side of the road, massaging her calf muscle.

Rats had slipped twice during the climb, the second time falling heavily against a tree and scoring a deep cut on his left arm. It was bleeding freely, dripping from his fingers into the dust.

Sis was hurt, too. Something, she couldn't be sure what, had bitten her left hand. From the knuckles to the wrist, it had swollen to almost twice the normal size. She said even brushing against a fern sent electric bolts of pain shooting up her arm to the elbow.

She sat beside Mei.

'I don't feel so good.'

Mei turned to her friend and placed the back of her hand against her forehead. It was burning hot.

'You've got a fever. Don't worry, the truck'll be here soon,' she said, feeling less confident than she sounded, 'and they'll take you straight to the sick bay when we get back to school.'

Sis offered a half-smile, then lay back and closed her eyes.

'Maybe they'll give us a day off training tomorrow.'

'Maybe.'

Somehow, Mei doubted that's the way the school authorities worked. But she kept the thought to herself.

Thirty minutes later, during which time Sis had fallen asleep and Rats had fashioned a makeshift bandage out of a strip of his tunic, Mei heard the distant rumble of the truck. It came round the bend belching black smoke and pulled up with a hiss from the air brakes.

The driver, cigarette dangling from his lips, leaned out of the cab window. He tilted his head sideways so the smoke from his cigarette didn't go in his eyes.

'What are you waiting for? Get in the back. Or do you want me to leave you there?'

Mei helped Rats to his feet and then between them they supported Sis as she staggered around to the back of the truck. A couple of the others already inside held the canvas flaps open, and somehow Mei and Rats managed to boost Sis inside before climbing up themselves.

Beneath their feet, the truck's transmission whined and clashed as the driver muscled it into gear and then, with a lurch and another gout of black smoke from the exhaust, they were off.

'OK?' Nine asked Mei.

'Yeah. You?'

'Yeah.'

'What's wrong with Ten?' she asked.

Mei turned to look at her friend. Sis was slumped over in the corner with her back to the cab. Her face was pale and sheened with sweat and her breath was coming in short, shallow gasps. Her hand was now a dark red and even fatter. It looked like a rubber glove someone had inflated and tied off at the wrist.

'Something bit her. A spider, maybe? A centipede? I'm not sure.'

'She doesn't look so good. Should we tell the driver?'

Mei nodded. She stood beside Sis and hammered on the window separating them from the driver.

'Hey! Ten is really sick. She's been bitten,' she shouted. 'You need to take us back to the school now. Let someone else pick up the others.'

He shook his head.

'Not until I've collected everyone,' he yelled back.

Mei hated begging, but now that Nine had started things she realised she was genuinely worried about Sis.

'She's got a fever. An infection!'

'And I've got my orders!'

'Please!'

Now he did turn round in his seat.

'Sit, the fuck, down!'

Mei sat. She briefly considered climbing out the back and over the roof to the cab. She could overpower the driver and force him to take them back to school.

She dismissed it. She could see him checking his rear-view mirror. He'd just lock the doors and leave her hanging on for dear life. He might even try to scrape her off on a telegraph pole or a tree growing close to the road.

Finally, all the students but Psycho were aboard. The driver had gone up and down the same long stretch of road three times, but the last student was nowhere to be seen.

Mei began to hope he'd died. Maybe choked on a fishbone from the Fat-boy he'd stolen from them. Ha! Wouldn't that be poetic justice?

She hammered on the window again.

'Hey, take us back to school! Now!'

'No Three, no school!'

'He might be dead! You can't keep driving up and down for ever.'

With a shudder and a lurch that sent Mei crashing into the window, hitting her head, he brought the truck to a stop. She saw him jump down out of the cab.

Seconds later he was flinging back the canvas at the back of the truck.

He pointed past the others at Mei.

'You! Out!'

Rubbing the lump on her forehead, Mei squeezed past the others and jumped down onto the road facing the clearly very pissed-off driver. He had his hand on the butt of his pistol.

'Who the fuck do you think you are?' the driver shouted. 'You're just some degenerate street rat from the Shenzhen slums. You don't get to order me around in front of them.' He jerked his chin at the back of the truck.

Mei glared at him. If he thought she'd wounded his pride, then bellowing about it when the only thing separating him from the other students was a tattered piece of canvas meant he was even stupider than he looked.

She tried to stay calm and to keep her voice reasonable.

'I'm sorry. Sir,' she added, even though his rank didn't warrant it. 'But my friend, Ten, I mean, is seriously ill in there. You don't want to be the one who caused her to die, do you?'

By way of answer, he pulled the Type 54 from its holster.

'Did I bite the little bitch? No! Get back on the truck now. We're not going back until I've picked up Three.'

'But he could be hours!' Mei protested, desperate now to get Sis back to the school and into the sick bay. 'Even if he isn't dead, he might be hurt or just, I don't know, wandering about. He's not like the rest of us.'

'I don't care if he's flying a kite while dressed as Chairman Mao. My orders are to collect you all before returning home,' he said doggedly. 'Now, get back on the truck, or it won't be your friend leaving feet-first.'

He extended his arm, pointing the Type 54 at a spot between Mei's eyes.

Which he shouldn't have done.

Mei shot out a hand and twisted the gun out of his grip. She flung it away, then took a half-step closer and chopped him on the side of the neck.

She'd been expecting him to go down like a sack of onions, so when he merely staggered sideways and came back up in a fighting stance, she was momentarily puzzled. Did they teach the guards as well as the students?

Dumb question. Asking it. She shouldn't have been thinking at all. She should have been *doing*.

Like the guard.

He leaned back and kicked her in the belly, hard enough to drive the wind from her. Gasping as her already-empty stomach seemed to contract to the size and feel of a small, hard stone, she fell backwards on to the tarmac.

He dropped onto her chest, his knees each side of her ribs and delivered two ringing slaps – one forehand, one backhand – that brought stars sparkling into her vision.

She tried to buck him off her but she was still weak from the climb out of the gorge; that and the lack of food. Grinning down at her with teeth stained brown by nicotine, he drove his fingers into her windpipe and started squeezing.

Mei's pulse throbbed behind her eyeballs: they felt like they were about to burst. She grabbed his wrists and tried to pull them away from her throat, but he was leaning downwards and putting all his weight into it.

The world darkened. Her lungs were convulsing as she fought desperately to drag even a sip of air past the driver's crushing grip on her windpipe. The strength left her arms and they flopped uselessly by her sides. Her hearing became muffled as if she were underwater, swimming in the Little Mekong with Ping. Ah, they were good times.

'Come back, then!' Ping said with a smile.

No! This was bad. Wrong. She wasn't at home. Ping was! Mei was right here, right now. And she was dying. She had to fight.

Then the driver's eyes rolled upwards, revealing yellowy whites. He toppled sideways and lay still in the road beside her.

Standing behind him, a tyre-iron dangling from his right hand, was Rats. He held out his left and she took it, letting him pull her to her feet. She heaved in one deep breath after another. They made a weird *whoop*ing sound, and dragging the humid air in hurt her bruised throat.

'Bastard was going to kill you,' Rats said, throwing a contemptuous look at the unconscious driver.

Mei followed his gaze. Blood was flowing away from the prone driver's head, meandering across the gritty tarmac like the river through the gorge. Flies had already found it and were crawling along its banks, feeding.

Rats walked to the verge and retrieved the guard's pistol. Back with Mei, he offered it to her.

'We should kill him,' he said. 'Otherwise he'll report us. We'll get punished, plus he'll be on our case for the rest of our time at the school.'

Mei shook her head.

'No. They're already at least two down. I killed one and Psycho did another. But they were hunting us. Maybe they allow for casualties, but him? He was just the driver. We can't.'

Rats shook his head.

'Yes. We can. They don't care, Juice. You know that. The Frog, the Crane – all of them – they're just interested in training us to be killers,' he said. 'OK, so let's show them what good students we are.'

Then he screamed and toppled sideways.

Mei looked down in shock. The driver had come round and stabbed Rats in the foot. He was getting to his feet. This time, Mei didn't think.

She kicked his right elbow, breaking at least one bone. The crack sounded like the firewood Rats and Sis had collected to roast their fish. The knife fell from his hand with a metallic clink as it hit the tarmac. She swooped on it and a moment later had cut his throat in a single swipe, left to right, just like they'd been taught.

Mei jumped back as bright-red arterial blood spurted up to head-height in front of her. Arc after arc pumped out of the wound in his neck before his heart lost pressure as he died.

She knelt beside Rats, who was clutching his bleeding foot.

'Are you OK? Let me look.'

Gritting his teeth and hissing out the pain, he let go of his foot. The knife had gone straight through his shoe. Blood oozed through the slit in the black canvas. But it wasn't welling out of the top so the driver hadn't hit an artery.

'I think it's going to be fine,' she said.

She turned to look at the truck. Faces were peering through the slit in the canvas. She had time to think how obedient they'd all, correction, most of them, become before shouting up.

'Hey! Come and give me a hand.'

A couple of the others jumped down and soon Rats was inside and sitting beside Sis. Mei looked down at her. She was pale and sweating, and behind her closed eyelids, which looked bruised somehow, Mei could see her eyes flitting; right, up, down. Her hand looked really bad. The fingertips had turned black and the flesh right up to the elbow was purple and mottled.

'What about him?' Eight asked, pointing down at the dead driver.

'Help me get him off the road,' Mei answered. 'We'll roll him down the hill into the bushes.'

With the driver's body hidden in the undergrowth, Mei went back to the truck. She stood at the back and called up.

'Anyone know how to drive?'

'I do,' One said. 'I used to drive a tractor on the farm back home.'

Mei accompanied One to the cab and climbed up into the passenger seat.

Once they were underway, she fell silent. She needed to think up a story to explain the driver's absence.

33

One started the truck and slammed the gear lever into first. The truck jumped forwards and then stalled with a loud bang from somewhere beneath their seats. He tried again, keeping his right foot flat on the floor, drawing a demonic wail from the engine. This time, he managed to get the truck moving.

After they'd travelled five hundred metres or so, still in first, Mei yelled at him over the noise.

'How about changing gear?'

He grimaced and executed a clumsy shift that produced another agonising howl of protest from the gearbox. Mei visualised a metal monster eating itself, chewing off fingers and toes and grinding them between steel teeth.

Five minutes passed. Mei's teeth were aching from the vibrations shuddering through the cab; they entered her body through the thinly-padded seat, travelled up her spine and set up home in between her ears, so that the very bones of her skull seemed alive.

'Again!' she yelled. 'Change gear again!'

'I can't!' One yelled back.

'What do you mean?'

'The tractor at home only had two forward gears.'

She looked down at the shiny black plastic knob topping the long, rattling piece of metal that disappeared into the floor. Faint impressions in the worn plastic suggested some kind of technical diagram. For the gears, she assumed. She shook her head.

'Try it. I think you go up and over to the left.'

One nodded. He looked down and grabbed the stick. The engine note screamed, the metal monster ripped off more of its own flesh and ground it between its teeth. The noise remained.

One shook his head.

'It's no good. I just can't.'

The cab began to smell of burning after another few kilometres and Mei feared One would set the whole thing alight.

Somehow, the ancient truck's engine and gears held together, though, but at the expense of any kind of conversation in the cab. Mei navigated using landmarks she'd glimpsed through the flapping canvas on the way out.

The highway continued in an unbroken straight line for many kilometres. By the time they reached the turning for the school, Mei's head was aching from the noise of the truck's overstressed transmission.

Finally, they reached the school. One pulled up at the gate and waited for one of the guards to come down from the watch tower.

Mei took a few deep breaths. This was her part of the performance and it had to be good. She wound her window down after One indicated by pointing and shrugging his shoulders at the gate guard that his window was stuck.

'Where's Chen Ruoteng?' the guard asked, looking at her through narrowed eyes.

'We were stopped by bandits on the road,' Mei said. 'They took him away. They said they were going to ask the school for a ransom.'

The guard's frown deepened.

'There aren't any bandits round here. They were all cleared out before the school was built.'

Mei eyeballed him.

'Well, they're back.'

'How many of these "bandits" were there, then?'

'Six. They were driving pickup trucks. Fotons. One was a dirty white colour, the other was dark blue,' she said. 'They were heavily armed. Kalashnikovs – Russian-made, not Norinco copies. Plus pistols, probably Type 54s; it was hard to tell because they didn't unholster them. They also had a Type 80 general-purpose machine gun mounted on the blue truck.'

The level of detail she'd invented did what she'd hoped it would. He was nodding appraisingly as she listed off the bandits' weaponry.

'Did they hurt him?'

She shrugged as if to say, *What do you think?*

'They hit him a few times then they put him in the back of the white truck. I think he was basically all right, though.'

'They give you any name for their gang, or their leader?'

Mei shook her head.

'No names. But the guy giving the orders had really pale skin and blue eyes like the sky, and his hair wasn't black like ours. It was light brown. I think he had a Russian accent.'

There. That ought to confuse him. She could see the cogs spinning in his brain as he tried to work out what to do. Decided she couldn't wait any longer.

'Look, can you let us through, please? Ten is badly hurt. We need to get her to the sick bay.'

He stared at her for another few seconds, then went inside the guard post. Seconds later the gates rolled apart and One drove through. He brought the truck to a shuddering, smoky halt right in front of the main building.

The guard must have radioed the Bull to say the students were back, minus the driver. He was standing in front of the main door, brawny forearms folded across his chest.

Mei jumped down and went up to him.

'Master Long, bandits kidnapped the driver and stabbed Five through the foot. I gave the gate guard all the details. But we have to get Ten to the infirmary. She's really sick. I think something bit her hand.'

'Show me,' he said, striding off towards the rear of the truck.

When Mei saw her friend, she cried out.

Sis's arm was black from fingers to shoulder. Her face was sheened with greasy-looking sweat and dark-purple patches had appeared beneath her eyes.

'Stand aside,' the Bull commanded the students supporting Sis on left and right.

He climbed up into the truck and knelt to scoop Sis up into his arms. He reversed out and jumped down with her. Mei was dismayed to see the way Sis flopped in the Bull's arms like a rag doll.

'Twelve, come with me,' the Bull said, already striding across the courtyard back to the main door. 'The rest of you, wait there. Madam Minxia will be out to debrief you in a moment.'

Mei followed the Bull down the hallway. Halfway down, an orderly was mopping the floor with that pungent disinfectant all the students called 'Dragon Piss'. He stood aside, mop held at attention, eyes downcast.

Normally the Bull marched around the place like he was on his way to a battle. Full of drive, purpose and energy. But now, Mei detected something else in his hurried gait: he was frightened. And that frightened her.

He reached the infirmary and spun round so he could barge through the double swing doors backwards. She followed him in before the doors had even swung back into position. Swivelling around without breaking stride, he laid Sis on a bed.

'Medic!' he bawled. 'I want a medic, now!'

A white-coated doctor Mei hadn't seen before hurried out of the little office in the corner of the infirmary. Her eyes were wide behind gold, wire-framed spectacles.

'What happened?' she asked.

'Ask her,' the Bull said, jerking his chin at Mei.

'Well?'

'We were coming out of a river gorge on the training exercise,' Mei said. 'Sis, I mean Ten, said something bit her. She didn't see what it was.'

The doctor was examining Sis's blackened arm.

'Where was the bite?'

'Her hand,' Mei said, glad to be able to provide even this small piece of helpful information.

'Where on her hand, girl? Think. This is important.'

Mei looked down at her friend's hand. The fingers were swollen to twice their normal size. The puffy flesh looked like the skin of an over-ripe fruit, ready to burst under the slightest pressure.

She tried to remember what Sis had said when she'd first complained of having been bitten. What had she said? *Something bit me. Look!* And she'd held her hand up so Mei and Rats could get a good look. How had she held it? Palm out, that was it. And she'd pointed to the soft pad of flesh just at the base of her thumb.

'There!' Mei said, pointing at the spot on Sis's grotesquely inflamed palm.

'Right. Leave this with me,' the doctor said.

'Come on,' the Bull said to Mei. 'There's nothing we can do here. She's in the right place.'

Mei felt tears pricking her eyes. Partly for her friend who was moaning softly in her unconsciousness or sleep or whatever the fuck it was, but mostly because there was something in the Bull's voice that made her think Sis wasn't going to make it.

The Bull was ex-PLA. A commando. He'd surely seen plenty of his comrades die in battle, or of their wounds afterwards. That was compassion she heard in his voice and she wanted to scream at him to speak normally. To curse her and swear and threaten to tear her a new one if she didn't pull herself together.

She cast a final look over her shoulder as the doctor worked on Sis. Then the doors swung shut behind her, she was walking down the freshly-mopped, Dragon Piss-smelling hallway.

Before she had time to process what was happening, she was out in the blazing sunshine again, where the other nine students were lined up in front of the truck. Eight was swaying, and, as Mei rejoined the line, she fell sideways in slow motion, her knees buckling beneath her.

The Crane was lecturing them. Mei caught the tail-end of a sentence.

'…disappointed you couldn't deal with a mere six bandits after all the training we've given you.'

Mei slid into line beside Eleven.

'We're in deep shit,' Eleven whispered out of the corner of her mouth.

'Something you wish to say, Eleven,' the Crane barked. 'Step out here, now.'

Eleven stepped forwards, made a quarter-turn and marched over to stand in front of the Crane. She kept her head up, for which Mei admired her. It was hard to do that when you'd been caught out by one of the instructors.

To look down showed subservience, but also weakness. Both could be punished at the whim of whoever had called you out. But to look them in the eye was a sign of insolence, of a challenge to authority. Also punishable.

Most of the students chose the lesser of two evils and looked down. Mei never did. Nor did Psycho, who seemed to relish the chance to 'stick it to the boss class' as he insisted on calling his frequent rule-breaking.

She suspected he simply didn't care. Beatings never seemed to affect him. In fact she'd actually seen him smirking on one occasion as an instructor broke cane after cane across his back and shoulders.

'What did you just whisper to Twelve?' the Crane demanded.

Eleven straightened and stared directly into the Crane's eyes.

'I told Twelve we were in deep shit, Madam Minxia.'

Mei caught a suppressed snort from somewhere to her right. She thought it might have been Rats, or maybe Two, who they all called Baby on account of him being smaller than all the others.

The silence deepened as the seconds ticked by. Mei wondered what sort of punishment the Crane would inflict. She was just as fond of beatings as the other instructors, but sometimes she seemed to take a special pleasure in devising subtler punishments.

She cocked her head on one side, like her namesake eyeing a particularly easy morsel of food.

'Deep shit, eh?'

'Yes, Madam Minxia.'

Then she did something extraordinary. She laughed. A full-throated cackle.

'Deep shit! Well, I think that would just about cover it. You let your driver get taken by these so-called bandits. Three is still out there somewhere, maybe even dead. Ten is in the infirmary. And two of the guards still haven't reported back for debriefing.'

Mei tried to keep her face from betraying her. She'd been responsible for killing one of the disappeared guards. And she didn't like the way the Crane called the bandits 'so-called'. All feelings of hunger had utterly vanished.

'On the other hand,' the Crane said, raising her voice and spinning Eleven round to face the rest of the students, 'none of you was captured before the end of the exercise. You survived in the wilderness on your wits and in the middle of one of the worst storms this region has seen in thirty years. This calls for a celebration. I have asked the cooks to prepare a special banquet for you. The table is set up in the centre of the assault course. Go! Go, my little chickens. Eat as much as you can!'

Mei stared at the Crane. This was unbelievable. Far from being punished, they were being rewarded.

'Well, what are you waiting for?' the Crane shouted, smiling. 'That food won't eat itself, you know!'

The ten remaining students stumbled off towards the assault course as if in a daze, which, Mei supposed, was pretty close to the truth. Probably none of them had had any sleep, let alone food. Now that the promise of a meal had been made, her hunger returned like wolves fighting over a dead deer.

She rounded the corner of the main building sandwiched between Rats and Baby. And there, just as the Crane had promised, was a long, wooden trestle table piled high with food.

She saw bowls of dumplings, fried pastry parcels, platters heaped with noodles from which huge prawns poked out, stuffed pancakes, pieces of grilled chicken, and, unbelievably, what looked like chocolate cakes, dozens of them, glistening with sticky icing.

Rats was the first to reach the table. He reached for a dumpling and stuffed it into his mouth. Then he turned and spat it onto the ground, retching. The others arrived and grabbed whatever they could before they, too, flung the food to the ground, their faces wrinkled in disgust. Nine was actually crying.

Mei stood unable to believe what was happening. Her eyes were giving her one message, but her nose was delivering another. The stench from the banquet was making her eyes water.

They looked at each other in disbelief.

Rats spoke first.

'They soaked it in fucking diesel!' Rats said.

Mei could smell it. Now she saw it, too. The staining on the exposed areas of wood. The puddles of the stuff in the dirt beneath the table. Every single dumpling, pancake, noodle, chicken piece, chocolate cake and deep-fried pastry was drenched in diesel. They must have used a whole fuel can of the evil-smelling stuff.

34

With a roar, Rats upended the table, sending the entire poisonous banquet onto the ground. Mei looked around, back towards the school, fearful of the Crane's reaction.

That bitch! She hadn't needed to devise a subtle punishment for Eleven's insolence. It was already waiting for them. Or was it always part of the plan? To dangle a prize in front of them then snatch it away again. Part of the process of 'hardening', as the Crane called it.

She'd explained how the old-time swordsmiths toughened the blades they fashioned by repeatedly heating then cooling them, a process called tempering. The school authorities practised the same arts on their students.

The ten starving students trudged back towards the accommodation block. They split into two groups at the entrance and went to their respective dormitories.

Hugging her belly, Mei fell asleep at once. She dreamed of bowls of noodle soup in which chicken's feet bobbed, and a tall, long-beaked bird that kept stealing them before Mei could transfer one to her mouth.

She awoke at dawn and went to the window. The sky was

streaked with pink. On any other day she might have thought about how pretty it looked. But not today.

Today she could only think of food.

One by one, the other girls woke up from their drugged sleep. As usual, they dressed and went downstairs as a group to the canteen. Mei wondered how Sis was getting on. She thought she'd ask permission to visit her after breakfast.

At the thought of a meal, her mouth filled with saliva and her stomach growled. She genuinely believed that if the school authorities pulled another trick like the previous day, they'd have to fight off ten trained killers.

As it turned out, she needn't have worried. It was as if the preceding couple of days, and the diesel banquet, had never existed. Everything happened the way it always happened: the cooks served porridge and fruit. Noodles and fried rice. Nobody talked. They were all bent over their plates and bowls, eating in silence; fast, too, as though each of them feared his or her food might be whisked away by the Crane as another example of 'hardening'.

Finally, after multiple trips to the serving counter, Mei leaned back in her chair, her hands cradling her distended stomach. The relief she felt at finally being able to fill her belly was mixed with stabbing pains as her gut struggled to cope with this sudden arrival of so much food.

She looked across the table at Rats, who was busily spooning up his third or fourth bowl of porridge.

'Slow down,' she said, smiling. 'Or you'll bring it all back up again.'

He glanced up and shook his head. He had a blob of porridge stuck to his chin, giving him a comical appearance.

'No chance,' he mumbled through a mouthful.

Slowly, ten spoons were placed in ten empty bowls, chopsticks were laid down and plates pushed away.

'I'm stuffed,' Rats pronounced.

'Good,' said the Crane, who had, at that precise moment appeared behind him. 'Because today's test is going to be a lot of fun.'

Mei saw the way the corners of the Crane's thin lips crooked upwards and didn't like it. Somehow, she didn't think the Crane's idea of fun involved funfairs and candies, or flying kites in the public park.

'Report to the gym in ten minutes,' the Crane said.

Nine minutes later, the ten remaining students were lined up in the centre of the gym.

Fifty-five seconds later, the Crane entered, accompanied by the Bull.

'The megacity of Shenzhen lies one hundred and thirty kilometres to the south of this institution,' the Crane intoned. 'It is a tribute to China's economic transformation. But along with progress inevitably comes backsliding.

'Even though the Party provides work for all, a decent standard of living for all, education, housing and social care *for all*, there are still antisocial elements who choose to live outside the law.

'Our police service does an excellent job, but even they cannot cope with the rising tide of filth that threatens to engulf the city. Drug-dealers. Pimps. Rapists,' she cast a knowing eye at Mei as she said this, 'murderers, sexual degenerates, thieves. They spit in the face of Chairman Mao every day that they are alive.

'So, today, we will lend the Shenzhen Municipal Police our assistance. Unofficially, of course. You will be dropped in the city centre. You will each be issued with a Type 54 and a knife. Your task is to remove one of these undesirable elements from the streets of Shenzhen and bring back an ear as proof.'

Mei's stomach squirmed as she listened to the Crane delivering the briefing. Yes, she'd killed. But that had always been self-defence. Now they were being sent back into Shenzhen to do it for no other reason than the school authorities wanted it done.

She tried to imagine what it would feel like, tracking down a target with the specific intention of killing him. And then she realised that this was the entire point of the training she'd been receiving at the school.

Somehow, until this very moment, she'd been able to lose herself in the training exercises. They were, she had to admit, mostly enjoyable, as long as you didn't get into trouble. She glanced at the scar on the back of her hand. Looking back on the trip out into the wild, even that had been – well, not fun, not exactly, but she'd felt a sense of accomplishment for having come through it.

Could she do it? Find some lowlife and stick a knife in his belly, or put a bullet through his brain? She thought of some of the men who'd prowled the streets of Shenzhen in the bad areas where she and the rest of the gang had foraged. She thought of how they treated their women, or any girls they caught out there alone.

Yes, on balance, she decided she could absolutely kill one of them. After all, if they didn't want trouble, they didn't have to follow that way of life, did they?

She listened as the Crane outlined the details of their assignment. Once again, the school would be deploying staff to ensure nobody got any 'silly ideas', as the Crane put it, about leaving. Mei thought they'd better have people with more brains than the guards they'd sent out previously. The Crane almost immediately confirmed that exact point.

'We are welcoming back last year's graduates as your supervisors,' she said. 'You will not see them, but, be assured, they will see you. At all times, in all places.'

There it was, then. Any thought Mei had of escaping into the city's back alleys and lying low until everyone returned to the school vanished.

Mei hung back until the others had all left. Then she approached the Crane, eyes down and stood meekly before her.

'Yes, Twelve? You wish to ask a question?'

'How is Ten doing, Ma'am?'

The Crane pursed her lips. 'She had contracted a severe infection. She will not be taking part in tomorrow's exercise.'

Mei knew better than to press any further. She thanked the Crane and performed a smart about-turn. *Please let Sis be OK*, she thought. *Please!*

* * *

The following morning, Mei walked down Long March Street, alone-but-not-alone thanks to her unseen supervisor. The Type 54 sat snugly against her belly, tucked into her waistband and concealed by the loose tunic she wore. Her eyes were shaded from the strong sunlight by a broad-brimmed straw hat.

They'd been allowed to choose their own outfits from a room full of clothes at the school: jeans, T-shirts, peasant tunics, business suits. Mei had opted for a nondescript outfit that suggested a girl recently arrived from the provinces. It was an easy role for her to slip into.

Long March Street was a broad, curving avenue lined with fancy shops selling mostly Chinese goods, although here and there she saw Western goods displayed in the windows. Levi's jeans. Nike running shoes. Chanel dresses.

Mei knew who could afford them. Party people. People with connections. She wondered what Chairman Mao would make of Party officials and their pampered offspring strolling down a street named after his great strategy before entering a shop and blowing the kind of money most of the people passing by wouldn't earn in a year.

A flash of turquoise in a dress shop caught her eye. She stopped to look in the window. Posed on a mannequin with *gweilo* eyes that had Mei touching her own reflexively, was the most beautiful garment Mei had ever seen.

All thoughts of Chairman Mao evaporated. Who cared what he would have thought? The trouble was, Mei wanted these things, too. If she had that kind of cash, she would walk straight in there, ask the sales lady to try on the dress and then hand over a fat wad of yuan in exchange.

She shook her head. Ridiculous! How would she ever get the kind of job where that could even be a possibility?

She refocused her eyes, not on the dress, but on the view reflected in the plate glass. Checking who was behind her, looking for anyone who stood out, maybe by standing still, resisting the flow of people busily travelling from here to there down Long March Street's thronging pavement. It looked OK. Nobody was watching her from across the street. She didn't see anyone who looked out of place. Watchful where everyone else was too busy avoiding bumping into someone.

She scolded herself mentally. She wouldn't see her supervisor, would she? That was the whole point. Except, how could she expect to become a trained assassin for the Party if she couldn't spot and throw off a tail? The Crane had lectured them over many hours in counter surveillance tricks. One in particular had impressed Mei.

The Crane had led them to a corridor, about thirty metres long. She stood at one end, dressed in her normal outfit of blue tunic, loose trousers and black plimsolls.

'Watch,' was all she said.

Then she began walking down the corridor. At first Mei couldn't understand what she was seeing. The Crane seemed to shrink in on herself. In a single, flowing movement she shucked off her tunic, reversed it and pulled a thread in the hem. As she put it back on again, the inner lining fell down to the floor: the tunic was now a tatty old dress printed with flowers.

Stooping, she took another few hobbling steps. Mei looked at her feet, which now seemed to be causing her pain, like an old village woman with bunions. The plimsolls had disappeared, replaced by those funny old-lady shoes you saw on the streets of Shenzhen, scuffed black leather with squat heels.

When Mei looked at the Crane's face again, it was hidden behind straggly grey hair that fell forwards over her cheeks. She swept a hand up and across her head, leaving a crumpled cotton hat in place. And now her eyes were behind a pair of spectacles with blue plastic frames.

Bent-backed, shuffling along on in-turned toes, the old woman carried a bulging string shopping bag. She stopped at the far end and turned to face the goggling students.

'Hey, sonny,' she called out to Rats in a dusty croak. 'Could you come and help an old woman with her shopping?'

As if in a trance, Rats complied, walking the length of the corridor and stopping in front of the Crane. He reached down for the string bag.

And then he was facing towards his fellow students, bent over backwards, with a large-bladed knife at his throat.

'He's dead,' the Crane said, before releasing him.

They'd spent the rest of the day practising the quick-change routine using props that the Crane explained were designed and made right there in the school's workshops.

The angry parp from a lorry's horn brought Mei back to the present. She was still looking in at the turquoise dress. Could she try a prop-less version of the Crane's routine now?

Like the Crane, she was tall. She bent her knees and let her spine curve outwards, losing almost ten centimetres in the process. She bobbed down as if to pick something up off the ground, and when she stood up again, the tunic was tied round her waist, so the pistol was still covered. On the move now, and keeping a knot of pedestrians between her and the outer edge of the pavement, she cut one of the sleeves off the tunic. She tied it round her head like a scarf, tucking her hair underneath the fabric that sat tight against her forehead.

With her limping walk and bent back, she felt like one of the disabled people you'd see travelling between begging spots, even though begging was forbidden by law. She came to one of the narrow alleys between the buildings and shot down it, breaking into a run and dragging her hands along the grimy brickwork. At the far end, she slowed and turned right, resuming her act. Now her cheeks were smeared with the black mould she'd transferred from her palms.

She ducked into a doorway protected by a metal grille which a careless shopkeeper had left unlocked. From the shallow recess she peered left, waiting to see if she'd been followed. After a couple of minutes it became clear that she was alone. Good. Now she could continue.

This side of the block was much less fancy than that facing onto Long March Street. The pavement was littered with broken glass and cigarette butts, and peppered with dark circles where people had spat out their gum.

She touched the Type 54's butt beneath her tunic. She could feel the hilt of the knife against her waist on the other side. Which would she use on her target? The pistol? She wouldn't have to get close, but it would make a hell of a noise and that might bring unwelcome interest, maybe even from the cops. The knife would mean getting up close to the target, and the possibility of him fighting back, but it had the advantage of being silent.

On balance, she favoured the knife. She'd had training, after all, and the target wouldn't be expecting an attack in broad daylight. Especially for a country girl newly arrived in the big city and about as wide-eyed and innocent as it was possible to be.

The Crane had mentioned drug-dealers and pimps. Mei knew exactly where to find them.

35

According to the official city maps posted on the public information boards, the area was known as District 45, 13th Municipal Banner, Northeastern Shenzhen.

Its denizens called it the Meat Market.

Once, there had been a real market there. Drovers from the countryside would arrive early in the morning after a month-long trip, finally herding their cows, pigs or geese down the district's narrow streets and coming to rest at a square where buyers and sellers, wholesalers and restaurant owners would come to haggle over the beasts.

Slaughterers would ply their trade; slicing throats and either catching the blood in vast blue plastic troughs or letting it drain down noisome gratings, direct into the sewers. Now the trade was in other kinds of human needs and desires. Often just as violent as before, but the killing as a side-effect of the trade not its purpose.

The Communist Party issued regular communiqués trumpeting the eradication of this vice or that from the streets of Shenzhen, which were dutifully picked up, repeated and amplified by the popular press.

SHENZHEN'S STREETS DRUG-FREE FOR NINTH MONTH
IN A ROW!

WORKER SOLIDARITY AGAINST PROSTITUTION
DRIVES THIS DEMEANING TRADE OUT OF EXISTENCE!!

PARTY BAN AGAINST ORGAN TRAFFICKING TOTAL
SUCCESS!!!

Maybe the Party officials who issued those communiqués believed what they wrote. Nobody else did.

Not the buyers of drugs, sex, weapons, people, or parts of people.

Not the sellers, obviously. They were triads for the most part. Plus assorted criminal gangs who'd never bought into Communist ideology and regarded it with the same cynicism they and their forbears had shown towards the millennia of monarchical rule, the short-lived Republic with its military government, and then the era of the warlords. Some were run by army veterans; it was said with the collusion, or at least passive acceptance, of highly-placed Party officials.

And not the residents. For the Meat Market was home to several thousand ordinary workers who had to walk to work or the nearest bus stop through its dangerous streets. The city authorities had just announced the construction of the city's mass transit system, but ask around and most folk rolled their eyes, after checking they weren't being watched. *I'll believe it when I see it*, being the most common reaction.

Several gangs attempted to dominate the trades at the Meat Market. Chief among them, the Paifang Street Butchers, who specialised in prostitution and sex trafficking.

Mei had run into a couple of their foot soldiers during her time on the streets. Somewhere along the line, maybe generations back, these men had shed whatever humanity they'd been born with. Now they existed to make money for themselves and the levels above them. The women and children they sold were chattels, kept for as long as customers were willing to pay for them, disposed of once their appeal dwindled.

She thought if she could find one, she wouldn't have any trouble offing him and taking his ear back to the Crane.

Night-time was the easiest time to find them; it was when they conducted their hateful business, after all. But night-time was when the Meat Market came alive. There'd be hundreds and thousands of people out and about, buying selling, drinking, smoking, fighting. The chances of making a clean kill – and an escape – dropped dramatically.

But they had scouts. Men who wandered around keeping an eye open for fresh meat they could snatch off the street.

Girls new to the city who'd come in search of a well-paid job in a factory making clothes, or light-bulbs, or cars, or furniture, toy soldiers, kettles or pocket calculators. Kids like Mei, Brains, Spark, Panda and the rest, who thought they were invulnerable until they came face-to-face with the real masters of the city. Or drunks who'd collapse in the street and turn up dead in the river, eye sockets scooped clean, body cavities emptied of all but the intestines.

She bundled her tunic up and stuffed it down behind some bins. They stank of rotting fish, which she hoped would put off any scavengers from getting too close. Next, she pulled the white vest out of her waistband and rearranged it to cover the pistol. She looked down at her chest. Stuck it out a bit like she'd seen the street girls do. Then realised she was supposed to be a sweet little country girl and rounded her shoulders as if she were trying to make herself inconspicuous.

She strapped the sheath holding her knife to her right calf using a bit of rope she found coiled up beside the fish-stinking bins, then straightened.

'My name is La Shiwen. I am from a little village called Lingbei,' she said in a high, fluting voice, speaking to her reflection in a grimy window. 'I am looking for work. I can sew very well and also look after children.'

Then she wandered off, looking up at the highest windows of the buildings that towered over the street. Many of the panes were broken: black stars against the dusty glass. Faded posters advertising circuses peeled in thick, curling wads from the walls at ground level. And everywhere, official notices in red, black and yellow urging workers to unite in a common purpose of economic growth. Chairman Mao grinned out at her from their corners.

The smell of the Meat Market was an eye-watering mixture: rubbish from the noodle bars and fish restaurants so rotten it was fermenting; harsh tobacco smoke from the cheap, Party-brand cigarettes everybody smoked from the moment they awoke to the moment sleep overtook them; petrol fumes from the delivery trucks and motorbikes that raced around the narrow streets; and an underlying, queasy aroma of body odour, perfume and incense.

'Hey, looking for something?'

Mei started, then immediately cursed herself for letting her guard down. She looked at the man who'd asked the question. And she knew she'd found her mark. He was not much taller than she was, with a wispy moustache and beard. His hair was cut in a Western style and slick with some sort of grease.

'Yes,' Mei said, beaming as she adopted the rough country accent she'd heard her whole childhood. 'My name is La Shiwen. I am from a little village called Lingbei. I am looking for work. I can sew very well and also look after children.'

The young man looked her up and down. The tip of his tongue protruded between his lips, like a cat's. Mei fought down the urge to kill him right where he stood. There were too many people about and, besides, there was always an outside chance he was just someone trying to help a stranger. Yeah, right! Because that was *always* happening in the Meat Market!

'Work, eh? Well, you're in luck, La Shiwen from Lingbei. Because I can set you up with work right now.'

She offered what she hoped was a shy smile, looking at him from beneath lowered eyelashes.

'What's your name?'

'Al.'

'Just Al?'

'Yeah. You know, like the *gweilo* actor. Al Pacino?'

'I don't know him.'

'Why am I not surprised? It doesn't matter. Come on, let's go.'

He took her left hand in his and enfolded it in the crook of his right arm, leading her towards a cross street she knew led deeper into the bad places at the centre of the Meat Market.

'Where are we going?' she asked. 'What sort of work do you have for me? Is it with children?'

He laughed. He actually laughed!

'Yeah, yeah, children, why not? Girls, boys, whatever. We've got all sorts.'

'Does it pay well? They said in my village you can earn a ton of money in Shenzhen.'

'Oh, it pays really well. You'll be rolling in it by the end of the week.'

They reached the cross street, a stinking alley, really, so small it didn't even have a name. He led her towards the opening. She was concentrating on keeping her right hand free. He dropped his hand to her waist and she had to feign a stumble to dislodge it before he found her Type 54. Somehow she didn't think he'd react well to a country bumpkin with a pistol stuck in her trousers.

'Watch your step!' he said. 'The streets probably aren't as clean as you're used to in Lengfei.'

'Lingbei,' she corrected him.

'Whatever.'

'Where are the children? Is it a nursery?'

'You ask a lot of questions. Come on, it's not far.'

She caught an edge in his voice now. And she knew why. He was close to bringing a new little chicken to whoever ran the henhouse. He was probably paid a bonus for recruiting new girls.

A thought occurred to her. Why not actually embrace the Crane's mission wholeheartedly?

She could go with him all the way to his base, or – she shuddered as she mentally uttered the word – *brothel*. Maybe she could strike back against the traffickers for real. Not for the Crane. Not for the Frog. Not for the school. But for the real country girls – and boys – who came to the big city with eyes full of stardust and who ended up enslaved by gangmasters.

They emerged from the far end of the alley into a narrow courtyard. On all four sides, apartment blocks towered above them, their windows black with dirt from the factory chimneys that rose higher still. Several cats, black, brindled and grey, prowled among the rubbish piled up in the corners.

'Al' pointed at a door on the far side of the square.

'That's us,' he said. 'Come on.'

Mei hesitated. This was her last chance to complete the mission simply and get away. Should she do it? Knife him here, take an ear and run back the way she'd come? Or play the role to the hilt – just for a little longer? She looked down at her right ankle, wishing now she'd stuck the knife in her belt on the opposite side to the pistol. But it was too late for that.

From somewhere inside the building she heard a high-pitched scream. A child's scream.

She looked in the direction it had come from. An open window, partially shaded by a lopsided slatted blind.

'Hey!' Al said, sharp now. 'Let's go!'

He grabbed for her and she pivoted away, a mixture of instinct from her street-fighting days and the months of drilling and training at the school. As a result, his hand skimmed her waist, right over the butt of her pistol.

His eyes widening in surprise, he jerked back as if burnt.

His hand went to his own belt and came up with a narrow-bladed flick-knife.

'Who the fuck are you?'

Mei stepped towards him, left hand up. As she turned his right wrist over he yelped in pain. The knife fell from his unresisting fingers as she dug her thumb into a pressure point between his thumb and forefinger.

She flipped him onto the ground and followed him down, drawing her own knife from its ankle sheath. As he struggled, she covered his mouth with her left palm and stabbed him three times, very fast, in the side of his neck.

'My name is Wei Mei,' she said as his eyes flickered left and right before stilling and filming over.

She dragged his body over to a wall and dragged some soggy cardboard and dirty scraps of fabric over it. A bruised plum rolled free from a broken-down cardboard box. Not quite knowing why, Mei stooped to retrieve it and placed it on his chest.

Now was the time to go. She glanced back towards the mouth of the stinking alley. Then she remembered that scream. Frowning, she stood up and pushed through the door that led to the interior of the apartment block.

36

Mei stood at the end of a long hallway. She transferred the knife to her left hand and drew her pistol.

She screwed on the silencer, then brought it up to her chest as she'd been taught. Only fools wandered around with their gun extended in front of them. Too easy for a concealed enemy to chop down and disarm you.

She listened, first. Straining her ears to catch a sound that would lead her to the child who'd screamed.

At first she couldn't hear anything. Then, little by little, she began to pick up low murmurs of voices, the squeak of bedsprings and, from somewhere deep inside the building, a man's voice, raised in anger, followed by a door slamming.

She stopped at the first door she came to and tried the handle. It was locked. On she moved to the second. Also locked. In this way she traversed the hallway, trying each door. At the last door before the stairwell, she reached out and gave the knob a cursory twist, expecting it to be locked like all the others. Instead it turned easily.

She pushed the door open wide.

Inside, the room was red, thanks to a bulb shaded with a piece of scarlet material. A fat, sweating man was crouched over a small, naked form. The fat man turned, his face a mask of anger.

'Hey! I paid for an hour! Fuck off!' he shouted.

From beneath his right shoulder, Mei saw a small, frightened face peering out.

She shot him in the face. The young girl on the bed screamed.

'Get dressed, and get out,' Mei hissed at her. 'Go down the alley on the other side of the courtyard. Now!'

The girl nodded mutely and scrambled into some clothes. Mei left her to it and exited the room. She pushed through the door leading to the stairs and took them two at a time on silent feet.

As she reached the landing, a door opened and a man resembling Al came out adjusting his trousers. Mei had time to catch the black pistol in his waistband. He looked at her.

'Who—'

The Type 54 bucked once in Mei's hand. He fell back, half his head missing, brains splattered onto the wall behind him.

She opened the door to the room he'd just left. A woman, older than the girl downstairs by maybe five years, looked at her in shock. Her black eye makeup was smeared and her lipstick had been dragged across the corner of her mouth.

Mei told her to dress and go. As she got out of bed, Mei turned to her.

'How many of you are there in here?'

The woman shrugged. 'Normally seven, but Aimin is sick today.'

'How many men?'

The woman looked down. 'I'm sorry, I don't know. Too many to count, you know?'

Mei felt a pang of pity. 'No, I meant, how many like that guy?' She jerked her head back in the direction of the dead gangster.

'Oh. Not counting him, three,' she said, eyeing the pistol in Mei's right hand. 'They play cards and drink on the next floor up. The room at the end; the others are empty.'

Mei nodded her thanks. 'Listen. Once you're dressed, can you get the others out? The ones like you, I mean? Leave the customers to me. They won't cause any trouble.'

'OK, but won't Marlon and the others come looking for us?'

Mei shook her head. 'No. I promise.'

The woman looked Mei's pistol again, then back into her eyes. 'I understand.'

'Hey, what's your name?'

'They say I have to call myself Wendy, but my real name is Zhang Wen.'

Mei smiled at her. 'I'm Wei Mei.'

Mei left her to finish dressing and strode down the hallway. There were five more doors before the one at the end.

She went into the first room. At the scene that greeted her, she nearly screamed. Instead, she shot the two men as they whirled round to face her, once each in the groin, once each in the head.

By the time she reached the final room, the hallway was full of acrid gun smoke and the stench of blood. Lots of blood.

She twisted the handle and pushed the door wide. The room was empty, bar a dirty mattress and a hard wooden chair. Cockroaches scuttled into the shadows as the light from the hallway filtered into the drab little cube. Behind her, the young woman was rushing from room to room, issuing whispered instructions to get dressed and follow her.

Seven women, minus the sick Aimin, equalled six. The girl on the ground floor had already gone and Zhang Wen was leading the others to safety. Anyone left was a target.

Mei headed up to the third and final floor. Finding the rest of the men wasn't hard. As Zhang Wen had said, the floor was deserted apart from one room. And that was easy to find because the door was half-open, presumably so the gangsters inside could listen out for trouble. Although what sort of trouble would concern them given the horrors occurring right beneath their feet, she couldn't work out.

She stood with her back to the wall opposite the door, then kicked the door in. The men inside rocked back on their chairs, spilling playing cards, bank notes and glasses onto the floor.

They went for their guns, which was technically the right thing to do.

But Mei could have told them, faced with an enemy with their gun-arm up, your only hope of surviving the oncoming attack is to throw yourselves at them and hope to surprise them into missing.

Not that hard with enough resolve, athletic ability and specialist training in unarmed combat. Nor given the accuracy problems usually experienced by an average shooter armed with a pistol.

And if they'd been faced with an *average* shooter, perhaps that would have worked for them. They died with their right hands still many seconds away from gripping, let alone levelling their own pistols.

Mei lowered her gun. Then she frowned. What had Zhang Wen said? Three men. The room contained two.

Mei heard a lavatory flush and then the click of a door latching closed in the hallway. She spun round in time to see the third gangster as he emerged from the toilet. He blinked as the gun smoke hit him. As he saw Mei, he shouted something and went for the gun tucked into the front of his waistband.

The front of his white shirt bloomed red and he fell forwards, grunting out a dying breath and fell face-down onto the sticky plastic floor covering. From beneath his torso, a lake of dark blood spread out.

Mei turned and strode back to the stairwell. After checking the rooms were all empty, she backed out of the door leading to the courtyard just in case there were any more gangsters inside who fancied chasing after her.

The sting on the side of her neck surprised her: a hornet she thought, like the big stripy ones that used to buzz around the fruit trees back home. She clapped her hand to the spot where it had got her and felt someone else's hand already there.

Then she felt nothing.

37

Mei opened her eyes. They felt sticky. She rubbed sharp little crumbs of dried goo from the corners. Her mouth tasted of metal.

She looked up at the ceiling. Then pushed herself up onto her elbows. Groaning as a bolt of pain whipped between her eyes, she lay back down again. Closed her eyes. Slept.

She awoke for a second time and rolled her head to the left. A blue tin mug sat on the concrete floor. Trying hard to raise her head and wincing at the anticipated knife-thrust of pain, she found she could move easily.

Relieved, she propped herself up on her elbow and reached for the mug. It appeared to contain water. She raised it to her lips, then hesitated. What if it contained poison? Then she sighed. Someone had already poisoned her, dummy! That was no hornet. She'd been injected with knockout drops.

She took a trial sip of the water. Apart from tasting a little stale, it was OK, she supposed. Although she realised she had no idea if taste was a reliable guide to whether water was mixed with anything.

Seized with a sudden thirst, she drained the mug and set it back down on the floor.

Her stomach rolled over and for a second she thought she would bring the water back up again. Then it settled. She lay back down and felt around with her fingertips. She was lying on a mattress. Thin, but still, a mattress. So whoever had captured her didn't want her to be too uncomfortable.

And who, exactly, had stuck her in the neck and ghosted her off the backstreets of the Meat Market anyway? A minder from the school? Unlikely. Why would they do that? It didn't make any sense.

Her mind was fuzzy and it was hard to think straight. She decided to start with simple things. Her location, for a start. The ceiling and walls were unpainted plaster. A single high window admitted a little light. There was a door.

She realised she had no idea how long she'd been unconscious. She touched the crotch of her trousers. Dry. That was good. She hadn't wet herself, so she hadn't been out for that long. That meant she was probably still in the city.

She closed her eyes and listened. Maybe she'd pick up a clue as to where she'd been taken. But she couldn't hear a thing. No traffic. No noise of construction equipment. Nothing that gave her even the slightest hint.

Cautiously, she got to her feet. She felt a little dizzy and leaned against one of the unpainted walls until the feeling passed. Then she stood on tiptoe beneath the window. It was too high. All she could see was sky, mostly grey, with lighter patches of cloud.

Her pistol had been taken. She felt for her knife in its ankle sheath. Gone. Not ideal. But she still had her hands, knees, feet… and teeth.

Oh, yes, the Crane and the Bull had been insistent on that point. If you were close enough, bite your enemy. Thanks to the masseter muscle, the human jaw could exert enough force to chop through muscles, remove fingers and thumbs and rip out chunks of flesh.

Couple that power with a knowledge of anatomy and the shock value of such a primal attack and you could disable or even kill your opponent.

Behind her, feet scuffed on the concrete floor and she heard the metallic scrape as the intruder picked up the tin mug.

Mei whirled round, angry at herself that she hadn't heard the key turn in the lock.

A man stood there, smiling. Not Chinese. His eyes were those of a Westerner: round, and bright blue. And he had yellow hair.

He said something in a language she didn't understand.

'*Privet, Dvenadtsat.*'

He switched to Cantonese. 'Your face betrays you, Twelve. You did not hear me as I came in because the door was not locked. I just opened the door. You could have done the same.'

She stared at him. How did he know her number? He must be from the school. Although the way he spoke was weird. He was pronouncing all the words correctly, but it didn't sound right at all.

Then it hit her. This was all part of the exercise. Fear flashed through her. The only reason the school would send agents out to capture the students was to show them what would happen if they fell into enemy hands. And the Crane had been explicit on the point.

You'll be tortured. They'll want to squeeze every last drop of juice from you about your mission. From the target to your handler. Tell them anything, even the colour of ink used in your orders, and you betray not just the mission, but China herself.

So she was to suffer pain. Her job would be to resist for as long as possible. She steeled herself. She'd been in pain plenty of times before. Like when the Crane had stabbed her through the hand with a screwdriver. Mei had got through that all right, so she could get through this.

The man smiled. If he took another step towards her, she'd attack. A kick to the balls to begin with, then she'd leap onto him and tear out the artery in the left side of his neck.

'You wonder how I know your number,' he said in his weird way of speaking. 'And you are thinking I am from the School for Technical Studies, yes?'

She backed away a little, hoping he'd interpret it as fear on her part. That Sun Tzu saying came back to her again. *Appear weak when you are strong, and strong when you are weak.*

He held his hands out wide. Still smiling. He looked like a

simpleton when he did it, especially with those silly eyes the colour of summer sky.

'My name is Valeriy,' he said. 'Full name, Valeriy Pavelovich Ivanov. Is quite a mouthful, so you should just call me Val. What is your name? Your real name, I mean, not that demeaning number they gave you at the school.'

Mei blinked. All traces of her earlier discomfort had vanished. What the hell was going on? This guy was a Russian. She knew from his name: they'd studied all kinds of stuff about Russia because it was one of China's enemies. Even though they had Communism, they had debased it and were sliding into Western-style decadence.

Should she talk to him? Lull him into a false sense of security? He already knew her number, so giving him her real name would hardly add to his stock of intel, would it? She inhaled. Then changed her mind at the last second.

'Juice.'

He laughed at that and she saw he had teeth made of gold at the back of his mouth. Was that how the Russians stored their wealth? Weird.

'Juice? What kind of a name is that for a Chinese girl?' he asked.

She shrugged. He'd asked, she'd answered. She wasn't his friend and she wasn't going to fall for his phoney routine.

She glanced at his throat, visualising the path the carotid artery took from his collarbone, up his neck and into his brain. The trick with biting out a guy's arteries was to clamp down, twist and pull. Otherwise you just left teeth holes they could block with a field dressing or even their own hand.

He shook his head as if still amused by her name. Fine. Let him be. The lower his guard, the quicker he'd die.

'OK, Juice. Thank you. Now, before you commit to the attack you are planning, know this,' he said. 'First, it will not be successful. I see you looking at my neck. Maybe you plan to bite me there. Or strike with your fist. But before your teeth close on my skin, a knife I carry will be in your gut. A very painful way to die. And not necessary. Not today. Second, I am not your enemy.'

'Then why am I here?' she blurted, immediately cursing herself for her weakness.

'Come,' he said, beckoning her. 'Hungry? I have food, something nicer to drink than old water. Maybe you want to clean up, go to the toilet, yes?'

She said nothing, folding her arms across her chest, suddenly aware that, not for the first time, she was alone with a man: another one who thought just because he had that *thing* between his legs, it gave him the right to do whatever he liked to girls.

He frowned and tilted his head to one side.

'You are worried I am a bad man. Thinking about sex all time, yes? Maybe you have met men like that before,' he said. 'Maybe they try to rape you? Did you hurt them? Kill them? Good for you!'

How was he doing this? Every time she planned a move or even thought a thought, he seemed to know about it. Had the Russians found a way to read people's minds?

She relaxed. Just like that.

Because if he could read her mind then he'd have no need to torture her, would he? And what if he really was a friend? What if he'd come to rescue her from the school?

'Touch me and I'll kill you. Knife or no knife,' she said.

He shrugged.

'You're the boss. Follow me.'

What an odd thing to say. No way was he part of the school. She'd experienced their methods for securing obedience and the Russian, Val, wasn't doing it right.

He turned his back on her, leaving himself open to a stranglehold, a head-strike or a bite to the carotid. He seemed not to care. She cautioned herself: he also had a knife. She scanned his clothing, which was Western-style and baggy. It was possible he had a blade in there somewhere, but he'd have to be as fast as a snake striking to get it out and into play before she dropped him.

He led her down a corridor. They were in a block of flats, or maybe an office of some kind. There was nothing on the walls to give her any clues.

He stopped by a door, turned to her and smiled. This was it. She knew exactly what was waiting for her on the other side of that door. A seat with broad leather straps. A car battery. Pliers. Rubber tubing. Water. Knives. Pain. She braced herself.

Val nodded at the door.

'Toilet,' he said. 'There is lock on inside. No window, though, so you'll have to come out same way you went in.'

He stood back. Suddenly aware she really, *really* needed to pee, she shot past him into the little cubicle and slammed the door. Panting, she slid the bolt across.

38

When she'd relieved herself and washed her hands, she stood with her hand on the bolt. She'd been captured by Russian intelligence. That was the only explanation.

For all his smiles and his jokey attitude, Val was going to take her to Moscow. And then, who knew what they'd do to her? Hook her up to some sort of mind-reading device and empty out her brain?

No way was she going to allow that to happen. But he was her ticket out of China, wasn't he? And it was a long way between here – Shenzhen – and there, Moscow. She'd take the offer, then find a weak spot in their security and escape.

She opened the door. Val was leaning against the wall, smoking a cigarette. He held the packet out and raised his eyebrows. Mei shook her head. He shrugged.

'Come on, let's get something to eat,' he said, pocketing the cigarettes.

He took her to a kitchen, complete with table and chairs, cooker, fridge, pots of cooking utensils beside the stove. He pointed to a chair.

'Sit.'

Mei sat, struggling to process what was happening, but increasingly sure that attacking Val would be the wrong move.

'What do you want to eat?'

She frowned.

'Too used to getting what they give you, I suppose. How about eggs? You like eggs?'

'Yes. Please,' she added.

'That's my girl!' Val said, smiling.

Ten minutes later, she was eating the most delicious dish of scrambled eggs. Val had added herbs from a little clear cellophane packet, explaining that 'you can't get this in China. No idea why, it's just dill tops.'

He made tea and poured them both a cup. He slurped his noisily, making Mei laugh.

'Well,' he said, 'that's the first sign of humanity from you since we meet. And listen, I'm sorry for—' he mimed administering a hypodermic in the air beside his own neck. 'But I had to move you out of Meat Market fast and under cover. After your little house-cleaning operation, you would have been running around with target on your back.'

'Where are we?' Mei asked, wiping her mouth after putting her chopsticks down.

'Still in Shenzhen. Safe house. You know what that is?' Mei nodded. 'Of course you do. So, tell me, Juice. Who, or what, do you think I am?'

Mei sipped her tea. How much should she tell him of what she suspected? What would Sun Tzu have to say on the matter? She found she couldn't remember a single word from the book. Decided to trust her own instincts.

'From your name, I think you are Russian.'

He nodded. 'Yes, I am.'

'I think you are a Russian agent. FSB?'

He nodded again. 'Close enough. You were paying attention in class. Good. That is a sign of intelligence,' he said. 'Not just interested in all the shiny toys. What else?'

'I think the Russians have found a way to read people's minds. It's why I'm not being tortured.'

His eyes, which in the better light of the kitchen were a much paler blue than she'd originally thought, widened. Then he laughed again, louder than the first time and with what sounded to Mei like genuine humour.

'Read people's... Oh, dear God, that is good one! I wish! My job would be lot easier if we had such a tool.' He wiped his eyes on a white cotton cloth he drew from a trouser pocket. 'Tell me, Juice, what makes you think we can read minds?'

'Before,' she said, jerking her chin in the direction of the door into the hallway. 'You knew I was thinking of attacking you. Of going for your neck. Then you knew about the men who tried to rape me. They're dead,' she added, thinking it wouldn't be a bad thing if he respected her ability to fight. Just in case he was still having evil little thoughts of his own in that direction, though somehow she doubted it.

Val shook his head and ran a hand through that oddly pale hair of his.

'No mind-reading needed,' he said. 'Take the attack. You are trained to kill, yes?'

She nodded.

'So, your captor enters your cell. He appears to be unarmed. You have no weapons. But you can kill without weapons. You have been taught how. By Du Minxia, yes? By Long Yan?'

Mei nodded again, dumbstruck by the inside knowledge Val possessed.

'There are many targets on human body, but you looked at my neck. Bad move. I saw it. A real enemy would, too. You must disguise every part of your attack. Not just the strike itself, the reconnaissance, also.'

'But what about the other thing? About men?'

Mei couldn't help it, she was intrigued now. She wanted to know more.

Val cocked his head on one side.

'You know about body language?'

237

Mei shook her head. She sat straighter in her seat. This was like being back at school. Only now she had a new teacher.

'Tell me,' she said.

'We are always talking, even when our mouths are closed,' he said. 'Our bodies betray our thoughts, until we learn to control them. When a woman is captured by a man, in war or another time, she is always fearful of this happening to her, yes? It happens. You study history at the school?'

Mei shook her head. 'Only tactics. Plus a lot of bullshit about Chairman Mao.'

Val smiled at that. 'We all have our heroes. For us it's Marx and Lenin.'

'They tell us about them, too.'

'You ever hear about Rape of Nanjing?'

'Who was she?'

'Nanjing was place. Still is, I suppose. Japanese killed hundreds of thousands of civilians there and they raped all women,' he said, looking down at his hands. He had long fingers. Mei thought they would break easily in a fight.

Val sighed. 'Men behave like beasts in war. You were captured, so you expected I would mistreat you. Your fear came out in two kinds of body language. You looked at my, uh, groin? Is that the right word?' Mei nodded. 'And you covered your breasts. Like for protection. No mind-reading needed, just better training than you have been given.'

'Did you really have a knife?'

A slender flick-knife appeared in his right hand. He thumbed the button. The gleaming steel blade shot out with a *snick*. Then he closed it and vanished the knife into his sleeve.

Suddenly Mei had had enough of this fake-friends act. He'd stuck her with knockout drops and taken her prisoner. She needed to watch that she didn't drop her guard all the way.

'Why did you take me? How long were you following me for? What's going to happen to me?'

He pinched his nose, which was large and had a few hairs growing out of the end.

'We've known about School for Technical Studies for some years,' he said. 'Long enough to study its routines and especially its field training. We wanted to pick you up during wilderness exercise, but storm ruined everything.'

Mei couldn't help herself. 'You were there?'

'Yes. But my transport got washed away. I had to radio for extraction myself.' Val poured out more tea and took a sip from his cup before continuing. 'Do you know what happens at end of your training?'

Mei nodded. 'We go into the field as trainee agents, under the care of a graduate.'

'Correct. But before that, they take you to Beijing. And do you know what they do to you there?'

'What?'

'They make you so you never have to worry about your mind being read ever again.'

Mei felt uncomfortable. A shiver ran across her skin as if she were outside in the dark in just her pyjamas.

'What do you mean? More training? Counter-measures?'

'Do you know what brainwashing is?'

Mei wrinkled her nose. The phrase sounded silly in the Russian's badly-spoken Cantonese.

'Is it waterboarding? They told us all about that.'

Val shook his head. 'No, my dear Juice. It is far, far worse. Worse than any torture.'

Mei had experienced waterboarding in the yard. Just a few applications of a soaking wet flannel over her nose and mouth while she lay on a sloping plank of wood head-down, but it had been enough to convince her she'd not last long under hostile interrogation. What could be worse than torture?

'Tell me.'

Val extracted the cigarettes from his pocket and lit one. Again he offered. Again Mei refused.

Once he'd drawn in a lungful of smoke and then exhaled it noisily at the fly-spotted ceiling, he looked at Mei with what looked to her like pity.

'Your day begins at 3.30 a.m. Not with food. Not with shower. With atrocity photographs projected onto wall. Loud music is playing in your ears. You have headphones on. Your head is restrained so you cannot look away from the screen.

'A doctor injects a drug into your veins. You feel anxious, like a tiger is chasing you. Music stops. Instructions from unseen figure boom. Telling you you are nothing. You are nobody.

'They turn lights on. They are too bright. Pictures stop. Instructions stop. Food and water are brought to you.

'Doctor comes back. Administers more drugs. Now you feel dreamy, happy, like you are free of every fear, every worry you ever had. There are voices in between your ears. Telling you to believe things it is impossible to believe. People can fly. Fish walk around on dry land. Mothers and fathers are children; children, mothers and fathers.

'More photographs, more loud music, more drugs. Lights go out. You sleep. Then they wake you with the soundtrack of a massacre. Of a firefight. Of buildings being demolished with high explosives. You do not sleep. At 3.30 a.m. it starts again.

'Every day is same. Every day is like this. Until one day, they let you rest. You sleep for days. They feed you, wash you, cut your hair, give you books to read, walks in the fresh air. Everything seems clear to you. Everything seems fine. You are happy. Relaxed. And also, empty.

'Then doctor is back. He injects you again. Now you have sessions with psychologist. He hypnotises you and puts ideas into your brain. It is like planting seeds in newly-tilled garden. Fertile soil in which they can grow. No diseases or pests to attack them. They flourish. They grow tall and flower, set seed and reproduce. There is no room in garden for anything else. They scrub out every trace of *you* and replace it with *them*. *That* is brainwashing.'

Val stopped talking and Mei blinked. Somewhere along the line, while he'd been talking, she'd drifted into a trance. She felt like she'd been dreaming and wide awake at the same time.

'What just happened?' she asked, feeling woozy.

39

Val smiled at her.

'How did you enjoy your eggs?'

'They were delicious. Why?'

'Did you like the dill tops?'

'The herbs?'

'Yes, the herbs.'

'They were lovely.'

Mei smiled back at him. He was nice-looking, really, despite the big nose.

'They weren't dill at all.'

'What were they, then?'

'Cannabis. What they call "Peace Weed" on the streets here.'

'You drugged me?'

'Only a little. Just to show you how easy it is to change the way you feel. Don't worry, it will wear off soon.'

'I'm not worried. I've smoked plenty.'

Val smiled. 'I bet you have. How long were you on the streets?'

Mei shrugged. 'Few years. From when I turned thirteen. Then the Crane picked me up after I killed that Party boy.'

Val chuckled, the sound seeming to come from deep in his chest.

'That's what you call Madam Du, is it? The Crane?'

Mei nodded, touching the tip of her nose before making scissors out of her fingers and miming a crane's beak.

As the effects of the Peace Weed wore off, Mei pondered what Val had told her about the next phase of the training. Was it really possible? Could they wipe your mind clean of everything but the ideas they planted there? Of course it was! Why was she even asking the question? They were already drugging them up with sleepers every night. Who knew what shit they were capable of?

'What happens after they brainwash us?'

Val shrugged, stubbed his cigarette out in an ashtray that had appeared by his left elbow.

'You're a killing machine. You have no conscience, no mind of your own, no sense of right and wrong. Only what they tell you,' he said. 'They order you to slaughter a pregnant mother, you do it. Kids, you do it. Scientists, academics, executives, writers, priests, activists: if they tell you they're a target, you do it.'

Mei narrowed her eyes.

'Sounds pretty bad.'

He nodded. 'It is. Worst thing you can imagine.'

'But you're different. The Russians, I mean. The FSB is going to let me retrain as, what, a teacher? Or are you just here to get me back to my village unharmed? Maybe fix me up with a nice farming boy to marry? Is that the plan?'

Val shook out another cigarette. He tapped the end on the back of his hand, then lit it. He squinted through the smoke as it curled up, partially hiding his face.

'Were you always a smart one, or was it three years on the street that did it?'

Mei paused before answering. Just a little. 'What do you think?'

Val smiled.

'We could use somebody like you, Juice,' he said, then frowned. 'No. Cut the bullshit, Valeriy. We *need* somebody like you.'

'Why? Don't you have any trained killers in Russia?'

He offered her a half-smile. 'Smart *and* funny. Of course, we have people who do what they're training you to do. Probably who do it better,' he said, directing a thin stream of smoke towards the ceiling. 'But we don't brainwash our people, Juice. They do it because they love Mother Russia.'

'OK. So?'

'So, we want to know what goes on inside the School for Technical Studies. I want to offer you a deal. Come back with me to Moscow. Tell us everything there is to know about the Crane and the rest of them. How many students there are, how they train you, what they feed you, what they tell you. Especially, what they tell you. About Russia, about America – about all their enemies.'

'What do I get out of it?'

'A job.'

'Killing for Russia instead of China?'

'Not always killing. You'll come and work for me at the FSB. You'll receive all-round training in espionage, you know that word?'

'No. Tell me.'

'Sorry, it means spying. You'll have a proper place to live. An apartment in Moscow. Your own clothes. Books, CDs, whatever will make you happy. You could travel to all sorts of countries. See a little of the world beyond Shenzhen. Meet interesting people.'

'And then kill them.'

He shrugged. 'Sometimes.'

'What if I say no? What if I go with you now then lose you in the crowds and go home?'

Val shrugged. 'Is that really what you want? To return to shitty little village in the sticks, where cows roam streets and dogs steal food from babies? Nothing to do but work and drink and suck up to local Party boss and get married at eighteen and then look after your baby while your husband ploughs rice field?' He spread his hands wide, so that the cigarette left a trail of smoke in the air in front of him. 'Don't let me stop you. It's just, when I looked at you, I thought I saw a bit more spark.'

Mei started. Out of nowhere, memories crowded in of running the streets of Shenzhen with Spark. Laughing as they outpaced angry stallholders, or cops blowing whistles and brandishing their batons. Sitting on the carpark roof, smoking Peace Weed and listening as Brains pointed out the constellations.

And then she thought of Mummy Rita. Had Fang been back to threaten her again?

Mei looked at Val. He was right about her. She *did* have a spark. But that spark wasn't available to the highest bidder. It was hers and hers alone. It had kept her alive so far and it would help her get back to the village.

'OK.'

He sat straighter in his chair, and stubbed out his cigarette.

'OK, as in…'

'OK, yes. Let's go. Now. Take me to Moscow. I can't wait to get out of this shitty country.'

'Good girl. You are making wise decision.'

'What you said to me earlier. In Russian. What was it?'

'*Privet, Dvenadtsat?*'

'Yes, that.'

He smiled. 'It means, "Hi, Twelve".'

'Which word is "Hi"?'

'*Privet.*'

She tried out the awkward-sounding word.

'*Privet?*'

He corrected her pronunciation. She tried again. After three tries, Val declared her to be 'speaking like a true Russian'. Then he hustled her out of the door.

'Plenty of time to learn properly when we're back in Moscow.'

The building turned out to be a regular apartment block. Val led Mei down a clean but drab corridor to a flight of concrete steps. The balcony beyond gave onto a square of grass enclosed on three sides by more blocks.

As they descended, she watched a group of children playing with a ball on the grass. A simple game of catch. She felt sad all of a sudden. It was so long since she'd done anything as carefree as that.

Even back in those frantic days on the streets, their lives had been *full* of care.

Care not to run into a rival gang that liked to fight with knives instead of just fists. Care to get enough to eat without catching a beating from a stallholder. Care to stay out of the way of the cops, with their heavy black boots and grinning beatings.

It must have been back in the village, playing with Ping. The last time she was able to just *be*.

They were on the third floor, turning at a half-landing every seven steps. A woman shouted from somewhere across the square.

'Children! Inside, now!'

The children moaned. Mei smiled; little ones never felt they had had enough playtime.

At ground level, Val turned to Mei.

'My car is parked opposite the apartments,' he said, pointing at the open side of the square. 'Wait until you hear me hoot the horn three times, then come.'

While Val was gone, Mei stared up at the apartments. Most had plants growing in pots on their narrow, steel-railed balconies. Many had clothes-dryers, drooping under their loads of wet washing.

Something soft brushed against her leg. She looked down. A cat the colour of ginger powder twined itself in and out of her ankles. She bent down to stroke it but it hissed at her, baring its needle-like fangs and arching its back, its puffed-out fur doubling in size.

'Suit yourself,' she said, straightening.

She mimed firing a pistol at it. 'If the Crane brainwashed me, I'd have to kill you, no question. She'd make me.'

The cat glared up at her, yellow eyes aflame, then stalked off, tail in the air, arsehole proudly displayed.

Mei grinned. Three blasts on a car horn echoed across the grassy square. It was time to move.

40

Mei trotted across the grass and left the enclosed square. She looked up and down the street, not recognising the neighbourhood. Somewhere far out from the centre where she and the gang used to hang out.

On the opposite side, a grassy bank led up to an elevated roadway. Beyond it, a line of grey concrete tower blocks stood, like giants waiting for a bus.

A few hundred metres down from the giants stood a dirty grey car. As she drew nearer, Mei saw the chrome badge on the back end, made of three interlocking ovals. She recognised it from posters she'd seen in Shenzhen. A Toyota. Japanese.

Val was leaning against the driver's door, smoking another cigarette.

He held up a hand in greeting as though they were meeting by chance.

Mei looked past him. The street was empty. No traffic. No pedestrians.

If she was going to make a run for it, this was her last chance. He'd chase her, but on foot she'd be faster. No way could anyone who smoked that much be fit enough for a sprint. And if he got behind the wheel, she'd just duck into an alleyway and lose him.

Yes. This was her chance. Fuck the school. Fuck the FSB. Fuck them all! She was going home.

She was only twenty metres away from the car. Remembering what Val had said about body language, she tried not to signal her intentions. She slowed down a little and relaxed her shoulders. Looked straight back at him and smiled.

He smiled back.

Then blood spurted from his mouth.

Eyes wide, he fell back against the car. She saw the bullet wound blossoming red on his shirt front.

Now she heard the gunshots.

Val's left cheek vanished, leaving a red mush through which his teeth showed.

She watched, stunned, as he staggered towards the rear of the car and collapsed. He was reaching into his jacket. His hand came out gripping a black pistol.

Blood was sheeting from his ravaged face, soaking the front of his suit jacket. His blue eyes were wild, swivelling in their sockets like a panicked ox stuck in a bog.

The noise of gunfire shocked her back into herself and she threw herself to the ground.

Val looked over to her. His face was grotesque, like one of the anatomy models they'd studied at school.

His jaw was moving. Was he trying to say something? She couldn't tell.

He made a pushing motion with his hand. Body language! He was telling her to run.

Then the top of his head exploded and Val toppled sideways. As he hit the tarmac, his shattered skull released a torrent of blood that ran down the road and into the gutter.

Mei dived to the ground and scrambled underneath the Toyota. Heart pounding, she scanned the far side of the road looking for the shooter. Her hand went to her waistband, but, of course, Val had taken her own pistol when he'd captured her. When even was that? Hours ago? Days?

Val's outflung hand, bloodstained now, had come to rest half a metre away from the car. His pistol lay beside it. If she could reach it, she'd have a chance. But it would mean stretching her own hand out, from beneath the Toyota's protective cover.

But what else could she do? Stay here and wait to be shot like a rat? No. Wasn't going to happen. Not now. Not when she was so close to freedom.

She inhaled sharply, one, two, three times, then reached for the pistol. Immediately, bullets struck the tarmac, kicking up sprays of sharp debris that stung the exposed skin of her right arm.

Mei grabbed the pistol by the barrel and pulled it back. She flipped it round, then aimed out from under the car and fired twice. More as a signal of intent than with the thought she'd hit the sniper.

They returned fire. Three shots in quick succession that hit the bodywork, low on the exposed side. Heart pounding, Mei ducked reflexively. Although she knew that, as body language went, ducking out of the way of a high-powered rifle was about as pointless as it got.

A fast pattering sound by her left ear was accompanied by a sharp smell. Petrol! She twisted her head round to see where it was coming from. Clear liquid was falling in a steady stream, splashing the tarmac. She swore. The sniper had hit the fuel tank. Probably not a lucky shot, either. Whoever it was knew exactly what they were doing.

The fuel spread out in a shallow puddle, met her belly and started soaking into her clothes. This was bad. She was turning into a human torch. One spark if a round hit something hard enough and she'd go up like a New Year's firework.

Another bang close by, followed a split-second later by the report of the rifle. They'd just hit the front tyre. That corner of the car dropped by twenty centimetres or so, and she had to snatch her legs out of the way to avoid being trapped.

She had time to wonder why the sniper wasn't using a silencer. And then the pieces fell into place. The quietness of the street. The lack of traffic and pedestrians. And the mother back at the safe house who'd hurriedly called her children inside. This was a set-up.

The sniper shot out the rear tyre. The car lurched downwards again. Mei slithered over as far as she could before hitting the kerb. She could roll out from under the Toyota and return fire from the cover it provided. But then what?

Val hadn't fired at all. She had twice. The pistol was a Tokarev, the Russian original on which the Norinco Type 54 was based. It should have an eight-shot magazine, maybe nine if it was a variant. If Val had come out with a full magazine, she had six or possibly seven rounds left.

What the hell could she do with seven rounds against a sniper with presumably a whole box of ammunition? A kill-shot was out of the question. Even if the sniper stood up and waved, holding up a target, the Tokarev's range was pitiful, its accuracy worse. She might as well *throw* the bullets.

The stink of petrol was stronger and her front felt cold as it hit her skin.

All the sniper needed to do now was put an incendiary round into the fuel tank and blow the Toyota – and Mei – into the next world.

Mei gritted her teeth. No way was she going to die here, cowering under a Toyota while an unseen enemy decided when to torch it.

She had an idea. The car had slumped over so that the side facing the sniper was just a few centimetres off the ground. That meant she was invisible. She scraped her way out from under the car, in a crouch so low that she was entirely hidden by the door on the pavement side.

With the memory of Val's skull bursting, she kept her head tucked well down into her shoulders. On her back she shuffled away from the Toyota, holding the Tokarev in both hands, arms straight along her body.

At some point soon the sniper would regain line of sight through the car's windows. Mei had no doubt the sniper's rounds would penetrate two panes of glass and kill her on the spot. But she wasn't going to give them the chance.

She aimed at a spot thirty centimetres below the filler cap on the rear wing and emptied the magazine. The first six rounds punched holes in the bodywork. Then she hit the fuel tank. This close the round was still hot enough to trigger an explosion.

The fireball blew out towards her. She felt its intense heat scorching her face, even as she rolled away and brought her arms up to shield herself from the blast.

She couldn't afford to wait. As black smoke billowed into the air, she got to her feet and sprinted up the grassy bank towards the tower blocks, zig-zagging randomly just as she'd been taught.

'A good marksman can anticipate a regular evasion pattern,' the Bull had bellowed at them as they ran in crazy patterns in front of him while he fired a rifle over their heads. 'Don't give him that chance.'

She risked a look back over her shoulder as she sprinted away from the burning car. The smoke and flames were boiling up, providing perfect cover. And the sniper hadn't fired again. She was in the clear.

She reached the elevated roadway. After checking for oncoming traffic – none, again, weird! – she raced across, heading for the space between the two nearest tower blocks.

Ahead, a window shattered. The report of the rifle reached her a fraction of a second later.

Mei swerved to her left, then right. She threw herself to the ground as she reached the front wall of the block. Scrambling along like a lizard, she desperately wanted to reach the far end of the alley and disappear around the corner.

Once she was out of range of the sniper, she could stop. And think.

Another round ricocheted off the wall over her head. Concrete dust showered down on her.

She reached the far end of the block and hurtled round the corner, the lizard chased by a predator reaching safety at last.

She realised she was still holding the Tokarev. She was out of ammunition and, for a moment, considered leaving it. Then she stuck it into her waistband. Even empty, a pistol made an effective club, and a pretty good threat, too.

Head down and panting so hard it felt as though her lungs might burst, she hung her head between her knees.

What was happening? Who was shooting at her? Val was Russian. Was it the CIA? British Intelligence? They both hated the Russians and the Chinese.

A shadow fell across her.

'Hello, Freak,' someone said.

She looked up into a familiar face.

41

The sun beating down on the school parade ground was mercilessly hot.

Mei stood in line, sweating in the heat beside Sis, Rats and the others. Psycho hissed at her. She turned. He was leaning forwards out of line and had turned to face her.

'*Privet*, Freak,' he said, grinning.

The grin was visible all the way round the side of his face where the bloody flap of his cheek hung down over his jaw, revealing all his teeth.

She screamed. The parade ground shimmered and slid sideways. She smelled disinfectant. She opened her eyes. The infirmary.

The doctor leaned over her.

'Quiet, Twelve! You were having a nightmare. It's the sedatives. Just a side-effect, that's all.'

Mei propped herself up on her elbows. Pain pierced the front of her head as if someone were threading a wire between her temples. She groaned and slumped back onto the thin pillow.

She raised a hand and gingerly felt around on her forehead. Her fingers rippled over a huge lump on the right side. Psycho! He'd been there. Back at the apartment blocks. He must have pistol-whipped her.

The doctor crossed the room and lifted a telephone. He muttered a few words. Mei couldn't make out what he was saying. Then he nodded. This time she did hear him.

'Yes, Director.'

He put the phone down and returned to his desk.

'Doctor?' she called out. 'Where is Ten, please? I thought she was in the infirmary.'

'She died,' he said, without even turning away from his paperwork. 'The infection entered her bloodstream.'

'But…'

Now he did turn, a scowl twisting the corners of his mouth.

'But what?'

She wiped the tears that had sprung to her eyes.

'Nothing, Doctor. I'm sorry for disturbing you.'

Poor Sis. While Mei had been lying drugged in Val's safe house, she'd died and been buried, or burnt or whatever the school did with dead students. She'd never see her again.

She sniffed and dragged a sleeve across her running nose. Forced herself not to care. Nothing to be done, then, was there? Sis had joined Spark and the other dead kids Mei had grown up with and then lost.

A few moments later, the door swung inwards and the Frog strode in. He crossed the room to her bed and peered down at her.

'Doctor Weng says you are ready.'

She looked up into his bulgy eyes, her own still wet with tears. Ready? For what?

'Sir?'

'Get dressed. Then come to my office.'

He turned on his heel and was gone, leaving a strong smell of his stinky aftershave.

Five minutes later, trying to ignore both the pain in her head and the nausea it produced, Mei knocked on the Frog's door.

'Come!'

She took a deep breath and entered, pushing all thoughts of Sis down as far as she could manage. Emotions would get her killed.

The Frog pointed at the chair in front of his desk.

'Sit.'

Mei did as she was told. As long as he stayed on that side of the desk, and let her remain on this, she thought she could cope with whatever dressing-down she was about to receive.

But after all, as far as the school was concerned, she hadn't done anything wrong. Had she? She would just tell him the truth: that the FSB agent had drugged and kidnapped her.

'Explain yourself,' the Frog said.

Mei nodded. 'I had just completed my mission, Director. I killed five morally corrupt men in an underage brothel in the Meat Market,' she said. 'I was preparing to take my proof when a man injected me with something that knocked me out. I came round in a windowless room. I was bound. He said he was an FSB agent and was taking me back to Moscow with him.'

'And then?'

'Then he ordered me to meet him at his car.'

'Why did you not run away, the first chance you got?'

'He said he had accomplices covering the other exits. They would kill me if I attempted to escape.'

The Frog brought his hands together under his nose.

'Were you bound when he took you from this windowless room to the car?'

Mei realised she was heading straight into a trap. The sniper had seen her unbound.

'No, Director. He untied me.'

He nodded. Blinked slowly, which brought out even more strongly his resemblance to a frog.

'Have you enjoyed your time at the School for Technical Studies, Twelve?'

'Yes, Director. Very much. I feel I am almost ready to make a full contribution to China's continuing battle against its enemies, within and without.'

'Just so. And your training?'

'Yes, Director.'

'You are always near the top in all the combat modules, both armed and unarmed, yes?'

She lowered her head. It would not do to show any pride in her achievements. Not here. Not now.

'I believe Madam Du and Master Long are content with my scores, Director.'

'Mm. And yet, faced with an enemy armed only with a pistol, you made no attempt to counterattack,' he said. 'No attempt to use any of the techniques so painstakingly drilled into you by Madam Du and Master Long and your other instructors.'

'I tried, Director. Truly, I did. But he was more effective. I am sorry I failed you.'

The Frog banged his fist on the table making Mei jump.

'It is not me you have failed, stupid child!' he shouted. 'I am a small cog in the machine that is China's security apparatus. Perhaps not even that. Just the spindle on which that small cog rotates. It is China you have failed.'

Unable to stop herself, and bitterly regretting it, Mei began to cry. It could have been from the stabbing pain behind her eyes. Or the fear of what he would do to her. But what truly frightened Mei was the shame she felt at knowing that in some way she believed the Frog was right.

'Stop your bleating, Twelve. You do not fool me with your childish playacting.'

She sniffed and wiped her nose with her palm.

'I am sorry, Director.'

She looked up to catch him eyeing her up and down, his eyes lingering over her breasts. She surpassed a violent urge to shudder. If he did *that thing* to her again, she would just have to bear it. Better that than a bullet in the back of the head.

'You are compromised, Twelve. You have spent too long in the company of an agent from a hostile state to be returned to your previous duties,' he said. 'However, I have good news for you.'

She frowned. Good news? What could he possibly be talking

about? The only good news she could imagine was the end of whatever punishment he had planned for her.

'You are puzzled, I can see that,' he said. 'Did you think you would be punished?'

Something odd had happened to his voice. She tried to work out what. Then it came to her. He was trying to sound friendly.

'Yes, Director. After the sniper – from the school?' He nodded, smiling with those wide rubbery lips of his. 'After they tried to kill me. I thought—'

'Part of our surveillance team. And you were never in any danger, Twelve. Just a precaution,' he said, still speaking in that jolly favourite-uncle voice. 'You will notice they placed their shots with extreme accuracy. If we had wanted you dead next to the FSB agent, you *would* be dead.'

'Then, forgive me, Director, but I don't understand. Please explain it to me.'

'Your training here is over. There is nothing else we can teach you.' That was a lie. Mei knew it. Her pulse kicked up, sending a fresh wave of pain into the front of her head.

The Frog was still speaking. 'I am transferring you early to Beijing, to complete the next stage of your training. Tomorrow a senior official from the Intelligence Bureau of the General Staff will arrive to collect you. This is a great honour. Your chance to rise to the very top of your profession early. To join the elite agents defending China against her enemies, within and without. What have you to say to that?'

She knew what was expected of her. She spoke words. About how she was not yet worthy but she would strive to become so. That serving China was her whole life's purpose. She was more grateful than she, a mere country girl, could convey to him, lacking the formal education required.

But as she mouthed these sickly phrases, her mind was whirling. Beijing? The Intelligence Bureau of the General Staff? A senior official. Something Val had said came back to her, shouldering its way through the pain threatening to split her head in two. *'They scrub out every trace of* you *and replace it with* them.*'

So *that* was her punishment. No need to shoot her, or administer another beating. She was too valuable an asset. But they were accelerating her training so all traces of any possible disloyalty could be cleaned away.

The Frog drew his head back into his neck, frowning.

'Are you feeling all right, Twelve? You look pale.'

'It is just the after-effects of the sedative, Director. I am sure I will be fine to travel tomorrow.'

He smiled, nodded.

'Very good. Return to your dormitory and pack your things. You are excused all duties for the rest of the day. You will eat with your fellow students this evening and tomorrow morning, but I strongly advise you not to talk about your transfer. It will only provoke feelings of envy. Do you understand?'

She bowed her head again.

'I understand, Director.'

'Good girl.'

Mei thanked him again for the wonderful opportunity he had arranged for her and left his office, closing the door quietly behind her.

The hallway was silent. She supposed everyone else was out training, or in a lecture hall somewhere.

Back in the dormitory, Mei sat on her bed.

She had less than twenty-four hours to escape the school.

If she failed, she'd be taken to Beijing and have her mind scrubbed as clean as the toilets in the washrooms.

Why did she feel so calm? Why wasn't she trying to fight down a wave of panic?

The answer came to her. Because she wasn't going to fail.

Her bag sat on the floor beside her feet. It contained so little that it really didn't matter whether she took it with her or not. Just some spare clothes, her own copy of the Crane's unarmed combat book, and a toothbrush.

But if the Frog conducted an inspection, she wanted him to see that she was obedient. No trouble.

Because Mei was planning a mountain of trouble.

42

Mei got to her knees and lifted the end of her bed until she could prop it on her shoulder.

The steel frame dug into her flesh, sitting right across the bone, but she didn't mind the discomfort.

She dug her thumbnails into the gap above the rubber bung at the end of the leg and worked it loose. As it came free, a stream of white tablets tumbled out into her cupped hands. One or two bounced out onto the floor.

She lowered the bed to the ground, then scooped up the tablets onto the bed covers, making a hill. After collecting the few strays and adding them to the pile, she paused.

How many would she need? She wanted to make sure everyone would be out, but she didn't want to kill any of the students. Maybe Psycho, but, even then, this wasn't how she'd do it.

There were ten staff, an equal number of guards, plus another ten or so orderlies, kitchen staff and cleaners. Add nine students and that made thirty-nine. Call it forty. One sleeper per person for a good night's sleep. Two each should be enough, surely. She wrinkled her nose. Because who'd want to be caught mid-escape just because they'd undercooked it on the dosage?

Three each, then. No, four, just to be on the safe side.

She counted out a hundred and sixty pills and hid them inside her pillowcase. The remainder she stuffed in her pockets. One quick trip to the toilet later and they were gone.

Outside the girls' dormitory, a fire extinguisher sat in its cradle bolted to the wall. She fetched it back inside. She lay the sleepers on the floor and started rolling the fire extinguisher back and forth over them.

The sleepers made a satisfying crunch as she worked them into a fine powder. After five minutes she was finished. The little hill was now a little sand dune.

She tore the centre pages out of the Crane's book and laid the double-width sheet by the dune. Carefully, she brushed and scooped until all the white powder was heaped in the centre of the paper. She folded it up into a parcel and pocketed it. The residue she scuffed away under her shoe, turning it grey so it blended with the flooring.

* * *

The smell of simmering chicken stock filled the kitchen. Mei approached the head cook. He was tasting the stock, lifting a big metal spoon to his lips and slurping noisily.

'Excuse me?'

He turned. Scowled.

'What do you want?'

'Director Gao put me on punishment duty. I am to help you prepare the evening meals.'

He rolled his eyes.

'What did you do?'

'Insufficient effort.'

He snorted. 'Yeah, well, I don't want you slacking in here, my girl. Here.' He handed her the spoon. 'Start adding the chicken. Keep it all moving.'

She nodded and took the spoon from his pudgy fingers.

He moved away and started shouting at one of the kitchen assistants.

Mei looked down into the huge pot of swirling yellowish-brown liquid. She saw her face reflected in it, a wobbling collection of features in which those softly-rounded eyes dominated.

She looked over her shoulder. Her pulse was racing. If he saw her, she was finished.

Stirring with her left hand, she turned a little to mask what her right hand was doing. She drew out the thick package from her pocket and slid it across her hip, around her belly and over the steaming surface of the stock.

'Hey!'

She nearly dropped the paper packet to the floor. Hurriedly, she shoved it back into her pocket.

'Yes, Cook?'

She tried to sound calm, obedient, yet she was sure he must hear the quaver in her voice.

'I told you to add the chicken. Get a move on or it'll be undercooked. Or do you want the whole school to come down with food poisoning?'

'No, Cook. Sorry.'

While he watched, she grabbed a handful of chicken pieces, cold and fatty, and dropped them into the stock. Another. He grunted his satisfaction and wandered away.

She glanced at him a couple of times, but he was on the far side of the kitchen, lighting a cigarette. She reached into her pocket, breathing lightly, trying to ignore the pounding in her chest.

Closing her fingers around the packet, she looked round again. The cook still had his back to her. She pulled it free of her pocket and shook out half the contents into the boiling stock, intending to save the rest for the rice.

Then she dug her fingers into the pile of pale-pink meat and grabbed a third handful. In it went. She stirred steadily, watching as the white powder spiralled around and around among the chicken pieces then gradually faded from sight.

The cook finished his cigarette and flicked the still-glowing butt out of the door into the yard. He came back to where Mei was stirring the pot of chicken and noodles. He peered in. Mei prayed he wouldn't want to taste it. He seemed content merely to smell.

'Good. Now you can help prepare the staff food.'

Mei had always thought everyone at the school ate the same meals. This was a revelation.

The cook led her to a second food preparation area. Here were thick steaks, dark red and marbled with fat, reddish-brown juices leaking from underneath into channels carved into the wooden board on which they rested.

'Slice those thinly,' the cook said.

Left alone again, Mei breathed out a sigh of relief. If she hadn't kept half of the powder back, her plan would have failed before it had even begun.

An hour later, the cook dismissed her.

'It's finished now. You can go.'

She nodded, thanked him and left, heading back to the dormitory.

* * *

For what Mei knew would be the final time, she sat beside Eleven at the table. Rats faced her.

'Where have you been, Juice? We were worried about you.'

'I got wounded in the exercise in Shenzhen. I had to spend a couple of days at the city hospital.'

It was a simple lie: the best kind. Easy to keep straight.

'Shit! Wounded where?'

She put a finger to the point of her chin.

'I think it was Seventeenth of August Street.'

He grinned.

'No, dummy! I meant—'

She laughed, though the effort cost her. She immediately felt like crying.

'I know what you meant. I got into it with a drug dealer. He stabbed me in the side. It's just a flesh wound but there must have been something on his knife. It got infected.'

'Did they look after you OK?'

'Yeah. It was fine. Though the food wasn't as good as we get here.'

'I'm starving. They had us on the assault course all day. I could eat my own bodyweight in noodles.'

She smiled. 'So how did your time in Shenzhen go?'

He puffed his chest out.

'Pretty good. I saw this guy mugging an old grandma. He bashed her over the head and took her purse,' he said. 'I chased him onto some waste ground and did him there. Two to the head. Blam, blam! They said I was the first to finish. Check out the Ratman!'

He flexed his biceps, which Mei suddenly realised had grown to an impressive size during their time at the school.

The others joined in, regaling her with their own stories of how they'd passed the test.

Out of nowhere, she felt a wave of sadness wash through her like a river swollen by spring rain flooding a village. She'd killed, too, of course she had. It was how she'd ended up here, after all. But she'd never enjoyed it. Never got a kick out of it. The school had turned killing into a game.

Maybe that was the point.

It was all part of their goal of turning children into machines who would kill whoever they were ordered to. Man. Woman. Old. Young. Powerful. Weak. Nothing mattered except the mission. The orders.

And now, thanks to the dead FSB agent, she knew what came next. A trip to Beijing. Where everything that made you who you were – your memories, your ideas, your beliefs, your personal code of morals – was blasted into nothingness by loud music, atrocity videos, drugs and psychological conditioning.

All of a sudden, she wanted to jump onto the table and tell them all what was waiting for them. To scream at them to resist. To come with her.

The cook called out.

'Queue, now!'

The students jumped up from the wooden benches and formed a straight line, each person the regulation forty-five centimetres away from the next, facing front, not talking.

It was too late.

43

As they returned to the table, bowls heaped with chicken noodles, Mei screwed her face up and laid a hand across her belly, low down.

'I have to go to the toilet,' she said, placing her bowl in front of her seat.

'Now?' Rats said. 'We just got food.'

'It's now or sit here and crap in my pants,' she said.

He wrinkled his nose. 'Better go, then. Though I can't guarantee your food will still be there when you get back.'

Mei had no intention of going back. She left the canteen and returned to the girls' dormitory, where she lay on her bed, folded her hands behind her head and stared at the ceiling.

When the other girls got back, chatting about the day on the assault course, Mei joined in with the conversation, asking them who'd done best, who'd fallen into the notorious 'mud bath' and who'd got their arses handed to them by the Bull.

Soon, though, there were more yawns than words.

'Shit!' Nine said. 'I can hardly keep my eyes open.'

'Me neither,' Seven said before yawning so widely Mei heard the hinges of her jaw crack.

The other girls stumbled around for a few more minutes then, one by one, crashed out, none making it out of their clothes or even under the covers.

The dormitory filled with their combined heavy breathing and snores as the quadruple dose of sedatives took effect. Mei daren't risk a trip along the hallway to check on Rats and the other boys, but she knew what she'd find if she did. They always ate more than the girls, so they'd all be out cold, too.

When did the staff eat? That was the question. She doubted it was as early as they made the students consume their evening meal. They probably sat around drinking whisky and smoking for a good while. Relaxing in their common room or watching films on their VCR.

Mei wasn't sure what Chairman Mao would have had to say about that. Somehow, she didn't think Old Fatface would have been smiling his shit-eating smile and handing out autographed copies of his little red book.

She was glad twice over she hadn't eaten at suppertime. Obviously, because if she had, she'd have been knocked into the deepest sleep of her life too. But also because the hunger pangs currently chewing on her stomach lining were doing a fine job of helping her stay awake. She had a good few hours to go before she could put the next part of her plan into effect.

She left her own bed and went to sit on the stripped mattress where Sis used to sleep. She laid her palm on the head end and stroked the coarse fabric.

'Maybe you were better off out of it, Sis,' she murmured.

She passed the time running through the layout of the school in her head. Even though the guards would be incapacitated, she didn't want to risk going out the front.

It would only take a surprise inspection by the next-level supervisors of the school for everything to go to shit.

She envisioned herself climbing down on the far side of the gates only to be caught like a rabbit in the blinding white headlights of a truck carrying a general or an intelligence officer from the 2nd Bureau.

No. That wasn't going to happen. Mei had another route

planned.

* * *

She checked the time: 3.00 a.m.

Time to go.

Rising from her bed, she looked down at her bag. She wouldn't need it.

She looked along the two rows of beds. The others were so deeply asleep she doubted they'd have woken if she'd smashed the window and climbed out while singing the national anthem.

Casting a final glance at the girls she'd spent so many months with, she opened the door and stepped out into the corridor.

Low-level security lights glowed green along the bottom of the walls, every two metres. Mei didn't need them: she could have found her way blindfolded. Had, indeed, on one training exercise meant to simulate escaping from a smoke-filled building.

It was time. And yet, just when she should have been taking her first steps to freedom, something pulled her in the opposite direction. She wanted to see Rats one last time. Just to say goodbye.

The boys' dormitory was down the corridor and around a corner. Keeping to the edge of the passageway, she made her way there, straining to catch even the faintest noise of someone stirring. But all she could pick up was the rushing of the blood in her own ears.

She turned the knob and went inside the long, narrow room. Just as in her own dormitory, the space was full of snores, snuffles and the occasional fart. She tiptoed down the space between the beds until she came to Rats. He was lying on his back, mouth gaping.

Gently, she pushed his jaw up with the tip of her forefinger until his lips met. He smacked them together a couple of times and then rolled onto his side.

She leaned over him and placed a light kiss on his forehead.

'Goodbye, Rats. Take care of yourself.'

She'd almost reached the door when she looked down at the

final sleeping form. It was Psycho.

Like Rats, he lay on his back. He made no sound as he slept, and his face was blank. She moved closer, hardly breathing. All she could think of was the cruelty he displayed whenever he got the chance. The way he'd cut Nine's femoral artery. How he'd stolen the Fat-boy she'd speared when they'd been on the wilderness exercise. And knocked her out just after the school sniper had killed Val.

'So, I'm the freak, am I?' she whispered.

Then she reached down, lifted his head up and tugged the pillow free. Slowly, though if he hadn't woken yet, she doubted this would bother him, she pressed the pillow over his face. And then she clutched her fists around the edges and drove it down hard, putting all her weight onto it.

She'd thought he might struggle, but the sleepers were so strong he might have been already dead. She counted to ten, fifteen, twenty, and then, suddenly, she yanked the pillow away.

She couldn't do it. Even to Psycho, who surely deserved it. Murdering someone in cold blood wasn't for her. That was the school's way, and she'd have no part of it. Panting, and wiping sweat off her forehead, she dropped the pillow to the floor and left the dormitory on silent feet.

Outside, she leaned against the wall. Her pulse was bumping uncomfortably in her throat. She needed to be calm to function at her best. Nothing less would do.

She paused, closed her eyes, and consciously slowed her breathing. Tensing and releasing the muscles in her feet, calves, thighs, abdomen, hands, arms, shoulders, neck and face, she focused on achieving the state the Crane called, 'relaxed alertness'. This was the state of mind-and-body readiness they had to achieve before a kill. Adrenaline caused muscles to tremble, throwing off a shooter's aim. Fear caused field of vision to narrow, cutting down information reaching the brain.

'You are not fighters,' the Crane told them, over and over again. 'You are killers. There is a big difference. You do not need the flight or fight reflex. You must conquer your body's natural reaction to stress.'

Mei practised what she'd been taught. Gradually, she felt the tension leaving her. In its place, that state of total calm in which every sound seemed magnified, even visual impression on her retinas imprinted as if in glowing colours.

She was ready.

Running on the balls of her feet, her rubber-soled plimsolls making no noise on the shiny floor tiles, she covered the twenty-metre length of the corridor in a few seconds and turned left to the stairwell.

She peered down over the handrail. Nothing, and nobody stirred. She caught a distant snore.

At ground level, she left the stairwell through a security door. The door to the courtyard was forty metres away. Offices lined the corridor. They ought to be empty. If anyone had decided to work late, they would have succumbed to the sleepers by now, of that, Mei was sure.

She reached the door and crouched. Putting her ear to the wood, she strained to catch any sound coming from the other side. Nothing. It wasn't guaranteed that the courtyard was empty. The wood was thick, after all. But she thought she would probably hear the clump of boots if any of the sentries had somehow managed to stay awake.

She stood up and turned the doorknob. It barely moved, and although she pushed against the door, it stayed firmly shut. No! This wasn't supposed to happen. They never locked the doors.

What was going on? Had the Frog somehow got wind of her plan?

Impossible. And anyway, why go to all this trouble? He could just go to the girls' dormitory and march her – *frogmarch her*, she thought and suddenly had to suppress a giggle that threatened to burst from her lips – to the punishment block. Lock her in a cell until the morning, when the Bureau official would arrive and haul her off to Beijing.

She tried the door again. Maybe she hadn't twisted the knob all the way. No. It was definitely locked.

She'd have to find another way out.

44

The fourth door she tried as she worked her way back down the corridor opened. She went inside and closed it quietly behind her.

She tried the window. It was locked. She hissed out her frustration. Who locked a window? The answer came just as easily as the question. A person working at a school that trained children to be assassins, that's who. Especially when their office was on the ground floor.

She briefly considered leaving and trying the next office along. But what if that door was locked, as the first three had been? Or what if it wasn't, but the window was? Or worse, what if the member of staff was in there? What if they'd skipped dinner and were working in the glare of their desk lamp? What would Mei say?

'Hello, Comrade Peng. I am just escaping. Could you let me past so I can climb out of your window, please?'

No. This was insane enough as it was. No more offices. She was here, now. And it was from here that she'd leave.

She marched up to the window, pulled the curtain down and wrapped it around her right elbow. Taking a deep breath, she drew her arm back and then smashed the glass. The noise as the shards fell out onto the concrete path leading to the courtyard was enormous. It sounded to Mei as though she'd pushed a bin full of empty bottles off the roof.

No time to worry now. Frantically, she unwound the curtain and threw it aside. Then she knocked out the sharp-pointed fragments sticking up from the window frame and climbed out into the still night air.

Her shoes crunched on the broken glass lying scattered by the wall. She took a quick look around to see if anyone was coming. She breathed a sigh of relief. Nothing but silence.

Running lightly on her toes, she ran along the path to the courtyard and headed for the admin block. Once there, she just needed to skirt round its northern wall and then head out to the far edge of the perimeter. Near the spot where she'd eavesdropped on the Crane and the Bull all those months ago.

Then everything changed.

She heard footsteps.

Not running footsteps. That was something. But as she froze and listened, she caught the off-kilter rhythm of two people coming at a fast march. Guards!

45

Now she could hear their voices. Irritable, tired, maybe even bored. Why were they even awake? With the amount of sleeper-dust she'd stirred into the food, they should have been unconscious for hours yet. Days, even.

'It'll just be a cat or something.'

'A cat? Are you serious? When was the last time you saw a cat out here?'

'OK, not a cat. A wild animal.'

'Inside the wire? Are you serious?'

'Listen, the students've all had their bye-bye pills, haven't they? So it won't be one of them. Are you saying it's one of the staff? Out for a laugh, smashing windows like a street kid with a pocketful of pebbles?'

'No.'

'What then? Ooh, I know. A CIA agent. He's going to kill everyone and then fly out on a jetpack.'

'Fuck off!'

Laughter. 'How about you fuck off?'

'I wish the director would fuck off. Docking us our dinner just because we were having a smoke.'

Mei had her answer, at least.

She willed herself to move. Caught in the open like this she'd be shot for an intruder if they didn't recognise her. And if they did, she'd be hauled off to the director. And that would *not* go well.

She unstuck her feet and sprinted towards the door of the admin block. The corner was too far away. They'd see her before she reached the sanctuary of the shadows.

Just as the guards rounded the other corner, she pushed through the double doors into the gloom of the reception area.

She crouched behind the doors and peeped through the narrowing gap between them.

The guards were strolling towards the accommodation block. From the direction they were coming, they wouldn't see the broken glass. Not unless they did a complete circuit of the building.

They took a quick look up at the front wall of the block then conferred with each other, heads bent together like friends sharing some piece of juicy gossip.

One of them pointed to the admin block. The other followed the direction of his extended finger. Mei shrank away from the door. For a second she'd thought the first guard had seen her.

No! That was impossible. How could he? She risked another glance. The second guard was nodding. Then they both started walking towards the entrance. Shit! They must have decided they needed to check the main offices. She backed away then turned and ran down yet another pitch-black corridor.

She skidded to a stop outside the Frog's office. A crazy thought came to her. She wanted the pistol she'd seen him take from the drawer on her first full day at the school. The one he'd told her to shoot him with. She wouldn't use it during the escape – too noisy – but it would come in handy for protection once she was outside the wire. She might even be able to use it to flag down a ride.

The Frog would be out cold, thanks to the powdered sleepers in his fancy steak stir-fry and she could have a last poke around before leaving. First she had to get in. She tried the handle. Locked, of course. No surprises there.

But she was not without resources. They'd spent a week learning how to pick locks. She pulled a hairpin out and seconds later had defeated the pathetic bit of hardware keeping her out of the Frog's private domain. On the far side of the door, the *safe* side, she closed it as quietly as she could and breathed a sigh of relief as the lock latched closed again.

Hearing the guards enter the block, she fled to the far side of the office where she scrunched herself into a ball underneath the Frog's desk. Heavy boots clumped down the corridor, before pausing at the door. Her heart was thumping and she knew no amount of readiness training was going to calm it. Not with two heavily-armed men just a few metres away from discovering her.

Their voices entered the room through the flimsy wooden door.

'We should go in and check it out.'

'You're joking, right? You want to break in to the director's office in the middle of the night? He'll make us cut our own dicks off.'

'What if there really is an intruder? And he's hiding in there?'

'This is insane! You really think there's a CIA agent in there? You've been reading too many spy comics. Come on. Let's go!'

Mei held her breath. The footsteps moved away. A few minutes later, they passed the door again. She heard the double doors open and then close. Now she could calm her racing heart. Now she could breathe easily.

Mei crawled out from beneath the desk and sat in the Frog's deeply-padded chair. The desk bore a computer, a bamboo pot of pens and pencils and a black phone. She opened the top drawer of the desk. There was the Frog's Type 54 pistol. Lying on top of a stack of brown cardboard folders.

She dropped out the magazine and checked it. Full. She slid it back and latched it before laying the pistol on the desk. Then she started poking around through the other drawers.

There was nothing much of interest. More pens and pencils. A packet of paper tissues. Some peppermints. A well-thumbed copy of Chairman Mao's Little Red Book. More folders containing dull-looking documents with loads of official stamps.

She opened the bottom drawer and drew in a quick breath. Bundles of paper money, each secured with a rubber band. Yuan, yes, in big denominations, but also the currency she'd seen sometimes in Shenzhen when she'd rolled a rich foreign tourist. American dollars.

She stuffed a bundle of each in her trouser pockets. But she hadn't made this risky detour to rob the Frog. That was just good fortune. So what *was* she looking for? She didn't know. It was just the temptation of being in the Frog's office.

She ought to be going, she knew that. But there was plenty of time. It was still before 4.00 a.m. and nobody would be waking up for hours yet, not after the massive dose of sleepers she'd given them all.

Then she knew what it was that had drawn her here. Not the pistol at all. What she wanted was her own file. They'd been told early on that the school maintained a personnel file on every student, past and present.

Mei wanted to leave no record of her existence at the school. Maybe they could still track her down without it. But it felt like the right thing to do. To make their job harder. And maybe they'd just give it up as a bad job and move forwards without her.

Where would the Frog keep such sensitive files? Probably not in his desk.

She spotted a dull metal filing cabinet in the far corner of the room. It was the only other item of furniture apart from the visitor chair on the other side of the desk. It stood to reason that the current crop of students would be in the top drawer. She pulled it out. At the very front, a little plastic tab stood proud of the folders. It held a little typed card:

2001 INTAKE

Was it really going to be this simple? Mei could hardly believe her luck. She walked her fingertips over the tops of the folders. Clipped to the top of each was another plastic tab bearing a number: 1 through 12. At 10, she stopped. She pulled it out.

The first document was a basic profile. Name, where recruited. Boring stuff. But it was the small colour photograph pinned to the corner that made her catch her breath. Sis was looking straight out at her. No smiling, but there was that lovely warm look behind the eyes.

Across the front of the sheet was a single word, stamped in red:

TERMINATED

Beneath it, in hand-written characters, someone had written, 'Unfit for further training due to injury.'

But Sis had died of her infection in the infirmary. That's what the Crane told them. The awful realisation hit Mei. They must have not been able to save Sis's hand. Without it she'd have made a very poor assassin. So they'd killed her.

She ground her teeth together. At that moment, she wished she could blow up the school and everyone in it. Not the students. But everyone else. Starting with the stinking, groping, sadistic bastard who ran it.

Dropping Sis's file back into the drawer, she found her own and pulled it free.

She returned to the Frog's plumply-upholstered chair and switched on the little lamp. Then she opened her file.

Just like Sis, there she was, scowling out with a look of pure defiance. The look that made Mummy Rita throw her hands up and exclaim, 'I don't know what to do with you, girl. You're like a wild animal.'

As she read, she saw herself as the school had seen her...

Subject is member of delinquent street gang.
    Multiple antisocial, anti-Communist tendencies.
    Multiple criminal activities.
    Extremely fit.
    Moderate fighting ability — would respond well
to training.
    Mixed racial heritage — one Western parent?
                    .   .   .

277

There it was again, that reference to a foreigner as her parent. Must have been her dad, 'cause Mummy Rita was most assuredly all Chinese.

She read on, discovering that the Crane had been watching her, on and off, for a whole year, culminating in the fight at the construction site.

Further documents outlined her progress at the school and her performance in the exercises and training missions they'd undertaken.

Mei became so engrossed in these dry reports that when the door handle began to turn, she didn't notice.

46

'What are you doing in here?' the Frog yelled.

He strode towards the desk, glaring at Mei.

'Those are confidential Party documents,' he snapped. 'You'll pay for this, Twelve.'

Mei's heart leaped into her throat. Adrenaline dumped into her system sped her pulse rate up, sending blood rushing to her muscles. She shoved the chair back and snatched up the pistol.

She pointed the gun at the Frog's fat-lipped face.

'Stop. One more step and I'll shoot you.'

Her voiced sounded wobbly and far away in her ears.

The Frog stopped and held his hands out wide. Then he smiled.

'If you shoot me, you'll sign your own death warrant. Someone will hear.'

'They're all out cold. I drugged the food,' she said.

He cocked his head. 'Very resourceful of you. But you didn't get *my* food, did you, Twelve? The chef prepares all my meals separately. I have to be careful, you see,' he said. 'One never knows when an enemy of the state might try to assassinate me.'

Mei noticed the hammer was down.

She thumbed it back. The metallic click was loud in the electric stillness of the office.

'There's only two guards left awake. I can take them out with this after I've killed you.'

'It's a training weapon,' he said with a smirk. 'Remember our first meeting? Those rounds you no doubt checked have no propellant. Try it.'

He stood in front of her, arms folded across his chest.

She thought about the guards she'd only just avoided. The Frog was right. If she shot him, they'd come running. They had machine guns. She had a pistol. She was trained – mostly. But so were they. And they could just wait it out until everybody woke up.

Then she thought of Sis. Murdered because she couldn't work as an assassin for the Frog and his Party cronies. And Mummy Rita, who she desperately wanted to see again. And the threat of brainwashing that Val had told her about.

She looked the Frog in the eye. And she squeezed the trigger.

The firing pin snapped home with a dry click. She kept on squeezing.

Click, click, clickclickclick.

The Frog didn't so much as flinch. He just stood there, smirking. Waiting for her to finish.

He backed away from her, reaching behind him. When he found the door handle, he drew a key from his pocket and locked the door from the inside. He never once took his eyes off her.

She came round the desk. She was going to have to kill him here with her bare hands. That, or die and be buried in an unmarked grave somewhere in the scrubby waste ground at the back of the main building.

She hurled the Type 54 at the Frog's face. Now he did flinch, twisting his head to one side as the squat black pistol spun through the air between them. Her aim was true, but his reflexes were fast and the gun only struck him a glancing blow across the right side of his head.

He hissed in pain and brought a hand up to his temple. It came away red.

Mei launched herself towards him, aiming a kick at his groin.

The room rotated around her and for one disorientating second she thought she was falling upwards onto the ceiling. Then she crashed down onto the floor. The Frog had snatched her right foot out of the air, twisted it, and sent her sprawling.

He was on top of her, hands at her throat. But his face was weirdly calm. No bared teeth, no wrinkled brow or feral eyes. Then he grinned.

'You're a little tigress, aren't you, Twelve? I like that.'

Mei bucked and twisted, but the Frog had planted his knees either side of her chest, high up: her attempts to throw him off were fruitless.

She could feel the blood pressure bulging her eyes out of their sockets. Sparks were shooting everywhere and her vision was telescoping to a small circle.

Summoning all her strength, she snapped her left fist up and connected with the Frog's temple, right on top of the cut from the pistol.

He screamed and momentarily loosened his grip. It was enough. She drove her clawed right hand into his eyes. His screams intensified and he fell backwards.

Mei was on her feet, coughing and struggling for breath. She staggered back against the edge of the desk. Then the Frog was coming straight at her.

She'd opened a deep cut over his right eye, almost severing the eyelid, which hung down amid the sheeting blood.

He barrelled into her and she brought her knee up in a sharp, percussive strike that would mash his balls into his pubic bone and put him down on the ground where she could finish him off.

But at the last second, he swerved so that her knee met the thick quadriceps muscle of his left leg. Then he drove a fist hard into her solar plexus. With a deep groan, her wind left her. The strike was perfectly placed. She could feel the paralysis in her diaphragm. Knew there was no way to recover except waiting for it to pass.

He threw her against the desk and she fell backwards, sprawling across the pristine surface and cracking the side of her head against the computer. The Frog drew back his fist and punched her between the eyes, smacking her head down onto the wood.

Dumb thing to do, she had time to think as she heard his finger bones breaking. But the Frog's own adrenaline was a better anaesthetic than anything they had in the infirmary. And now his mouth was drawn back in a snarl.

'Bitch!' he hissed into her face, so that saliva spattered her cheek.

The punch had made her groggy, and she still couldn't breathe. Frantically, she tried to draw air into her lungs. Managed a pathetic whoop and a whisper of air. Tried to push him away.

The Frog was wrenching at her trousers. He got the belt undone then ripped the fly zip down.

He slapped her hard across the face, forehand then backhand. Then he yanked the crotch of her trousers down until he could stand on it and drag them down around her ankles.

Now he was undoing his own belt while holding her left hand down on the desk above her head.

She snatched another breath. Then another. The paralysis had left her chest and she dragged great whooping breaths into her lungs, like scooping up handfuls of cool spring water after a day's march through the forest.

His hand was on her underpants. Dragging at them.

No! This was not going to happen!

He was shoving and thrusting at her, trying to get his legs between hers.

She had seconds left.

She scrabbled her right hand about behind her over the desk. Her fingers upended the bamboo pot with a clatter.

The Frog leaned over her, so close she could smell the fish he'd eaten for dinner.

'I'm going to shoot you myself,' he said. 'But first, I'm going to—'

She brought her hand up and over her head in a fast, low arc and drove the pencil she'd grabbed deep into the Frog's left eye. The sound was like stepping on a thin, dry twig. Crack!

This time he didn't scream. Instead, his lips relaxed and he uttered a funny little sound – Ohh! – like he was surprised. He tried to reach up to pull the pencil free but she hit it with the heel of her hand, driving it deeper.

She felt the lifeforce leaving him and rolled him off her. Struggling out from underneath him, she grabbed his head with both hands, raised it up and then smashed it down onto the desk. The pencil made a crackling, squelching sound as it slid the rest of the way into his brain.

Mei stepped back and let the Frog's inert form slide off the desk and onto the carpet, where he lay, face-down, blood pooling around his head.

Gasping for breath, fingers shaking, she pulled her underpants and trousers up and cinched her belt tight around her waist.

She took the key from his trouser pocket and unlocked the door. She was about to leave when she remembered her file. She retrieved the folder and stuffed it inside her shirt. And even though it was useless, she took the pistol, sticking it into the back of her waistband.

Leaving had been simply a matter of timing her run to avoid the two remaining guards and then climbing the fence. She'd stuffed some basic supplies from the kitchen into a nylon daysack. From the side of the road, Mei looked back at the compound of buildings and training grounds that had been her home for the last eight months.

She felt a tug of sadness in her belly that she hadn't been able to say a proper goodbye to Rats. But soon he'd be shipped off to Beijing with the others and then he wouldn't remember her anyway.

Wiping her eyes, she moved off the tarmac into the trees and started walking.

Overhead, the moon emerged from behind a cloud, casting its ghostly light over the landscape. Thin beams of pale grey illuminated the path through the forest.

Somewhere in the distance, a wolf howled, as if calling to her.

47

Hours passed.

She was desperately tired; the fight with the Frog had taken more out of her than she was ready to admit.

But she couldn't risk stopping: the options facing her were simple. Escape. Or die. She concentrated on putting one foot in front of the other, keeping to the trees, even though, this far out in the boonies, the chances of anyone being on the road were zero.

As the sun came up, she estimated she'd put fifteen kilometres between her and the school. Her feet were hurting and she'd scratched herself on a long, grabbing bramble.

Maybe it was safe to rest now. She pushed deeper into the trees until she found what she was looking for. A tall, ancient sawtooth oak with a deep V created where two branches had diverged centuries earlier.

She climbed up. Thick moss grew in the cleft. She settled down into its embrace, pushed her back against one of the cradling branches using the daysack as a pillow, and was asleep seconds later.

She awoke to the sound of birdsong. Glancing up at the sun, she estimated it was seven, maybe eight in the morning. After drinking some water and eating a little bread, she climbed down.

As she made her way back to the road, she realised that without a ride, she wasn't going to make it back to Shenzhen. For a start, she had no idea where she was. And the original drive out to the school had taken hours. So there was no way she could walk it, even if she did know which direction to head in.

That meant trying to flag down a truck. And that meant danger. If the sleepers she'd dosed up the food with had worn off then it wouldn't be long before they discovered the Frog's body. They'd see she was missing. After that, there'd be guards on the road, scouring the countryside for their runaway student.

Would they contact Beijing? Get full military backup for the search? She frowned. Probably not. After all, what could they say?

We let ourselves get drugged by a student who then killed our director and walked out the front gates?

Maybe the central authorities would send more help, but Mei wouldn't be the only one lined up in front of a firing squad.

She smiled grimly. Maybe that wouldn't be such a bad way to go.

What? She kicked angrily at a stick in her path. What was she *saying*? Of *course* it would be a bad way to go! It would be a *shit* way to go!

After pushing through a final stretch of thorny scrub that grabbed at her clothes and whipped long, spiny creepers at her face and hands, Mei reached the roadside.

She looked up and down the highway. White wisps of mist coiled above the tarmac, but it was already clearing as the sun climbed higher. She wiped sweat from her forehead. It was going to be a hot day. All the more reason to catch a lift.

An hour went by. Mei kept walking. A song that Mummy Rita used to sing to her when she was cooking popped into her head. The thought of her soft, deep singing voice crooning the old familiar words made her smile. She joined in.

'My true love went a-hunting,
to bring me back a plump, brown hare.
We ate it by the fireside,

and he caressed me softly there.
My true love went a-foraging,
To bring me back red berries, sweet.
We ate them by the fireside,
and there our souls did meet.'

It was corny, but Mummy Rita had a way of closing her eyes and swaying as she sang the last lines that made the young Wei Mei believe it was a true story not just an old folk song.

She knew that Mummy had been married before they moved to the village. Her husband's name was Dennis. But she'd once told Mei that Dennis wasn't her father.

Sometimes, at night, when Mummy thought Mei was asleep, she'd creep from the bed and go outside to sit on the porch. Soon, the pungent smell of her cigarettes would waft inside, and then Mei would hear Mummy crying.

The distant sound of an engine snapped Mei out of her daydream.

She turned to look behind her. A dust plume was rising from the shimmering heat haze and drifting left to right. Her pulse jacked up. Was this her chance to get back to Shenzhen? Or a truck full of machine-gun-toting guards from the school?

If only she'd thought to bring binoculars. But that would have meant delaying her escape further while she broke into the stores.

She retreated into the scratchy scrub by the side of the road and watched as the truck drew closer. She couldn't tell if it was military, yet. Too far away.

The school's trucks and those that delivered supplies were all painted in the same shade of sludgy green as the Frog's official uniform. Red stars on the hood and side panels. She'd have to try and identify it that way. Green meant keep hidden, any other colour and she'd jump out.

The truck drew closer, maybe less than half a kilometre. At this distance it was impossible to tell whether it was a government vehicle.

Mei crouched in the undergrowth, ignoring the sharp prickles that scratched her hands and face. Compare to what was waiting for her back at the school, these were the soft caresses of Mummy Rita's 'true love'.

Now the truck was three hundred metres away.

Mei's pulse thudded in her ears. If she left it too late to jump out, she'd miss her ride altogether. But if she went too early, she could end up staring down the barrel of a Type 56.

Two hundred metres.

One.

It looked brown. She squinted, trying to make out the familiar five-pointed red star on the hood. Nothing. It was safe. A farm truck, maybe. Or one of the long-distance ones shipping manufactured goods around the country. Maybe even one bringing raw materials to one of the huge factories in Shenzhen.

She pushed her way out of the thorn bush and got to her feet. Raising her arms above her head, she started waving; calling, too, even though she knew the driver couldn't hear her.

It wasn't slowing. She dashed into the middle of the road, screaming now.

'Stop! You have to stop!'

The driver blew the horn, a great, mournful blare that sent a covey of white-feathered birds screeching out of a tree at the roadside.

She planted her feet wide apart and put her hands on her hips.

And then she closed her eyes.

The horn blasts joined up into a single angry bellow like an enraged water buffalo finding people strolling down its favourite path in the forest.

Mei felt the wave of warm, dusty air barrelling down the road in front of the truck. Grit speckled her cheeks. She felt the vibrations of the onrushing truck coming up through the trance into her feet.

Then a terrific noise, like a dragon hissing, filled her ears. A squeal of tyres on hot tarmac. The stink of burning rubber and diesel fumes.

Mei opened her eyes.

Towering over her was a chrome grill, flanked by huge

headlights like the glassy eyes of a giant fish. The cab of the truck was still shuddering, rocking on its springs.

She ran round to the side, where the driver was leaning out and yelling at her, his lips working around a lit cigarette.

'What the hell are you doing, girlie? I could have killed you! Are you literally off your rocker?'

'I need a ride. Where are you going?' she asked him, having to crane her head so far to meet his angry gaze it was hurting the back of her neck.

'Shenzhen. Not that it's any of your business. Got a load of parts to deliver to the Geely car factory,' he said.

He was lonely. Mei saw it at once. Heard it, too, in his voice. How he volunteered the information about his load.

'So are you going to let me up?' she asked.

He took the cigarette out of his mouth and looked down at her through the smoke.

'You're not one of those delinquents, are you? Going to stick a knife to my throat and ask for my wallet? Anyway, on my wages, I've got nothing worth taking.'

She smiled. 'I'm not a delinquent. I just need a ride to Shenzhen. I'm trying to get back to my mum.'

He stared down for a few more seconds. Then he nodded.

'Come round to the other side.'

She hurried round the front of the truck. The passenger door swung open and she hauled herself up and inside the cab. She slammed the heavy door behind her and settled back in the oversized padded seat.

The driver put the truck into gear and pulled away with a hiss as he released the brakes and a rising groan from the engine.

48

They arrived in Shenzhen at just after two in the morning.

After chatting with the driver for half an hour, Mei had drifted into a sleep so deep it felt like unconsciousness. He woke her with a nudge of his elbow.

'Hey, we're here. Wake up, Mei.'

She opened her eyes, blinking in the bright light from the sodium street lamps illuminating the factory entrance.

Peering out of the huge windscreen she spotted a road sign. They were five kilometres from downtown. She thanked the driver and climbed down, pulling her daysack after her.

'Thank you,' she said. 'You're a lifesaver.'

He smiled back. 'First time I've been called that. Take care of yourself, OK? Lot of bad people in Shenzhen this time of night.'

Didn't she know it. Half of them were her friends.

She swung the heavy door closed. With a cheerful double-blast from the airhorns that echoed back off the factory buildings, the truck lumbered through the gates, trailing acrid exhaust fumes.

* * *

At 6.45 a.m., Mei clambered aboard the first train out of Shenzhen station, having paid for a first-class ticket with some of the Frog's yuan. Hers was the seventeenth stop on the route.

At 8.01 a.m. she was standing on the platform. She was the only passenger to leave the train. A cleaner sweeping up cigarette butts with a besom broom gave her a cursory glance, then, finding nothing worthy of her further attention, went back to her duties.

At 9.55 a.m., Mei alighted from the single-decker country bus that did a long, winding circuit through all the surrounding villages, belching choking clouds of blue smoke from its holed exhaust.

The journey from the bus stop to Mummy Rita's house normally took ten minutes. Mei did it in five, running all the way, the daysack bumping on her back.

Mei saw Mummy Rita first. She was stooping over a gourd vine in her vegetable patch. And she was singing.

'My true love went a-fishing, to bring me back a nice fat carp.'

Mei sang the second line.

'We ate it by the fireside, and there he stole my heart.'

Mummy Rita jerked upright as if pulled into position by a puppeteer. She whirled round, eyes wide.

'Mei, is that you?'

Tears running freely down her cheeks, Mei ran forwards, arms wide.

READ ON FOR AN EXTRACT FROM TRIGGER POINT, THE FIRST BOOK IN THE GABRIEL WOLFE THRILLERS...

CHAPTER ONE

Close protection.

A lucrative business for a man with an SAS background. Especially one fluent in half a dozen languages, and trained by a Chinese master in ancient Oriental disciplines. A man like Gabriel Wolfe.

He shook hands with the businessman who'd just hired him for a trip to Mexico City, then headed out of the discreet office building off Trafalgar Square.

Walking to Waterloo Station, he hooked right into a dim, slime-walled tunnel beneath the pedestrian bridge over the Thames. As he reached the midpoint, the semi-circle of brighter light at the far end darkened: three men with shaved heads and sharp suits were coming towards him.

The man in the centre had a cocky swagger to his walk and was about Gabriel's height. Slim build but fit, jacket straining across his shoulders.

To his right, a giant, well over six feet. Heavy too, with the kind of muscle only steroids can build. To his left, a smaller man, not so keen on the gym, more of a beer and chips guy, soft flesh on his face and pudgy hands poking out of his shirt cuffs.

The leader moved into the centre of the tunnel, making Gabriel's passage a choice between walking over a wino's meagre estate of flattened cardboard and filthy overcoats, or squashing himself against the slimy wall to let him pass.

The other two spread out to left and right. He could smell their aftershave from yards away. Gabriel aimed for a gap on the leader's left but the man mirrored his move, delivering a good bump to his shoulder.

"Oi," the man said. "What do you say when you knock into someone?"

The other two laughed. Confident, smug, self-assured. Clearing his mind, Gabriel remembered the words of Master Zhao. *Do not seek the battle: run like the mouse. But if the battle comes to you, fight like the wolf whose name you bear.*

That suited him fine. He'd seen enough fighting to last him a lifetime. And enough death to last him for all eternity. He wanted to give these idiots a chance. He wanted to get the early train.

"I'm sorry for bumping into you. Now, if you don't mind, I have a train to catch."

The leader hooted with laughter and mimicked Gabriel's voice.

"'Now, if you don't mind, I have a train to catch.' I don't think so, shorty. I want to hear something like a proper apology. Like maybe on your knees."

No. That wasn't going to happen.

"OK, you've made your point, and I've said sorry. I just want to go home."

"And I just want you to say it properly, don't I?"

The others loved that one and cackled. Gabriel noticed they'd adopted a balanced stance, weight on the balls of their feet, fists curling and uncurling, muscles bunching and tightening under their jackets. He tried again.

"Please, let's not do anything we might regret, OK? We can all just walk away from this. I don't want any trouble."

"You pissing coward. Nobody's walking away from this. I tell you what. Why don't you give that old wino all your money then we'll give you a little something to remember us by?"

The old wino turned his booze-reddened face towards Gabriel. Maybe hoping he was about to get a windfall.

This wasn't going to end well, Gabriel thought. They reminded him of the big-boned army brats at one of his schools in Hong Kong. The ones who'd taunted him about his mother, who was half-Chinese, before punching him to the ground and stealing his lunch money.

"If you insist," he said, removing his jacket, "but let me put this down to kneel on."

He folded the jacket with the lining outermost, knowing that everyone was watching, before laying it in a pad to his side. His shirt concealed a hard-muscled frame kept in shape through thrice-weekly visits to a gym run by an ex-sergeant he knew.

The gang almost looked disappointed that the verbals were over and only the beating remained. The leader smirked and clenched his fists, but what happened next took him by surprise. From his crouching position, Gabriel straightened lightning fast, took a step to his left, and punched the giant hard in the throat.

The big man never expects to get hit first: he's relaxed, watching and waiting. So the surprise doubles the effectiveness of the blow.

He toppled, cracking his head against the wall on the way down. Then Gabriel took two quick steps to his right, at the same time pulling the top off the fountain pen he'd palmed with his left hand as he took his jacket off.

The lead thug blinked and focused on the object sending tendrils of fear into his balls. Gabriel let the point of the steel nib hover a couple of millimetres from the man's right eye. The pudgy man hung back; Gabriel barked at him, using his best parade ground tone.

"Stand still!"

He'd mustered out of the SAS as a captain and could bring the tallest, biggest, toughest men into line with that voice. The two thugs stood still. Very still. Behind them, Gabriel could see a young couple, tourists maybe, walk into the tunnel, notice the standoff and about-turn.

He leaned close to the leader's face, then whispered in his ear.

"I used this in the Congo to relieve a warlord of his left eye. We had to practice on dead pigs in training, but men's eyes are easier." The man gulped, his prominent Adam's apple jerking in his throat. He wasn't to know Gabriel was lying. "So be a good boy and be on your way, and I won't use it on you. You can still get out of this in one piece."

He withdrew the pen and stepped away from the shaking thug. *That should do it*, he thought.

"Bastard!" the man screamed before throwing a wild punch at Gabriel's head.

By the time the fist arrived, Gabriel had moved to one side. The heel of his hand connected with the underside of his opponent's chin, clattering his teeth together with such force that two upper incisors shattered on impact. As the man staggered back, clutching his bloody mouth, Gabriel moved again.

No need for overkill, just some summary justice.

One, two, three quick jabs with outstretched fingers to the man's throat, his gut, and, as he collapsed onto the pavement, the back of his neck.

The last blow landed directly above the basal ganglion, a knot of nerve fibres that functions like an on-off switch for consciousness. As the thug passed out, the final thing he saw was Gabriel leaning over him.

"The nearest A&E is St Thomas's," he said.

No need to worry about the pudgy lieutenant. He'd scarpered as soon as his leader's swing failed to connect. Gabriel reached into the leader's jacket and withdrew a brown leather wallet stuffed with twenties and fifties. Three hundred pounds at least.

He returned to the old wino slumped against the tunnel wall and held out the bundle of cash.

"Here, he said with a smile.

Wide-eyed, the wino started counting the money before stuffing it deep into his pocket.'

Thanks, guvnah,' he rasped. 'I saw what you done to those bastards. You're a gent.'

298

Gabriel shrugged. 'Find yourself a room for the night, and maybe avoid this spot for a few days?'

* * *

As Gabriel approached his front door two hours later, a frenzied barking let him know his burglar alarm was still operational. Half inside, he was almost pushed over by the brindle greyhound snuffing and nuzzling at his trousers.

"Seamus! Did you miss me, boy?" he said, scratching the dog behind the ears. "Has it been too long since Julia let you out?"

Julia was a good friend, one of very few; a fight arranger for the movies who'd burned out in Hollywood and moved back to her childhood home.

He poured himself a glass of white burgundy and looked across to the answering machine he had to rely on owing to the patchy phone signal in his village.

The red light was blinking. One new message. It could wait. Gabriel needed a walk and so did Seamus by the look of his tail, which threatened to come off if it wagged any harder.

* * *

The next morning – after waking from a dreamless sleep with no nightmares, a sign of a good day to come – Gabriel pulled on jeans and a jumper and headed downstairs for breakfast.

He made tea, breathing in the distinctive aroma of what he called "the house blend": one third Kenyan Orange Pekoe, one third Earl Grey and one third English Breakfast. It was a tangy, floral smell that reminded him of his father's morning routine. Always the same, never changing.

His father, a trade commissioner in Hong Kong, always drank tea from a bone china Willow Pattern cup, threads of vapour curling up and catching the morning sunlight slanting in over the bay through the apartment windows. Those moments together were the best time. Before school and its torments.

With the same clockwork regularity that he did everything else, the elder Wolfe would fold his paper, dab his lip with a linen napkin, and stand.

"Well, old boy, duty calls. Queen and country. Mustn't keep the old girl waiting, eh?"

With a ruffle of his son's unruly black hair, his father would leave for his office, whistling a snatch from *HMS Pinafore*, *The Gondoliers*, or *The Mikado*. Gabriel still couldn't hear a Gilbert and Sullivan operetta without being whisked back to those precious mornings. Then he frowned, because, once again, his memory was refusing to replay the darker moments from his childhood.

He'd been expelled from seven or eight schools for fighting, for disrespect, for "lack of discipline." In the end, his parents had entrusted their only child's education to a family friend.

Zhao Xi tutored their much-loved but wayward son for seven years, instilling in him the self-discipline Gabriel's parents hoped he would and the ancient skills that they knew nothing about. Along with karate, meditation, and hypnosis, they'd worked on *Yinshen fangshi*, which Master Zhao, as Gabriel learned to call him, translated into English as "The Way of Stealth."

His father had assumed he would go to university – Cambridge, like he himself had done – and the Diplomatic Service. Gabriel had other ideas and had told Wolfe Sr he intended to join the army. Not just any regiment either – the Parachute Regiment.

From there, he'd applied to and been badged into the SAS, where the emphasis on personal performance rather than strict adherence to arbitrary codes on everything from uniform to the 'correct' gear suited him.

He replayed the phone message from the night before. The caller's voice was warm. Cultured.

"Hello, Mr Wolfe. Sir Toby Maitland here. I need a chap with your sort of skills. Come and see me, would you? Rokeby Manor. It's the big house behind the racecourse. Please call my secretary to fix an appointment."

ACKNOWLEDGMENTS

I want to thank you for buying this book. I hope you enjoyed it. As an author is only part of the team of people who make a book the best it can be, this is my chance to thank the people on my team.

For being my first readers, Sarah Hunt and Jo Maslen.

For their brilliant copy-editing and proofreading Nicola Lovick and Liz Ward.

The members of my Facebook Group, The Wolfe Pack, who are an incredibly supportive and also helpful bunch of people.

My cover designer, Nick Castle.

And for being a daily inspiration and source of love and laughter, and making it all worthwhile, my family: Jo, Rory and Jacob.

The responsibility for any and all mistakes in this book remains mine. I assure you, they were unintentional.

Andy Maslen
Salisbury, 2022

ABOUT THE AUTHOR

Photo © 2020 Kin Ho

Andy Maslen was born in Nottingham, England. After leaving university with a degree in psychology, he worked in business for thirty years as a copywriter. In his spare time, he plays blues guitar. He lives in Wiltshire.

Printed in Great Britain
by Amazon

81167316R00180